The Quest

Heather von Prondzynski

Attic Press
Dublin

First Published in 1992 by
Attic Press
4 Upper Mount Street
Dublin 2

British Library Cataloguing in Publication Data
 Prondzynski, Heather von
 The Quest
 I. Title
 823.914 [F]

 ISBN 1-85594-038-8

 Cover Design: Cathy Dineen
 Origination: Attic Press
 Printing: Guernsey Press Co. Ltd

This book is published with the assistance of the Arts Council/An Chomhairle Ealaíon.

"'I think being a woman is like being Irish,' said Frances, putting aside her work and sitting up. 'Everyone says you're important and nice, but you take second place all the same'"
Iris Murdoch, The Red and the Green.

CHILD

To Ferdinand, with love

Heather von Prondzynski was born in Stockton, England. She completed a PhD in French at London University and subsequently lectured at Trinity College, Dublin for ten years. As Heather Ingman, she has had many stories and articles published including literary reviews in UK and Irish newspapers. Heather has two sons and is currently working on a new novel. She divides her time between Yorkshire and Mullingar.

Although the place names in this book refer to real places, the characters and events are entirely fictional.

Chapter One

Her thirtieth birthday provoked a crisis in the life of Maggie James. This was not entirely a surprise - she had felt it coming on for months. Too many things had been piling up at the back of her mind, unexamined. Like the fact that her interview for tenure at the university was due shortly, that thirty had been the age she had set for starting a family, that Conor with whom she had hoped to start the family, had not been much in evidence of late, that in fact she was beginning to suspect the existence of *another woman*.

She stuck a toe out apprehensively from under the duvet. The start of a new day always gave her butterflies in her stomach. It generally took until lunchtime for them to settle down. Morning sickness would be a doddle, she thought, compared with early morning panic.

She padded over the landlord's synthetic deep pile carpet to the window. Though it was May, the sky above Dublin was grey. Grey houses, grey canal, grey trees - it was like living inside a metal box. She had once heard Fergus McKenna argue that the grey granite stones of the buildings had had a determining effect on the national character, inducing a deep depression which drove the Protestants to morality and the Catholics to drink. She turned away and peered at herself in the mirror, at her tangled brown hair and asymmetrical green eyes. She stuck out her tongue. Just for once, she thought, it would make a nice change if a different face looked back at her - say, shimmering long blonde hair and dark, alluring eyes.

She glanced around the bedroom and screwed up her mouth. Dismal hardly described it. The landlord's orange-weave curtains matched his orange carpet but clashed horribly with her bright pink duvet. The wallpaper, presumably white in the beginning, had turned grey over the years and acquired yellowish stains from the residency of a previous tenant. Some experimental scrubbing in a discreet corner had merely had the effect of removing the wallpaper.

The flat, the best she had been able to find at short notice, was the kind of place secretaries up from the country rent for working in Dublin during the week, their real life taking place at the weekends back home. It had that uncared for, lonely look an apartment gets when it sees tenants come and go at short intervals. She had tried to make an effort. She had stuck up posters, reproductions of Renaissance paintings, Botticelli's *Venus*, Clouet's portrait of Francis I, Perugino's *Madonna and Child*. But it still looked temporary and studentish, right down to the books lying about in heaps on the floor (Nolan had been stingy with the shelving) and the unwashed coffee mug on the rickety bedside table. Hopefully indeed it would be temporary. But that all depended on Conor.

She went into the tiny kitchen and boiled the kettle for a hot-water bottle. In face of a crisis, she thought, retreat to bed. Curl up in foetal position with, since Conor was down the country interviewing, her arms round the hot water bottle. And think. Of that evening a couple of weeks ago when she had called round to his house (which used to be her home too, till he had suggested this temporary hiatus in their relationship) to use Conor's washing machine.

It was a new house on an estate to the south of the city. Thousands of such houses, semi-detached boxes Conor called them, had been built over the last ten years to accommodate the city's expanding middle class. They had been sprawled on the floor in the living room reading their way through a backlog of Sunday papers when the phone rang. Conor sprang into action, doing a neat dance to get between her and his brand new chocolate coloured Telecom Éireann phone and giving her in passing a peck on the cheek (extremely unusual and therefore arousing instant suspicion).

'Hello. Oh, it's you.' His voice shot several degrees up the Centigrade scale. 'Hang on a minute.' He unplugged the phone. 'I'll take this upstairs,' he said, trailing flex out of the living room and shutting the door behind him.

Maggie had remained sprawled amongst the newspapers, feeling anxious. Conor who, unusually for an Irishman, was tall, with curly brown hair and eyes that crinkled at the edges when he smiled, had recently woken up to the fact that women considered him attractive. Maggie found this tiresome. She thought of opening the living room door and tiptoeing to the bottom of the stairs (it was no use going up the stairs; they creaked), but this seemed too base, even for her. So she contented herself with lying flat on her stomach and concentrating very hard on any sounds that might drift down through the cracks in the ceiling, relying on the sloppiness of modern builders to solve a sticky moral problem.

Though Conor had spoken in a very soft voice (in what might almost be described as a coo, in fact) certain phrases made their way down to her. Such as

7

'Are you all right?' 'Did you tell him?' (voice raised excitedly here). 'What did he say?' (lower, a little nervous?). Several understanding 'Mms,' and finally 'I'll phone back later.' At this point, Maggie wondered about rushing out to remove the fan belt from her car, obliging Conor to invite her to stay overnight and putting the kibosh on that second phone call.

But it was too late. Conor slid back into the room, carrying the phone under his arm. If she had had to choose one word to describe his expression, she would have chosen sheepish. She rose from her disadvantageous position on the floor.

'Anyone interesting?' she asked in a light, careless tone, pretending to squash a yawn.

'A friend.'

She raised a tactical eyebrow and waited for him to expand. He sat down to finish the papers.

'Anyone I know?' Once they had shared friends.

'Someone who has an idea for an article. Not important. I'll ring them back later.' The careful disguise of gender did not escape her notice. He glanced up from his newspaper. 'Do I hear the washing machine stopping?'

A stronger woman, she felt, would have questioned him further, pressed the point home, kicked his head in. 'And quite right too,' whispered her mother's voice in her ear. But being a coward and more her father's daughter than her mother's, Maggie preferred to let things slide. No invitation to stay the night being forthcoming, she had gone home early.

She hugged the hot-water bottle closer. Conor with another woman. It was unthinkable. Meanwhile craftily, whilst her back had been turned, her thirtieth birthday had sneaked up on her. She considered it a low down trick to play on a woman who wasn't even married and whose womb had recently begun to cry out for a tiny occupant. How many child-bearing years did she realistically have left? The newspapers, from which she derived most of her medical knowledge, spoke of women whose menopause had begun as early as thirty-five. That gave her five more years. Or was this being over-optimistic? The same newspapers also told of women who had tried for ages to have children, without success. The later one left it, the more difficult it became, apparently. 'Sublimate,' said her mother's voice. 'There are plenty of women around quite content to be childless. You have your career to think of. Look at me - I might have been high up in the tax office by now if I hadn't had you.' 'Work, work, work!' said her father. 'This doesn't make a rounded personality. When are you going to start taking it easy? Once you get tenure, you'll be in a perfect position to have a child. Get out and find a suitable father. What about this Conor? He seems a decent enough chap.'

'You're right Dad,' she thought.

At ten fifteen on her thirtieth birthday, Maggie James sat up in bed, shook the duvet down over her ankles and made a number of resolutions. One, to throw away her packets of Ovran and let her hormones settle down. Two, to make an all-out attempt to win back Conor. Failing that, to put resolutions three, four and five into operation. Three, to look for a suitable father for her child, preferably (to make a contrast with Conor), someone mature; or did sperm weaken with age? Resolution three (a), stop relying on newspapers and consult a medical dictionary. Four, find out the identity of the other woman in Conor's life. Five, take revenge on her or both of them, depending.

This blow for action inspired her to get up.

She tugged on a pair of jeans, ate her way through a bowl of All Bran and drove into college. Maggie had an ambivalent attitude to her job. At times like these, with crises looming on her horizon, she found it something of a relief to escape the present and delve back into the remote and often bizarre problems of the past. She would remind herself that after spending six years of her life studying history in London and three teaching it at Trinity College, Dublin, she was ill-equipped to do anything else. At other times, it seemed to her that the main advantage of being a history lecturer was that it enabled her to avoid rush hour - and that Trinity's chief function was to provide a refuge for social inadequates.

'There are three types of academics,' Fergus had told her upon her arrival, fresh and innocent, from London. 'Those who construct a scaffolding of theory upon theory and clamber up it to the dizzy heights of Fellow, Associate Professor, Professor, and even, if they're lucky, Dean of the Faculty. I used to be one of those myself. Then there is the second type - the ones who fall over themselves dodging students in the corridor, go to the pub at lunchtime and forget to come out for that seminar at two. But the worst type is the third - the academic who, having failed to think up a theory which will lead him through the ranks of Fellow, Associate Professor et cetera, involves himself in administration and college politics. These are the empire builders, to be avoided at all costs. Obsessed with minute 2a, paragraph 4 (amended), they spend their lives circulating bits of paper about expenditure, the new office carpet and who should be allowed to park their car in college. Well, there you have it, kid,' he had said, slapping her on the back. 'Choose which one you want to be and go for it.' This was the only piece of advice any of her colleagues had ever given her. She still hadn't worked out into which category she fell.

Maggie parked her somewhat battered Renault carefully between two white lines in order to escape the attention of the little gnomes who haunted Trinity's car park, pasting large white notices over people's windscreens, saying *Park In The Space Provided* and, in case one had not yet twigged, *Between The White Lines*. The gnomes had perfected a type of paste resistant to spit, fingernails and French swearwords.

She walked down a grey corridor in the Arts Building. These corridors had apparently been designed specifically so that students' minds would not be distracted by views of the city, sunlight or air. The lack of windows made artificial lighting necessary even in the middle of summer. The air circulated from office to office through tiny vents. With it also circulated cigarette smoke, flu germs, the common cold. Maggie had once performed the experiment of placing a piece of paper over the vent in her office. When she had taken it down at the end of the day, it had been black. She shuddered to think of the state of her lungs; by now, they must be thoroughly toxic and what would that do to an unborn child?

She was walking along, meditating upon such matters, when she caught a glimpse of Professor Gardener bearing down on her, hair neatly greased back, trousers flapping wildly above his ankles. She dodged round a convenient corner till he had passed by. He was to be avoided before lunchtime. Something to do with blood sugar levels.

As she skulked in the corridor, pretending to

11

examine the notices (they were incomprehensible - this was the sociology department), Julian Fordham came out of his office and practically fell over her.

'Hello, Maggie,' he boomed. Everything about Julian was big. Big nose, big hands, big feet and a large bottom accentuated by the baggy cords he was wearing. She had often been embarrassed by his loud, upper class English voice for, in a country where the people were soft spoken, it emphasised the fact of his foreignness and seemed by extension to reflect on her too. As an English person in Ireland, she was always trying to play down her origins, whereas Julian appeared to delight in exaggerating his.

'Hello, Fordham,' she said. 'Done a day's work already?'

He smiled modestly and a lock of hair fell over his eyes.

'Started late today. Seven thirty as a matter of fact. Had a bit of a binge last night.'

She tut-tutted. If they ever built an underground passageway from the car park to the computer terminal, people like Julian would never see the light of day.

'Feel as if I've been hit on the head by a Ukrainian parking meter. Need to get some blood into my alcohol stream. Off to the CR for coffee. Coming?'

The CR was the Common Room. Julian often spoke in abbreviations. Maggie supposed it saved him valuable research time.

'Can't, I'm afraid,' she replied. 'I have to teach.'

He smiled sympathetically and walked off.

Julian fell into the first of Fergus's categories; he was one of the serious ones. She had once caught him staggering towards the car park with two outsize briefcases stuffed full of books. 'You'll get accelerated promotion if you walk three times round the Front Square carrying that lot,' she had remarked. For one sticky moment he had looked as if he was going to take her comment seriously.

Musing on the vagaries of her colleagues, she poked her head round the departmental office door. No one there. She hopped in, collected her post and tunnelled her way down several more corridors to her office. Maggie was not greatly fond of her office. It had a scratchy grey carpet and drooping plants. She was always hoping they would surprise her one day by lifting up their heads when she walked in. But like everything else in the building, they suffered from a shortage of light.

She sat down at her desk. Most of the mail went straight into the waste paper bin. Publishers' circulars (*Calvin's Use of Adverbs*, a snip at £59.99); the minutes of the latest Faculty meeting, not attended by her; a memorandum from the Dean advising colleagues to re-use envelopes, write on both sides of the page and, following eighteenth-century practice, down the margins as well. The xerox had been so reduced (to save paper) that it was barely legible to the naked eye. At times like these, Maggie wondered whether the cuts were going too far. Soon paper would be forbidden altogether except in emergencies.

She was cheered up, however, by an invitation from Moira Molloy, whom she knew slightly, to a fund-raising event the following evening. It was in aid of the refuge for battered wives that Moira ran. She decided to give resolution two a shove along the road by inviting Conor.

A scuffling and whispering outside her door

indicated that her seminar group was bracing itself for entry. She hurriedly scattered a few books across her desk and shouted 'Come in.'

Fionnuala swept in first wearing an exquisite, flounced Michael Mortell skirt with a wide leather belt and a silk shirt in a delicate shade of egg-shell blue. The belt alone was equivalent to a week of Maggie's salary. She decided that Fionnuala would have to produce real evidence of possessing a II.1 brain: she reserved the right to penalise for overdressing to her classes.

Behind Fionnuala came Niall in his usual green cloak, smelling of crisps and sweaty socks. Finally, there was Seamus in sports jacket and tie. These were in honour of Fionnuala whom he had been trying to seduce all term. Maggie checked for signs of success. The pimple on the side of his nose, the dark rings under his eyes, the melancholy droop of his eyelids all indicated failure. He had even cut himself shaving - a piece of cotton wool hung off the corner of his mouth. A crisis was clearly in the offing. He would need careful handling. She didn't want any breakdowns in her class, not with exams approaching and her promotion interview coming up. Something would have to be done.

'Whose turn is it to give a paper?' she asked, having temporarily or permanently mislaid the attendance sheets for all her groups.

'Me,' replied Niall, with little care for the rules of grammar. From beneath the folds of his green cloak, he produced a tin of tobacco and some cigarette papers. He hooked an ankle around the waste paper bin and dragged it towards him. An expression of acute distaste crossed Fionnuala's face.

14

Whilst Niall rolled his cigarette and assembled a random collection of notes seemingly composed on the backs of envelopes, bus tickets and assorted paper napkins, Maggie glanced idly over the rest of her post. She spotted a scribbled note from Professor Gardener informing the department of an emergency meeting at four. The Professor being of a nervous disposition, emergency meetings happened about every two weeks or so. She wrote, 'Fergus', over it in large letters. It was Maggie's duty to inform Fergus of any important departmental business. This enabled him to dispense with reading his post altogether.

Niall began speaking. They were launched on the topic of free will and tolerance in sixteenth-century France. By the end of the hour, Maggie had come up with a solution for Seamus. She proposed that he and Fionnuala work jointly on the paper for next week's seminar. She was immediately rewarded by a bright, conspiratorial grin from Seamus. She avoided meeting Fionnuala's eye. As they left the room, she heard Seamus invite Fionnuala to go for coffee with him in the Buttery to discuss the paper. She smiled to herself. Unlike that creep Calvin, she was a firm believer in free will and in assuming responsibility for one's life, a role Calvin and his followers had, in their defeatist way, assigned to God.

Sometimes Maggie wondered why she, a non-believer, had chosen to devote her life to the history of the civil wars in France with their complicated technical debates on free will versus predestination, chance versus providence, Calvinism versus Catholicism. In England it was considered bad taste to bring God into the conversation and in the tutorials she had occasionally been called upon to give as a postgraduate in London, the students had stared at her as if she had dropped in from another planet.

In Ireland, however, a country she had arrived in purely by chance, because there happened to be a job going in her field, she had found that such matters were hotly debated, the decline into secularism was feared and providence still firmly believed in. At the close of every conversation, her landlord for instance would say, 'See you on Thursday, please God,' or 'We'll get that fixed for you next week, God willing.' (When next week came round, God generally turned out not to be willing.)

In a country where Protestants still got up and raved about the Pope being the Anti-Christ, her subject had begun to seem very up to date. This did not altogether please Maggie. For she had particularly chosen history as the subject most remote from the understanding of people like Charlotte and Giles, both grimly determined to be modern. Charlotte and Giles had never seen the point of reflecting on the past, particularly not on old quarrels long over and forgotten by the rest of the world. She had chosen it, originally, to annoy them.

Her parents, on the other hand, were proud of what she did. She had satisfied her mother's ambitions by having the professional career, salary and status she herself had been prevented from having because of the times and the lack of child-care facilities. Maggie pictured the glow of pride on her father's face when the letter had arrived offering her a place at university. She had been the first in their family, indeed the first in their street, to go into higher education.

Her imagination dwelt on her past. She had had a very ordinary, quiet sort of upbringing in the London suburb of Mill Hill, then a lower middle-class area with an atmosphere of faded gentility. Her father had worked as an accounts clerk, staying with the same firm for over thirty years. On his retirement, they had presented him with a gold-plated carriage clock now proudly displayed on the mantelpiece in their front room. Because she was an only child, her parents had had a little more money to spare than their neighbours. She and her mother had gone regularly to the theatre and ballet. Each summer the three of them went on a fortnight's cruise to places like Egypt and Morocco. The history of her upbringing, as she pictured it, was one of security, warmth and love, but then all history, as Maggie well knew, is subjective - which was another reason why she had chosen to study it, its subjectivity seeming to suggest an area in which she could make her name quickly. Recently, though, she had gone off the idea of making a name for herself. There were other, more conventional, ways to live on in people's memories.

With this in mind, she made two phone calls. One to Fergus who was at home and grumbled loudly in her ear at having to come in specially for the meeting and the other to Conor who was neither at home nor in his office. She left a message on his answering machine to say that she would call round that evening. It has almost got to the point of having to make an appointment to see him, she thought. 'And where's my birthday present, sod?' she growled into the tape.

On the way to the Common Room for coffee, she passed another member of her department, Dr McGregor. He had dry, sandy hair that rose up stiffly from his forehead, freckled skin and a firm Ulster jaw. He slithered against the wall when he saw her, giving a blink and several wriggles of his eyebrows by way of acknowledgement. Stephen McGregor had been born in the Shankill Road at least sixty-one years ago and had worked his way out of Belfast by means of various scholarships and state grants. 'One of those autodidacts you wish hadn't bothered,' Fergus had once remarked. Maggie felt that McGregor disliked her intensely, suspecting her, amongst other things, of wanting to introduce changes. She had to watch him, however. He was not as stupid as she would have liked him to be. Also, he was quite powerful in the university. So she nodded politely and passed on.

On the Common Room stairs, she said a cheerful hello to Bridget O'Doherty from the history of art department. She had yet to make her acquaintance, but Maggie liked the look of Bridget, a big, blonde Canadian woman. There were few enough women around Trinity and Maggie often got lonely for a little female company. Bridget, seeming a little surprised to be addressed by her (at Trinity it was the custom to wait to be formally introduced before venturing to have personal relations), muttered something which Maggie took to be an 'hello' but which might possibly have been 'sod off'.

In the Common Room, various middle-aged men, all wearing the same kind of badly creased suit, were absorbed in their usual pastimes of playing chess, grunting behind the *Times Literary Supplement* and hawking into their coffee. She caught sight of a group of her colleagues huddled in a corner, obviously plotting. She hoped it was to do with the meeting at four rather than with her promotion prospects. She flashed them all a warm smile just in case they were thinking of booting her out.

She sat down with her coffee and spent several minutes working out a conversation between herself and Calvin on the subject of free will and babies. He told her sternly that babies were a matter for God's providence. She explained to him that contraception had allowed women to take over the role of providence and decide for themselves when to bring a new life into the world. Barring the odd accident, God had now become virtually redundant in this area. Calvin thundered on for a while about predestination and eternal damnation. 'You never were able to see any other point of view but your own, were you?' she retorted. 'If you don't behave, I'll take you off the course next year.' An empty threat, she thought, if Trinity had already decided to drop her.

On her way to the departmental meeting, she collided in the corridor with Fergus McKenna. They were both late.

'Definition of a departmental meeting,' she whispered, as they slid into the room. 'It takes minutes and wastes hours.'

He raised an eyebrow. 'Quite good. For you.'

She sighed. The Irish thought they had a monopoly on humour where the English were concerned.

'Now that we are all finally here,' said Professor Gardener, unnecessarily pedantically, Maggie felt, 'perhaps we can begin to address ourselves to the matter of the new appointee.'

'Oh good. Politics,' murmured Fergus, with a metaphoric rub of his hands. He was a short, sturdy man with grey, cotton-wool hair, a copper-coloured beard and a mouth that was tilted at a strange angle. Like most small men, he tried to make up for his lack of physical stature by thrusting out his chest. He strutted rather than walked. Lately, Maggie had begun to suspect him of wearing shoulder pads in his jackets. Today, however, there was no chance of checking out this theory because he was dressed simply in an open-neck shirt and brown trousers. Like so many of her colleagues, Fergus had little imagination when it came to clothes, apart, of course, from the recent, intriguing matter of the shoulder pads.

'I have circulated a shortlist,' began Professor Gardener and then stopped.

A man in white overalls had come in without knocking and now proceeded to stroll around the room examining the walls.

Professor Gardener coughed. 'Er ... can I help you?'

The man glanced briefly at him over his shoulder. 'No, no, just taking a look at the walls.' He thrust his hands into his pockets and began to hum. From time to time he stopped humming and pursed his lips.

Professor Gardener tried again. 'Er ... we are holding a meeting here ...'

'Yep.'

The Professor gave it up. They all sat back and watched the man's ponderous progress around the room. Luckily it was a small room. He exited without a word.

'As I was saying, I have circulated a shortlist,' Professor Gardener continued, 'of what are, in my opinion, the ten most suitable candidates for the job. Without prejudging the issue, I think...'

'What list?' interrupted Fergus. 'I haven't seen any list.'

'If you would take the trouble to look occasionally into your pigeonhole, Fergus, you might feel less like an outsider at these meetings,' replied the Professor, shuffling his papers irritably.

Maggie pushed her copy of the list across the table so that Fergus could see it.

'Ah ha, the Apple Macintosh,' he said approvingly.

Professor Gardener looked smug. 'I have been practising at weekends.'

Dr McGregor frowned. 'I hope we aren't being asked to acquire secretarial skills now.'

'No, no.' The Professor hastened to assure him. Like many people at Trinity, he was afraid of McGregor. 'It's just something I wished to learn for my personal use,' he said smoothly, making it sound like bee keeping or jam making.

'Press on with the quill, McGregor,' murmured Fergus. He was not afraid of McGregor.

On the other side of the room Norman got up from the table and began flipping through some magazines on the shelves behind. This did not necessarily mean he was not listening, despite appearances to the contrary. Norman, who worked in the French department, had been lent to them for the year as part of the Dean's new scheme for inter-disciplinary co-operation. He was supposed to be working out a bridging course between history and French. As was the case with most of the Dean's proposals, it was an idea that pleased no one, neither the French department who had to manage without him for the year, nor the history department who were uneasy about a member of another department sitting in on their meetings (the word 'snooping' had been used). Nor, though this was a lesser consideration, did it please the students who wanted to study, not French and history, but French and business studies, or marketing, or computing.

21

Norman was a dark-haired, middle-sized, powerfully built man who looked like an ex-policeman. Possibly he was an ex-policeman. He worked out three days a week in the university gym and was the fittest person in Trinity. Yet Maggie often thought Norman's appearance was misleading. When you expected him to land a punch, he strayed off instead into discussions on phenomenology and hermeneutics, structuralism and semiotics, post-structuralism, Marxism and psychoanalysis. Norman had run the entire gamut of fashion in literary criticism. He was currently onto feminism, which was as far as literary criticism had got. Maggie wondered what it felt like to have a personality so much at odds with what might be expected from one's physical appearance. Then she thought, I should know I'm a woman. People have been inflicting their stereotypes on me for years. She was a little afraid of Norman's tongue. He was liable to be sarcastic, particularly about the way the history department was run.

'I don't wish to prolong this discussion any longer than necessary,' began Stephen McGregor, wishing to do exactly that, 'but if I may say so, I think there has been remarkably little time for us to prepare our views on this most important issue. This is the last new post we are likely to have in the department for a number of years and we all know that mistakes have been made in the past.' Was she imagining it, or was his square Ulster jaw pointing in her direction? 'For instance, I would have liked to have seen the full list of candidates circulated, together with their cvs.'

'All three hundred?' The Professor looked stunned.

'Spare us,' murmured Lallie on Maggie's left. Lallie was absorbed in drawing large cats over the list of candidates' names.

Norman looked up from his magazines. 'Let's try these ten first, shall we? That should be quite enough to be going on with for one afternoon at the rate you lot progress.'

The Professor glanced round the table. 'Everyone agreed?' Everyone nodded.

With one exception.

'I would like to register a formal protest at the way this matter has been conducted.' Dr McGregor slammed down his pencil. The Professor shivered. 'Make a note of it, Ron.'

Ron, a thin, balding man with glasses, dutifully noted it down. Dr McGregor always registered at least one formal protest per meeting. It was as well to get it over with as soon as possible.

'If I er... er... might just er... er... offer my er... opinion,' began Dr Hammett-Greene, blinking round at the assembled company. 'I er... think this chap fwom Essex looks an awfully good bet. Thwee publications and a weview in the TLS.'

'Journalism!' snorted Dr. McGregor.

'I think we should have a woman,' said Lallie, completing the ear of a very fat Persian cat.

As the only other woman present, Maggie felt duty bound to nod her support.

'I don't think we could operate positive discrimination if that's what you mean,' replied Professor Gardener. 'It wouldn't be fair to the male candidates - and so on and so forth.'

Lallie rolled her eyes and returned to her cats. Maggie had a sneaking admiration for Lallie. At the start of each new year, she stood in the Front Square urging students to march for bigger grants, more crèches and contraceptive machines in the lavatories. She was radical, vegetarian and lesbian, and she had been trying for years to organise a Women's Studies degree at Trinity. She had not yet succeeded. She had her weaknesses - cats, good clothes and expensive perfume. She came to her classes beautifully turned out and smelling of Chanel No.5. She was the only woman Maggie knew who actually possessed a winter coat.

On the whole, Lallie had a better life than most of the women around college, for Trinity was slightly in awe of her and left her alone. In the early days, a lecturer from another department had committed the error of attempting to play footsie with Lallie at High Table. During the course of the meal she had gradually worked his shoes loose and by dessert they were sitting on the table in full view of everyone. Shortly afterwards, the lecturer had taken early retirement. Lallie was the type of woman Maggie herself would have liked to have been, if she had had the courage.

'Anyway,' put in Fergus, 'this process of pre-selection is entirely arbitrary. However much we huff and puff over it now, we won't know until the interviews whether any of the candidates are satisfactory.'

'What do you mean, arbitrary?' demanded Dr McGregor, his Ulster hackles rising. 'The whole basis of academic life rests on the notion of merit and selection.'

'I think...' began the Professor.

McGregor ploughed on. 'That's the trouble with this department. It's intellectually flabby.'

Silence bounced off the walls. Norman glanced up from his magazines with interest. Maggie looked at her watch. Five o'clock. She suspected Fergus of having orchestrated this deliberately in order to be in the pub at his usual time.

'Well weally!' exclaimed Dr Hammett-Greene.

Ron paused in his minute taking and looked perplexed.

Professor Gardener gazed down at his notes, pretending not to have heard.

'Perhaps it would help the discussion if I drew up a shortlist of three candidates,' he said finally.

Murmurs of 'Yes' 'Yes' from around the room and people began rising to go and dig their allotments, collect the kids from school, feed the cats. Dr McGregor registered another formal protest at the general sloppiness of the department, falling standards in recent years, newfangled ideas.

'Have you finished then?' Norman closed his magazine and walked out of the room with a nod.

Ron chewed fretfully on the end of his pencil.

'Put inconclusive,' whispered Maggie. 'Discussion to be continued.'

'I put that last time,' he wailed miserably from behind his thick glasses.

'Never mind. No one reads them anyway,' said Fergus, comfortingly. 'Coming for a jar then, Maggie?'

Maggie nodded. She and Fergus were old drinking mates.

'You did that on purpose,' she said, as they walked along the corridor.

'What?' he asked, his air of injured innocence the result of long years of practice.

'You know what. Giving McGregor the rise like that.'

He grunted. 'Who was it said that a quirk of linguistics has made all the Northern Irish sound bad tempered?'

They walked (she walking, Fergus strutting) out into the street and round the side of Trinity to the pub. It was one of the few pubs left in the city that had not yet been spruced up. It had hard wooden seats and the lino on the floor was pockmarked and scuffed. Fergus preferred it that way, claiming that too much fancy decoration distracted from the serious business of drinking. Maggie, who would not have been averse to a bit more comfort, put up with the pub because of her fondness for Fergus. He had a quick mind, much quicker than her own. It leapt from topic to topic as if there was a small gnome inside pressing a button. Mostly she enjoyed this; just occasionally, though, she wished he would stay longer on one topic, allow for a little silent reflection now and then. But Fergus, she had come to realise, feared silence.

In former times, Fergus had been in the first category of academics, whizzing up the scholarly ladder. His book on the French Revolution had been hailed as brilliant. But six months ago, the Protestant, working-class kid from Dublin 22 had discovered sex. He had not yet recovered. Now, instead of writing the follow up to his book on the Revolution, his afternoons were spent making love to Anna, the wife of a prosperous barrister who lived in Foxrock. Fergus had moved out of the house in Lucan he had shared for eight years with his wife Gráinne and rented a flat in town. So far, Anna had been afraid to leave her husband and two children and join him. Maggie's role in Fergus's life, apart from the matter of the post, was to monitor his progress, provide a shoulder to cry on and give helpful advice from her reading of D.H. Lawrence and Proust.

'Well, how's it going?' she asked, swinging herself up on to a barstool and ordering a glass of Smithwicks.

He looked despondent.

'There are two categories of husbands. Eyes filling

and fists flailing. Anna's falls into the first category.'

'The worst kind.'

'Exactly. He's been so decent and understanding about it all, I could kill him. Every day, I say to her, come with me, stay with me. She's almost on the point of leaving him. But at the last minute the thought of ould eyes filling gets the better of her.'

'Hang in there, Fergus. She'll come with you one day.'

He grimly swilled the Guinness at the bottom of his glass and ordered another.

'How's your love life?' he asked, tugging his beard.

'So, so. Conor's being evasive.'

'Frig Conor. What you need is a good man.' Galvanised into action, he rummaged in his briefcase and came up waving a copy of *In Dublin*. 'Small ads.'

'I'm not that hard up, thank you.'

'You don't have to be. You can have great gas with these, take it from me.'

'Fergus! You haven't tried them, have you?'

He looked coy. 'Once, when I got fed up of kissing Anna goodbye at four o'clock and going back to the empty flat, I contacted "Attractive forty-year old female, separated, two children, varied interests, seeks male for friendship, outings. Discretion assured." We arranged to meet in the pub. "I'll be the one wearing a red carnation in my beard," I said. She didn't laugh. Her identification mark was a pair of looped gold earrings like those wheels they put in budgerigar cages. She worked in the Health Education Bureau. Over a glass of orange juice, she told me about her promotion prospects, the pension scheme and her younger son who was running riot for lack of a father. When we got into the car, I noticed a strange smell. "It's

27

tiger balm," she said, flapping her eyelashes. "I've put it on all over." I drove once round the block and dropped her home.'

'I see. This is all very encouraging.' Maggie peered over Fergus's shoulder. 'I can never understand why these people advertise themselves as non-smokers. Do they think they're railway carriages or something?'

He glanced down the columns. 'I didn't realise Ireland had so many professional, witty, solvent Jewish men interested in the arts. Sounds just up your street.'

'I don't know Fergus. Dublin would be risky. Chances are you'd meet your uncle.'

'Incest, the great Irish pastime.'

'It's called keeping it in the family.' She grinned.

'Yeuck.' He made the thumbs down sign. 'You want to watch it. You're developing the Irish disease - if you joke enough about life, it might go away.'

'I love the Irish. I love their wit.'

He grimaced. 'You'll never be entirely accepted here, you know, with your English blood and your English accent. When the chips are down, you'll always be regarded as foreign.'

'Perhaps you're right. Julian Fordham told me the other day that the highest proportion of schizophrenics in English hospitals are Irish. It's obvious the two races can't get on.'

'Clash of temperament. The Irish have seen civilisation and rejected it. The English, especially people like Julian, still believe in it.'

'Do they? They have very little reason to, with women afraid of breaking down on the motorway, pensioners raped and beaten up in their own homes, teachers assaulted in the classroom by ten-year olds.'

'That's what I like about you, Maggie.' Fergus

downed his Guinness. 'You always look on the bright side of life. Well, I'm off to spend a fascinating evening down at the laundrette. What are you doing?'

'I'll probably drop round to see Conor,' she said sheepishly.

'I suppose I can't dissuade you?'

'No.'

He shook his head. 'Look out for yourself, kid.'

'I always do.'

'Now that,' he said, wagging a finger at her, 'is what I am not sure of.'

But as Maggie turned into Conor's road and saw his car parked outside the house, her heart lifted. The trees gave her a friendly wave, the setting sun smiled down on her. The world was coming back together again. Resolution two was about to be put into action.

Chapter Two

Conor opened the door.

'Oh, it's you. Come in then.'

The way he said it made her wonder whether he was expecting somebody else. She followed him into the living room and glanced at the mantelpiece for signs of dusting (always a clue that visitors were imminent). She looked to see whether his desk had been tidied, sniffed the air for traces of air freshener. But the house was giving nothing away. Come to think of it, she had always suspected it of harbouring unfriendly feelings towards her.

The room had filled up since her departure. The Apple Macintosh had been brought down from the spare bedroom and, together with the printer, was taking up the whole of the dining table. A new compact disc player with giant speakers stood against the wall where her plants had been and he had rearranged his books to hide the gaps left by hers. She felt crowded out. Perhaps this was what he intended.

'Want a drink?' he asked, waving the gin bottle. She nodded. Since moving over to Ireland, drink had become rather a hobby of hers. She sat down on the brown corduroy chair they had bought together in Switzers one Saturday afternoon. Conor sprawled on the sofa opposite, a pose he had recently adopted for showing off his long legs to advantage. He was wearing an old pair of jeans and a shirt which she recognised as being the one with the tear under the arm. She felt a pang of guilt for never having found the time to mend it. Perhaps her relationships with men would be more successful if she spent more time on the things men said they didn't want women to do for them any longer, whilst secretly hoping they would.

'You're lucky to catch me,' said Conor. 'I've just come back from interviewing and I'm off in half an hour to the men's group. Pity, otherwise we could have done something for your birthday.'

'Never mind,' she said. 'At our age, what's a birthday more or less?'

'Why are women so obsessed with their age?' he grumbled. 'Especially women around the thirty mark,' he added, with all the smugness of someone who has a year to go before his thirtieth birthday.

'I don't know. Perhaps you could discuss that at your men's group,' she replied cattily.

The men's group had started up a couple of months ago amongst some of Conor's friends. It was supposed to help them come to terms with the inroads made on their masculinity by women's new found independence. What went on at their meetings was shrouded in a certain amount of secrecy, but Maggie could always tell members of the group by the way they hugged each other in public. It seemed to be some kind of masonic ritual, indicating 'We may be men but we need affection too.'

'Will you call round afterwards? We could go for a birthday drink.'

He hesitated. 'I er... have an article to finish by tomorrow. Sexually Transmitted Diseases.'

'How savoury.' Did you come round just to give the guy a hard time? she asked herself. 'I've had an invitation to a fund-raising do tomorrow night,' she said, as casually as she could. 'Moira Molloy needs money for her battered wives. Would you like to come?' She crossed her fingers. 'Drinks are on the house for the first hour.'

He untwined his legs, fetched his Psion organiser and pressed a few buttons. 'I've nothing particular on.' He sounded almost disappointed.

'Well?' she said.

He looked away. Her stomach lurched. And not from the gin.

'Don't - um - organise your life too much around mine.'

'What do you mean?' she asked, in a tight little voice.

He shrugged. 'You know how busy I am these days.' He glanced at her. 'I'll come if I can.'

Someone was tying a scarf very tightly around her throat. 'Good,' she croaked. 'It starts at eight. Give me a ring if you're coming.' 'That's it,' whispered her father, 'don't make a fuss, he hates displays of emotion.' 'Make a fuss,' said her mother. 'Ask him what he's so busy at.' Shut up mother, she said, firmly.

They chatted brightly for a few minutes about this and that, glue sniffing amongst teenagers in Ballymun, the growing number of Aids babies, what the government wasn't doing for haemophiliacs. Conor was a journalist on the *Irish Post* with a special interest in social problems. Christ, she thought, I used to live here. She patted the arm of the chair affectionately. I used to dust you on your tubular steel arms. I used to come downstairs on a morning and sit on you, sofa, eating All Bran and toast as if life would go on forever. We gave dinner parties that lasted till three in the morning and when everyone had gone home, we made love on the big cushion by the fire. The cushion was still there. She gave it a friendly kick. 'Better not go on,' said her mother. 'It will only end in tears.'

'Oh, I almost forgot. I've something for you.'

Conor went over to his desk and handed her a parcel done up in a bow. She opened it. It was a whiskey glass from the Kilkenny shop. 'Thanks,' she said, kissing him on the cheek (she supposed that was still allowed?). 'It's beautiful.' She felt tears prick her eyelids. 'Get out fast before you disgrace yourself,' said her mother.

He showed her to the door. She noticed that the knob needed some Brasso. Maeve from next door was walking her child up and down the garden path. 'Hello,' she said, with no conspicuous attempt to keep the curiosity out of her voice. I bet she'd know whether there's another woman, thought Maggie. Maeve had witnessed it all. The gleeful, wicked moving in, the parties, the curtains drawn in the bedroom in the afternoon, the raised voices (how could she not have heard those through the paper-thin walls?), the sobs, the tear-stained departure with armfuls of jeans and pans, and a solitary pink duvet.

'Take care,' Conor said, patting her on the arm. As if I was his sister or something, she thought. She drove out of the estate.

Back in the tiny rented flat she had now to call home, Maggie tipped all her packets of pills into the dustbin. At least that's one resolution achieved, she thought, as she stood in front of the open fridge door, spooning Yoplait yoghurt into her mouth. She ate on the move nowadays, hating the sight of a setting for one. As she was eating, the pay phone down in the hall rang. Nolan had his own phone in the basement and the ground-floor flat was vacant at the moment so any phone calls had to be for herself. Glad of a diversion, she ran downstairs to answer it. Perhaps he's had a change of heart, she thought, lifting the receiver.

'Hello, darling!' Maggie winced as the upper-class tones came shooting down the line at her. 'It's me, Charlotte,' the voice added, unnecessarily.

'Hello, Charlotte.'

'I called to wish you Happy Birthday. Twenty-nine, isn't it?'

'Thirty. Where are you phoning from?'

'Antibes. Darling, it's simply glorious here. Giles swam in the sea today. The first time this year. And now we're lying by the pool drinking champagne in your honour.'

'You drink champagne every day.'

'Oui, chérie, mais aujourd'hui c'est à ta santé qu'on boit.'

'Very nice of you.'

'When are you coming over? *Il fait tellement beau ici, tu ne peux pas savoir.* Why don't you fly out and join us? I bet it's pouring down in that grey little city of yours.'

Yes it was, but she didn't feel like telling Charlotte that.

'I can't come out now, it's the middle of term.'

'Oh darling, are you still working in the university? If it had been me, I'd have chucked that job in ages ago.' Yes, you would, thought Maggie, but how else, short of selling my body, am I to pay the rent? 'I don't know how you keep at it day in, day out. You must be desperate for some sun by now. Couldn't you explain that to them?'

Maggie sighed. 'It doesn't quite work like that, Charlotte. Perhaps in the vacation...?'

'Yes, do. Did you hear that? That was Giles clinking glasses. He sends you all his love.'

'Thank him from me,' she replied, politely.

'Now I must dash and change. We're off to a party. What are you doing to celebrate? I must say, darling, I was a teeny bit surprised to find you in on your birthday.'

'Oh, I'm going to a party too. Later.'

'Glad to hear it. Well, must fly. All my love.'

'Who was that?' asked her mother as she put down the receiver.

Maggie shrugged. 'Oh, just someone called Charlotte.'

'What was all that about a party? You shouldn't tell lies, you know,' said her mother, severely.

'You haven't met Charlotte. I have to keep my end up.'

She went back upstairs, washed Conor's whiskey glass and put it in pride of place on the kitchen shelf. Then, finding nothing better to do, she sat down in the armchair and continued reading Proust, keeping an eye out for tips for Fergus. But her attention wandered. What was Conor doing now? Was he really at the men's group and, more to the point, what was he discussing? How to end a relationship he had grown tired of? Well, he had got over the first hurdle - booting her out of his house - it would be easy enough for him to walk away now if he chose. For one thing, he had no biological clock to worry about. Tick, tock, tick, tock.

She thought of the woman she had seen, girl really, certainly several years younger than herself. Dressed in T-shirt and pink leggings, her hair tied back in a pony-tail, she had been sauntering down Grafton Street hand in hand with her daughter. It was so much a picture of what Maggie hoped for for herself that she had had to catch her breath. Envy was an emotion new to her and not one she particularly appreciated. Generally if she

35

wanted something, she went all out to get it, but one could not do that with children who required planning and responsibility.

It was all her parents' fault, she thought. If they had been different people, she wouldn't have felt this desperate need to strike out for a life of her own. 'Don't decry the benefits of a good education,' she heard her mother say. 'I would have given my right arm for the opportunities you've had.'

'Yes, and where has it got me?' she retorted. 'Sitting on my own in a rented flat on my thirtieth birthday, whereas by rights I should have a home of my own, a man and kids by now.'

'What's brought this on?' said her mother. 'Your trouble is you're never satisfied.'

Her mother was right. At thirty, it really was time to stop blaming other people for the way her life had turned out. I am becoming dreary and bitter, she thought, closing Proust and getting up to draw the curtains. All in all, she reflected later when getting ready for bed, it had not been an outstanding birthday.

The next morning, she sidled into the office to collect her post and walked back along the corridor, opening envelopes. Inside one was a notice requiring her to present herself before the Junior Promotions Committee in six weeks' time. She grimaced.

'Bad news?' asked Norman, striding along with his policeman's stride from the opposite direction, slapping the wall with his newspaper.

As if he was banging the heads of convicts together, she thought irrelevantly. She waved the notice at him. 'Junior Promotions.'

She half expected him to shrug and say something like 'Par for the course.' Instead he stopped beside her, took her by the arm and said, quite sympathetically, 'Rotten luck. I hate interviews myself. Anything I can do to help?'

'Um, well...' She floundered, unused to this new non-sarcastic tone from Norman.

'Let me know if you think of anything.' He squeezed her arm and walked on. Halfway down the corridor, he turned and said, 'What do you think - didn't do that too badly, did I?'

What was this, she wondered, an experiment in empathy? Perhaps Norman had joined a men's group too, though it seemed unlikely. She stared after him, puzzled.

Back in the office, the phone rang. Conor, she thought, with lifting heart.

'Maggie here,' she cooed into the receiver.

'Maggie, it's Fergus. What's the matter with your voice? Listen, things have reached a delicate stage with Anna. She needs careful handling. It's make or break...'

'Yes?' she interrupted.

'Well, I was wondering whether you could take my first-year class this afternoon?'

She groaned. 'When?'

'At three.'

'I suppose so.'

'Thanks Maggie, you're a good mate.'

'See,' sneered her father, 'no one thinks of you as a woman any more.'

'Don't say that, Fergus,' she said.

'Why not? It's meant to be a compliment.'

'Yes but... never mind. What should I do with your class?'

'Oh, show them a video. Don't exhaust yourself. They're not worth it.'

'Good luck, Fergus.'

She decided to compose a letter of resignation. If the interview went badly, she wanted to be first off the mark rather than hang around till she got the sack. She jotted it down in her notebook with several alternatives.

Dear Professor Gardener,

Delightful/Stimulating/Soul-destroying as it has been working in your department, I must regretfully hand in (tender?) my notice of resignation. I have just been offered a place in film school/the post of poetry editor at Faber and Faber/a modelling assignment in Trinidad. I did hesitate for several days over the offer of Chair of History at the University of New South Wales, but refused for personal reasons.

I shall always remember my time at college with great fondness/astonishment/loathing.

Signed yours ...

At four, Conor rang. He could make it tonight after all, and would even like a lift. He had sold his Saab and was waiting for his new Renault Espace to arrive from England. She agreed to pick him up at his office. She rushed back to her flat to change and have a bath. Her period had started earlier than it should have done, encouraged, no doubt, by the fact that she was no longer pumping her body with hormones. For the first time in her life she looked at the blood trickling out between her legs and thought not what a relief, as she had often done in the past, fearing she might be pregnant, but what a waste.

She inspected her meagre rack of clothes and chose her slinkiest, her only slinky, dress. It had a deep V at the back and was ambiguous at the front about the size of her breasts. One advantage of pregnancy, she thought, would be that she would at last grow decent breasts. Turning to go, she caught sight of an ugly red spot half-way down her left shoulder. In more ways than one, it looked like being an evening for keeping her back to the wall.

On the steps of the office block which housed both the *Irish Post* and the *Sunday Post*, Conor was chatting eagerly to a short, plump woman.

'Who was that?' asked Maggie, as he slid into the car and fastened the seat belt.

'A colleague,' he replied, with real or feigned indifference.

She decided to let it go - it was too early in the evening to start quarrelling. But she noted down the woman as a possible candidate for the post of *other woman*.

They spent ten minutes circling the tiny backstreets that ran off right from Dame Street towards the quays. Parking was not Maggie's strong point.

'There's a space.' Conor leant forward and tapped the windscreen.

'Where?' she asked, peering into the distance. She knew where he meant, of course; it was just that she hadn't the slightest hope of manoeuvring into it. And he knew she knew. They were playing games again.

'You've gone past it.' He gave an elaborate sigh and drummed his fingers on the door handle.

'Oh dear, have I? Never mind, I'll go round this corner,' she replied brightly, changing down into second with a crunch (the first day of a period always made her physically uncoordinated).

'For God's sake, Maggie, do you intend us to spend

the entire evening cruising around the backstreets of Dublin?'

She laughed at the suggestion, having caught sight of a space large enough for three cars. She parked in two goes, which wasn't bad she thought, considering. Conor opened the door and looked down.

'It's all right, I can walk to the kerb.' He grinned.

She tapped his knee affectionately with her car keys. 'Some Woody Allen you make.'

He put his hand on his heart. 'If only you were Annie Hall.'

There was a short silence while she considered this. Annie Hall never wore dresses.

'Don't you like this dress?'

'It's fine.' And, as she still looked uncertain, he added, with a trace of irritation, 'You look OK. Right?'

She followed him down the street. He was wearing pale cream trousers and a leather jacket. She began to wonder whether he had been unfaithful yet. And how it had felt and whom he had done it with and in what way - and whether he had stayed long afterwards chatting about this and that in his past. No, no, she thought, surely he could not have been unfaithful to me. Or if he had, it was most likely because he had been too drunk to realise what he was doing and then, she reasoned, she would have to forgive him since obviously some woman had taken advantage of him, which was not at all the same thing, was it?

She took his arm. He patted her hand absent-mindedly, then released it.

'Come on, we're late,' he said.

A tall, blonde woman with her hair bound in a tight plait was standing at the door of the restaurant.

'Conor!' she exclaimed. 'How good to see you.' She

hugged him warmly.

'Moira! It's been ages,' he responded, kissing her on both cheeks.

Maggie found this little scene very touching indeed. It occurred to her though that she had been the one to whom the invitation had been sent. She coughed into Conor's right shoulder blade. He released Moira (reluctantly?) and moved to one side.

'Hello, Maggie.' Moira held out her hand. Maggie had noticed this recently: people kissed Conor but shook hands with her. She wondered whether it was socially significant. She would ask Julian - he would be bound to have some statistics on it.

Moira was wearing white cotton trousers and a lacy Indian tunic. 'Stunning,' said her father. Whose side are you on?, retorted Maggie. Feeling the spot gathering to a head, she turned slightly so as to move her back out of Conor's angle of vision.

'Well, darlings, I have to welcome my other guests,' said Moira. 'Do go over there and get George to give you a glass of vino.' She waved a hand in the direction of the bar where a man with close-cropped, blonde hair and an earring was pouring out wine from a huge bottle. 'Conor, I want to have a talk with you later.' She pressed his hand briefly, shooting to the top of Maggie's list of suspects. 'Don't be so suspicious,' whispered her father. 'She probably means business.' 'Yes, but what kind of business?' asked her mother. Shut up, said Maggie firmly. I want to hear no more out of either of you tonight.

They made their way between little tables draped with pink cloths to the bar in the corner. George came round the side of the bar to hug Conor. One of the men's group, thought Maggie instantly.

'This is Maggie.' Conor waved a casual finger in her direction. 'Maggie, George. George, Maggie.'

'I've heard about you,' said George, giving her a limp handshake.

So they do talk about women at their meetings, she thought.

'All bad, I hope?' she said.

He stroked his nose.

'Not altogether bad. No, I wouldn't say all bad.'

Oh God, these men's groups always teach them to be so sincere, she thought.

George went back behind the bar and handed them both a glass of wine. Maggie spent several minutes trying to figure out whether his hair was dyed.

'...English?'

Conor nudged her.

'I beg your pardon?' she said.

'I was saying,' said George, a trifle hurt, 'that you're not Irish, are you? You look so English, like an English rose.'

Good grief, she thought, the men's group is sending them round the bend.

Conor grinned. 'Maggie likes to think she's one of us. Irish.'

'Oh surely not. She looks so cool and reserved. Very English.'

If he says that once more, thought Maggie, I'll hit him - and his hair *is* dyed, the creep.

'Not that there's anything wrong with that - we're all becoming more English by the day over here,' continued George. 'A good middle-class society which washes the car on Sundays.'

'Clearly you haven't been down the country recently,' replied Conor. 'The flashing Sacred Hearts are still good for another twenty years down there.'

'I was brought up and went to college in London,' began Maggie in her best South-of-England-wimp voice. 'But sure amn't I as Irish now as if I was born and bred in Dublin like yer man here?'

'Oh.'

'I had lunch last week with Angela,' put in Conor hastily. 'She's asked me to write an article on our men's group.'

'Angela Mahoney?' George looked impressed. Angela Mahoney was editor of one of Ireland's glossiest women's magazines.

'That's the one,' replied Conor smugly. 'She likes me. We have lunch once a month and she advises me on my next career move.'

George grinned in open envy. Maggie felt the time was ripe for giving them both a kick in the balls. Angela Mahoney zoomed up the class to gain a First Class (honours) degree. Moira slipped back to a II.1. The list of suspects was growing longer by the minute.

'How do you scratch a living, Maggie?' George popped open another bottle.

'I'm a lecturer at Trinity. History department.'

'Maggie has her promotion interview soon.'

How sweet of him to remember, she thought.

'Oh? How does that work?' asked George.

He doesn't really want to know, she thought. It's the men's group. They have to be seen to care. How tiresome.

'Well, when term ends, I shall be interviewed by...'

'There's Prue. Excuse me a minute.' Conor dashed off. Maggie, following him out of the corner of her eye, saw him head in the direction of a slim woman, of indeterminate age, who was standing in the doorway.

43

Was she too about to win a place on the list of suspects? She turned back to George.

'...interviewed by a big committee of small men sitting round a big table. If they approve of you, you're made a lifer which entitles you to thirty-one weeks holiday a year, the salary of a supermarket manager and the key to the Common Room drinks cupboard. If not...'

'You're out on your ear?'

'Something like that.'

George leant over the bar and, rather to Maggie's alarm, winked.

'Glad to see you two together,' he said.

Maggie felt her stomach begin to do strange things. Did George know something she didn't?

At this point, Conor arrived back. His arm had somehow got entangled in Prue's. Maggie awarded her a II.2 on the spot.

'Maggie and George, meet Prue. Prue runs a women's group in Tallaght.'

Prue had a small, pointed face, expertly styled blonde hair and skin which, to Maggie's chagrin, appeared to be entirely unblemished. She was dressed in a pink striped shirt, loose cotton trousers and a pair of blue glass earrings which swung wildly every time she moved her small, shapely head.

'I keep telling Maggie she ought to join a women's group,' said Conor.

Traitor, thought Maggie. He knew she was highly suspicious of any division of the sexes, especially in Ireland where the sexes had been divided for so long by the Church.

'We're always on the look out for new members.' Prue beamed and scrabbled in her tapestry holdall for

44

a notebook and pen. 'Where do you work? Oh yes, at Trinity, Conor told me. I'll send you some bumph. Anyone else there who might be interested?' She stood at the ready, pen poised, earrings bobbing.

Maggie scratched her nose. 'There aren't many women around actually. Lallie...'

'Oh yes, we know Lallie. It's not quite that sort of group.'

'Bridget O'Doherty from the art history department, have you tried her?' Maggie wanted to get to know Bridget. She had a round, calm sort of face.

'I'll put her on the list. We're planning a rally soon in protest at the continuing American involvement in Nicaragua,' gabbled Prue, her earrings swinging furiously from her neat little ears. 'I'll keep you posted. Oh, there's Moira calling. Must dash. I've promised to sell raffle tickets.'

'God!' Maggie fanned herself with a beer mat. 'Does she stop for tea, do you think?'

Prue was obviously one of those women determined to keep herself busy, thus avoiding the need to worry about the smaller questions of life like premature senility, the rising cost of funerals, delirium tremens. Maggie suspected that in Tallaght, where one out of every three households lived on social welfare, the women had more pressing concerns than the war in Nicaragua. Very likely Prue commuted out to Tallaght from some middle-class area like Ballsbridge.

'Prue's a grand woman,' said Conor, as if he read her thoughts. He poured out more wine. 'You wouldn't think to look at her that she has three kids, would you?' he added, with loathsome sentimentality.

Maggie felt he was insensitive, putting that particular question to her.

'Sure and isn't it a grand thing to be an Irish mammy?' she replied, gulping back her wine.

Conor looked at her with raised eyebrows. She had started to explain to him once about the thing that creeps up on women as they near thirty, the way they wake up in a cold sweat at five in the morning, counting the number of child-bearing years they have left. Conor had said that he was too young to have children, that his body wasn't ready for it. Lately, Maggie had taken to watching the children playing in her street. Sometimes she had conversations with them, even quite long conversations. Where will it all end, she wondered. She hoped she was not going to turn out to be a baby snatcher. That would be embarrassing.

They said goodbye to George and, whilst Conor queued for food, Maggie went off to look for a table. She found one at the side of the room and sat down. Jazz music was leaking from the whitewashed walls and some people were already dancing. Her eye was caught by a large man in a white suit, prancing around with his hands in his pockets. Good God, it's Julian, she thought. The suit was a distinct improvement on the clothes he wore around college. But who was he dancing with? She couldn't see.

Conor arrived back bearing plates heaped with moussaka.

'I didn't know you knew Moira so well,' said Maggie, as they began to eat.

He shrugged.

'I don't know her *well*. She wants me to do a piece on the refuge for the *Irish Post*. It seems like a good idea. You know when she first set up that refuge nobody knew what she was talking about. There weren't supposed to be any battered wives in Ireland. No broken homes, no separations. Now the place is full every night.'

'As George said, more like England every day.'

He shrugged again.

'There are two different countries - Dublin and the rest of the Republic. I couldn't live outside of Dublin for long. It would drive me crazy.'

'Back again, darlings.' Prue materialised out of the crowd, waving a book of raffle tickets. 'Come on now.' She leant over and playfully pulled Conor's hair, a thing Maggie herself was not allowed to do. 'I want you to buy lots and lots of tickets. First prize is a bottle of whiskey.'

Maggie looked up from rummaging in her bag for change and saw that the selling of raffle tickets necessitated Prue sitting on Conor's knee with an arm round his neck. To give him his due, he looked a trifle uncomfortable with this arrangement. Maggie decided not to rescue him. She had caught sight of an old friend over the other side of the room.

'I must go and speak to Maureen,' she said. 'I haven't seen her for ages.' She fancied Conor mouthed the words 'mean sod' at her. Or was that wishful thinking?

She elbowed her way over to where Maureen was standing with her husband Art. They looked older and tireder than everyone else. Art was still in his work suit and Maureen was wearing a glitzy cocktail dress with bows, the kind of thing that had featured in the window of Brown Thomas two summers ago. From beneath her thick fringe, she peered out at the crowd, a bewildered expression on her face.

'Hello, Maggie. There are some weird people about nowadays, aren't there? Look at them.' She pointed over to a group of young men with identical blue hair.

Since the birth of her first child six months ago, Maureen had hardly stepped outside the house. Maggie thought that by the way she was blinking nervously around her, Maureen might be developing agoraphobia. Maggie had heard of women like that who had to be dragged into the supermarket and left to scream among the Yellow Packs till they were cured. Maggie did not fancy doing this with Maureen, however - and should friendship be expected to stretch that far, she wondered.

'They all dye their hair nowadays,' she assured Maureen. 'It's quite normal.'

Maureen sighed. 'I'm losing touch.'

'You've more important things to think of, now you're a mother,' said Art soothingly.

Maggie thought again what she had thought before now, that a little of Art went a long way.

Maureen grimaced. 'Don't mind him - he thinks my brain cells dropped off in the labour ward. When are you coming round again, Maggie? I need some grown-up conversation.'

It occurred to Maggie that this was an ideal opportunity to watch motherhood in action.

'I'll ring you tomorrow,' she said,' and we'll fix a time. What have you done with Amber? Dosed her with sleeping pills? Locked her in a cupboard for the night?'

Art frowned. He took his role as father, as he took most things in life, very seriously indeed. He had a pale pink face, unabundant fair hair and was already acquiring a business man's paunch.

'Babysitter,' said Maureen. 'We have to be back at the stroke of midnight or she turns into a pumpkin and demands double rates.' She glanced at her watch. 'We'd

48

better get in a dance or two before Cinderella's whisked away from the ball.'

She and Art went off to dance. Maggie noticed that Conor was also up there, dancing with Prue. Surely the music didn't require Prue to stroke his arms like that?

Well, she had no intention of standing around any longer like a droopy wallflower. She edged up to the dance floor and tapped Julian in the small of his back. 'Hello, you. I see you've got dressed.'

Julian turned round, grinned and introduced her to his companion, a fair-haired boy with fragile bones and the dingy complexion of someone who lived too much in discos. She wondered briefly if Julian was gay and how many heterosexuals, apart from Conor, there were left in Dublin. No wonder she was finding herself up against so much competition from *other women*. Julian gave her a few interesting statistics on the number of battered wives in Ireland, the percentage that returned to their husbands, the effectiveness of barring orders. She thanked him very much and asked whether there were any figures for battered husbands.

'Don't be stupid,' he said, looking down his large nose.

It wasn't so stupid, she thought, she was a husband batterer herself - at least she had once punched Conor on the nose for dancing the whole evening with another woman. She had given it up now though. Physical violence only alienated him further.

Conor came up to them. 'Hi, Julian.' Maggie listened in vain for a note of suspicion, resentment, jealousy even. 'She's a bit overpowering, that Prue. You might have helped me out, Maggie.'

'I thought you were enjoying yourself,' she replied, airily. Prue dropped out of class altogether. Or was this

49

a cunning ploy? She hedged her bets and left her with a Pass degree.

They had a few more dances. Maggie with Conor. Conor with Maureen. Maggie with Julian - she liked the way he sauntered around the dance floor with his hands in his pockets. Conor with Moira - *three* dances. She did not like this. Maggie with Art. Maggie by herself. Time to go, she decided.

'Wonderful evening,' she said, prising Conor's arm away from Moira's waist.

'So glad you could come,' replied Moira, looking at Conor rather than Maggie.

That woman was decidedly a bit much. Maggie found it hard to believe she was entirely motivated by a desire to get a piece in the *Irish Post*. But she might be.

Since Conor was without his car and Maggie had taken pains to elaborate on the shockingly high price of taxis, he had agreed to spend the night at her place. She decided not to tell him she had come off the pill; it might be too much of a shock to his system. Some other time, she thought, as they took off their shoes and crept up the stairs to her flat. This was to avoid waking Nolan who had banned men between the hours of midnight and nine a.m. The anti-heterosexual rule, Conor called it.

They squeezed into the narrow single bed and Maggie took Conor's warm cock in her hand. He came almost immediately, with a groan.

'Sorry,' he said, 'I'm nervous.'

'What about?'

He rolled off her and lay on his back looking up at the ceiling. The room became remarkably still.

'How would you feel,' he began, 'if we had some

time off?'

Off? Off what? she wondered. Work? No, not in that tone of voice. She froze into the foetal position as terror flooded over her. 'What do you mean?' Her voice produced a squeak she had not known it capable of.

'Well you know - if we didn't see each other so often.'

'So often! I've hardly seen you these last few weeks...' She sat up in bed, clutching a pillow to her stomach. 'Why?'

'Well er...'

'There's someone else, isn't there?' She could almost hear the rounds of applause as she hit the jackpot (three pears, an orange and an apple) and the coins fell clinking into the drawer.

'Er well...' he said, ringing the variations.

'Who?'

'I can't say,' he replied.

'Why not? Is she famous? Are we being bugged? Is there a *Sunday Sport* reporter hanging from the window ledge outside?' She noticed, not for the first time, what a nice shade of brown his eyes were.

'Don't be silly. It's a complicated situation. It doesn't only involve you and me.'

In best Hollywood tradition, her foot was on the floor. She was in imminent danger of falling out of bed.

'I'm thinking of you as well, you know, your feelings.'

'I'm overwhelmed with gratitude,' she said. To avoid an ignominious slide to the floor, she crawled out of bed and sat in the armchair, clutching the pillow.

Conor sighed and put on his little-boy-lost look. Don't think I'm falling for that again, you bastard, she thought.

'I shan't be seeing her all that often,' he added, by

way of consolation she supposed.

'Why not?'

'Because of the situation. It's...'

'Complicated.'

'Right.'

She had always been a quick learner. She punched the pillow a few times. 'Why didn't you tell me this before?'

'It's just happened.'

'Just? You mean tonight?' Moira? Prue? Maureen? No, not Maureen. She was becoming deranged.

'No... a few days ago.'

'Is it anyone I know? Do you work with her?' What's this, she thought, Twenty Questions? Is she animal, vegetable or mineral?

'There's no point asking. I can't say any more.' He turned on his side and fixed her with his beautiful dark eyes. 'Anyway, you don't really want to know.'

'Yes I do.' No she didn't. Yes she did. Tears plopped onto the pillow. 'Why did you come here tonight then? Giving me hope?'

'Because I wanted to tell you properly.'

'You could have told me fully clothed. Why did you sneak into my bed under false pretences?'

'Maggie, I hope we can still be friends.'

'Is that a euphemism? You mean still sleep with me? Two women at once?' She wiped her face with the pillow.

He sighed again. 'I don't know. I'm confused.'

This can't be happening, she thought. She buried her head in the pillow. Conor came and put a hand on her shoulder. 'I'm very fond of you,' he said, making her feel like an old record, a favourite mug, a long-lost pen and several other things.

'Well, you can't have both of us,' she said to the pillow.

'What? I can't hear you.'

She lifted her head and said very slowly and clearly. 'You can't have both of us. Either her or me. Not both.'

'Who do you think you're punishing?' whispered her mother.

'Do you want me to go?'

'Sod you.' She hit him on the leg with the pillow. Being a gentleman, he did not flinch.

'Look, I think I'd better go. I'll call a taxi.' He began to dress.

She contemplated screaming, rolling on the floor, kicking him in the balls, but all those things had been done already. She had no more cards to play. She handed him his jacket.

He hooked his little finger through the tag and stood there, hesitating. 'I'm sorry, Maggie. I really am. It was good with you.' Pause. 'Look, I'll ring you tomorrow. Don't cry. Please.' He patted her arm.

The next thing she knew, she was hearing the door downstairs close behind him. Oh, Conor. Where did I go wrong? 'Don't blame yourself,' said her father. 'The man obviously doesn't know a good woman when he sees one.' 'Perhaps if you'd dressed up a bit more, done the washing up more often,' suggested her mother. I thought you were supposed to be a feminist, snapped Maggie. She rummaged in the kitchen for the whiskey bottle. There was not enough in it to drown a fly. She threw it into the rubbish bin and began hunting for the sleeping pills, eventually locating them in the shoe box. She took three.

Chapter Three

Maggie was woken next morning by the persistent bleep of her Texaco digital alarm clock. She threw it across the room. It continued bleeping. Groaning, she got out of bed to switch it off and staggered into the bathroom. She felt as if a dwarf had been hammering on her head all night whilst his mate chucked salt down her throat. She ran the bath water and got in. It was times like these that made her wonder whether Calvin had a point about lack of free will. Conor, where are you this morning, she wailed. Are you seeing her? 'Sit tight,' said her father. 'It will pass.' No, she thought, clutching the soap, I wanted his child. Yes. I did. The soap slipped out of her hand, over the side of the bath, along the floor and under the wash basin. She burst into tears. What kind of a life was it when even inanimate objects were against you?

She supposed it was her comeuppance for all the men in the past with whom she had broken so lightly, because they bored or irritated her or, in one case, because she couldn't stand the thought of yet another summer of hay fever. Sneeze, sneeze, sneeze, all day long and eyes as swollen and red-rimmed as Dracula's on a bad night. Serves you right, Maggie James, she thought, you've got what you deserve. She imagined them all (and not so very many of them either, considering her great age) standing there, laughing their heads off. They were probably all married by now and producing their two point whatever it was children. She had tried her best to please them, to pretend that one day she would want to stay at home and cook for them and look after their children. Only with Conor she had not had to pretend. He had wanted none of that from her. But in the end he had not wanted her, either.

Driving into work, she felt the tears roll down her cheeks as if they had a life of their own. The road in front of her, the houses on either side, quivered and shook. She blinked. The houses wobbled. She blinked again. The houses righted themselves. At the next traffic lights, she put on a pair of sun glasses and stuck out her tongue at the man in the car alongside hers who was staring with a certain amount of interest, possibly because it was raining. She thought longingly of Antibes, picturing the sunlight pouring down on the palm trees, the pink villa, the purple bougainvillaea and the swimming pool. Then she saw Charlotte and Giles lolling in deckchairs, sipping their champagne and the screen went blank.

As she walked over to the Arts Building, she caught sight of Fergus's wife, Gráinne, in the distance. Gráinne was a small, dark-haired, intelligent-looking woman who worked in the personnel department. Since Fergus had moved out, she had begun to look her age. For the first time, Maggie felt a sneaking pang of sympathy for her. Gráinne had done nothing wrong. Simply eight years of marriage could not compete against passion. Wicked Fergus, she thought.

Walking along the corridor, she reconstructed in her mind, from things Fergus had told her, that evening when he and Anna had first met. Fergus and Gráinne getting ready for the dinner party, Gráinne pulling his tie straight, brushing down his jacket. On the way in the car, exchanging the news of the day, Fergus making some old joke, perhaps agreeing between them on a signal when to leave if the party got too boring. Pausing to admire the house from the outside, being shown into the high-ceilinged drawing room. Anna standing by the window in a white dress, her thick red hair unbound and reaching nearly to her waist. The beautiful and cultured wife of a barrister, she had been a concert pianist before her marriage. Fergus's sharp intake of breath as she held out her hand in greeting. The dinner where he tried to dazzle them all with his wit and found his eyes constantly returning to hers.

Coming home, wandering restlessly from room to room, looking down at his sleeping wife and knowing things would never be the same again. And for Anna? Perhaps the feeling of being wanted again by a man for herself and not because she was a wife and mother. And now, after all, Anna wasn't sure she wished to give up these roles and venture into the unknown. Poor Fergus too, thought Maggie. He had transcended the class barriers between Dublin 22 and Foxrock (ironically it had been Gráinne who had prepared him for middle-class life, who had taught him to drive, insisted on a mortgage, weaned him off sausages and chips and onto paella and lobster); but he had found that life was not so free amongst the lawyers, the dentists, the retired colonels who inhabited Foxrock. There were more traps, more snares and conventions binding Anna to her life there. Maggie feared it would not be easy to disentangle her. And then, because it was impossible to keep her thoughts off him for long, she began to wonder whether Conor was finding himself in a similar situation - 'complicated' he had said.

'Not a bad bash last night.' Julian boomed down the corridor at her. 'Bit LMC.'

'What?'

'Lower middle class. I say, what's with the sun glasses? Been over-indulging?'

She laughed, a trifle hysterically. 'You know me and the booze, Julian. Can't keep away from the stuff.'

'Oh?' He looked at her with narrowed eyes, as if he was thinking of using her to illustrate the high incidence of alcoholism amongst white female academics over the age of thirty. 'I say, Maggie, I've been doing some research into the sociology of Christmas Day. How many families split up afterwards, who says what to whom over the plum pudding, you know the sort of thing. The point is, I was wondering if your friend Conor would be interested in it as an article for the *Irish Post*?'

'It's not exactly seasonal, is it?'

He looked surprised. 'Does that matter?'

'I think it does, in the outside world.'

'Journalists!' He sniffed and walked off.

One thing's for sure, she thought, Conor's new woman is not an academic. You wouldn't tangle twice with these kind of people.

In her office, with the plants looking on mournfully, she drew up her list of candidates. Angela Mahoney (First Class), Moira Molloy (II.1), Prue (Pass), the woman on the steps of the *Irish Post* (an Allowed degree). She looked at it uncertainly. It didn't seem much to go on. Still, revenge was one of her birthday resolutions. 'Go for it,' said her mother. 'Be careful,' said her father. English wimp, retorted Maggie, lifting the receiver. The conversation with Julian had given her an idea.

She dialled Angela Mahoney's office and got her secretary.

'Good morning. I'm a freelance journalist. I've written a piece on the increase in promiscuity in the Gaeltacht and I wondered whether you would be interested in it.'

'Well,' doubtfully, 'we do have a resident columnist who writes on matters of psychological and sexual interest. Conor Kavanagh. Perhaps you know him?'

'I've seen the name, certainly.'

'I could consult Ms Mahoney if you like, though it's not really our policy to accept unsolicited material. Who shall I say phoned?'

'Aurelia Le Grys,' replied Maggie, promptly. It was a name she had had occasion to use before. 'I was... er... rather hoping to have a word with Miss - Ms Mahoney myself, if that's possible.'

'I'm afraid she's out of the office.'

Lunch with Conor? In Conor's bed?

'When do you expect her back?' she growled into the receiver.

'In a week's time. She's away on a family holiday. Has been for a fortnight.'

'Ah. In that case, don't bother mentioning my name. I'll try to place the article sooner somewhere else. Thank you.'

'Good day.'

Maggie replaced the receiver, crossed Angela Mahoney's name off the list and did a little dance round her office. 'Miserable sods,' she whispered to the plants.

The phone rang.

'Hi,' she said breezily.

'Good morning, Margaret,' responded Professor

58

Gardener, at his most ponderous. 'I wonder whether you would mind stepping into my office when you have a free moment? I have been meaning to have a little chat with you.'

This sounded ominous. Rearranging the timetable? A small sherry evening? Using too much paper? Whatever it was, better to get it over with straightaway.

'I'll come round now,' she replied.

Professor Gardener's black head, shining with Brylcream, looked up from his desk. He waved a hand to indicate that Maggie should sit down. They were in for a long haul then. Not a sherry party.

Professor Gardener coughed, leant his elbows on the desk, arranged his fingers in the form of a church aisle and coughed again. There were two little red spots on his cheeks, always a bad sign. Maggie wondered whether to take off her sunglasses.

'It is about your interview for tenure, Margaret.' Cough, cough. 'I see it is scheduled for six weeks' time. Did you know?'

'I received notice yesterday, Professor.' She folded her hands neatly and, she hoped, meekly in her lap.

'Well the thing is, in any other year it would be a mere formality.' He glanced out of the window. 'But in the present economic climate - well you know how it is - there's a general feeling all round that we should be tightening our belts, pulling up our socks, only selecting really top-notch people and - and, so on and so forth.'

'I see. Have there been any complaints? I believe I've turned up for all my classes. On my cv you'll find I've published a number of...'

'Yes, yes. Your research is quite adequate. No one is

denying that. It's just...' he scrutinised his blotting pad, 'that, well, there have been a number of complaints - from some of your colleagues - that you refuse to co-operate in the administrative work of the department. Now, as you know, we all have to pull together and do our bit, especially in these recessionary times, however tedious it may sometimes be and - and so on and so forth.'

Maggie thought this might be a suitable moment to give the Girl Guide salute but she refrained and said instead, 'If you mean that I refused to copy out by hand all the marks for all the students at the end of last term, add them up and obtain an average for each - yes, I did refuse. It's a waste of time doing the job ourselves. It could all go on the computer and be finished in five minutes.'

'Dr McGregor informs me there are valid reasons why the computer cannot be used for this particular exercise.'

She thought she had detected the McGregor hand - of course computers represented the deadly threat of change.

'Well, I'm sorry, I thought the computer could be used.'

'I think we should bow to Dr McGregor's greater experience in these matters, don't you?'

'Certainly.' 'Hypocrite, liar, toad,' said her mother. She rose to go.

'And that's not all.'

She sat down again.

'There's a feeling abroad that you approach the academic life with a certain amount of... of levity, not befitting an institution such as this. That you are not, how shall I put it, entirely responsible in your attitudes? Take the matter of the pay claim last year. I gather you supported the union's call for strike action.'

'Along with several others. We felt it was time we received more recognition. As you know, university lecturers earn less than secondary school teachers and unlike them we are supposed to work through the vacations.' Her arguments on this point were well rehearsed. 'Anyway,' she added, 'I thought it was supposed to be a private affair, voting.'

He ignored this. 'Naturally due allowance will be made - it seems it was mainly the younger staff members who voted to strike, those whose loyalty to Trinity may not yet have had time to mature, and so on and so forth.'

'After all, it's not as if we actually went on strike. There were too few of us.'

'No, but you voted to, you voted to.' He leant forward impressively over the blotting pad. 'Others do not take such a... er... liberal view as myself. And with the pressure for cutbacks, especially in the more... historical subjects like your own...'

'This is the history department.'

'...in short, we are going to have to fight to keep you.'

He sat back in his chair, obviously exhausted after this painful and trying session. Maggie shuffled towards the door.

'Fingers crossed, Margaret.' He flashed her a toothy smile. 'We will do our level best to keep you.'

And so on and so forth, she thought.

She went back to her office, feeling battered and confused. 'Told you so,' said the plants. Oh Conor, Conor, where are you? she wailed. A tear rolled out from behind her sunglasses and down her cheek. What was left for her in life but to toady to McGregor in order to keep her job, in order to afford a baby? There should be a law against sacking women of child-bearing age, she thought. She put her head on the desk and had a small cry.

'Pull yourself together,' said her mother, sternly. 'I'm surprised at you.'

Wiping her eyes, she decided to go over to the Common Room for coffee. McGregor was there, gossiping with Dr Hammett-Greene. She could have sworn he turned his back ever so slightly when she came into the room. She went over to the percolator, poured herself some coffee, stewed to a turn, added warm milk, fished out the skin and smiled at Bridget O'Doherty who immediately buried her head in *The Listener*. Seating herself at the table in the centre of the room, Maggie flicked through the job ads in the English papers and indulged in fantasies of becoming sales rep for Apple or the sub editor of the inhouse magazine of a cement-mixing company. What price free will now? sneered Calvin. The delicate fragrance of Chanel No.5 made her look up. It was Lallie, looking elegant in a dark-green velvet suit.

'Oh hello, Lallie.'

Lallie pulled out a chair and sat down beside her. 'You're looking dismal today, Maggie. Anything wrong?'

Since Lallie was on the union executive and might be helpful if the going got rough, Maggie decided to let her in on her conversation with Professor Gardener.

'Disgraceful!' Lallie exclaimed, thumping the table and causing several elderly men in armchairs to rustle their newspapers in disgust. 'If they look like threatening you with the sack, I can promise you the full support of the union. I might even be able to persuade the students to stage a demonstration, perhaps a march to the Mansion House during rush hour. Though they're an apathetic lot nowadays - I remember in 1975 when they stormed the...'

'Thanks, Lallie,' said Maggie hastily. 'I hope it won't come to that.'

'It pays to have your counter-attack well prepared, believe me. Perhaps I should mention it to the students' rep?'

'Er... not till after the interview if you don't mind, Lallie.' Heavens, she thought, I don't want to be thrown out for starting a student riot.

Lallie gave her a stern look. 'You mustn't let them push you around. There's been too much of that going on lately. Just because they know jobs are scarce they think they've got us over a barrel. Stand up for what you believe in.' She tapped her on the shoulder. 'You were right to vote for the strike. Don't you give in.'

'No, Lallie, I won't,' replied Maggie humbly, wishing she had an ounce of Lallie's courage. 'Thanks.'

'Phone call for Dr James!' someone shouted across the room. For a second, Maggie's heart leapt. Then she remembered that Conor never called her Dr.

It was Fergus.

'Got any spare sheets?' he asked.

'What?'

'Sheets - you know - for beds.'

'Well, I'll have a look. Single or double?'

'Double.' He sounded smug. 'Anna moved in last night.'

'Good heavens! Congratulations!' she exclaimed. The elderly gentlemen rustled their papers again. She lowered her voice. 'How's it going?'

'Marvellous - except that she can't seem to sleep. She

was up making scones at four o'clock this morning.'

'Whatever for?'

'Nerves, pure nerves. She's afraid her husband will come round and beat me up.'

'And will he?'

'Not a chance - eyes filling, remember? Anyway, I'd be grateful for some extra sheets. The ones my wife so graciously lent me have holes in them. They don't make a good impression.'

'I'll see what I can do.' It never occurs to men that these kind of things can be bought in shops, she thought. They seem to think they are passed down from generation to generation like the Kabbalah. 'Anything else?'

'Well, the odd plate would come in handy.'

'Heavens, Gráinne did leave you short.'

'She meanly took advantage of my complete ignorance in household matters.'

'Serves you right. Thanks for taking my class by the way.'

'What? Oh yes, sorry. With all this going on, it slipped my mind. Thanks a lot Maggie, you're a real...'

'Mate. Yes, I know. Any time, Fergus,' she replied dryly.

Well at least one of us is happy, she thought, as she walked back to her office. She would miss her drinking partner though.

She looked down her class list and dialled the number Prue had given her.

'Hello, Prue, this is Maggie James. I don't know if you remember me - we met last night at Moira's do.'

'Darling! Of course I remember you. In fact, I was just popping some bumph in the post to you. How are you feeling today?'

This is it, thought Maggie. This is the *other woman*.

'I'm feeling all right,' she replied, stiffly. 'Any *particular* reason for asking?'

'Only I felt hostile vibes coming from you last night, darling,' Prue went on, in the breathless way she had.' I'm very sensitive about this sort of thing. I pick up on people's feelings super quick. Do you feel like talking about it? I'm a great believer in letting it all come out.'

Was she being facetious? Either Prue was cleverer than she had taken her to be or Maggie had got the wrong end of the stick.

'It was nothing, a slight headache,' she said hastily. 'Listen Prue, I was thinking of joining your group.'

'Super, darling.'

'Could you tell me a bit about it? I... I've never been to one of these things before.'

'Well, darling, we meet once a fortnight in Eithne's house in Tallaght. I'll send you the address. We have no chairperson or agenda or anything like that. We regard those as male ways of going about things. We try to organise our meetings so that nothing will inhibit the free flow of feeling.' Maggie pictured Prue's earrings jumping furiously around her neat little head. 'Some of the women are rather... well, shy would be the politest way of putting it. They need to be encouraged to speak. We do that by sitting in a circle so that no one is in a dominant position. Every so often we have assessment sessions to see whether everyone's needs are being met. What are your needs, darling? Why have you decided to join us?'

'Well... I... well, I felt I wanted to explore more about myself,' she lied. 'To try to come to terms with being a woman.' She bit her lip quite severely to prevent hysterical laughter breaking out.

'I have a feeling, Maggie, that you're trapped in a male work environment and finding the structures a little bit hostile, am I right?'

'Er... probably.' She leered ferociously into the receiver.

'Well, Maggie, you've come to the right place. A group like ours is just the sort of thing to give you the kind of on-going support you need. And we'll be glad to have you. To tell you the truth,' she lowered her voice here in the way people do when they are about to say something unpleasant, 'some of the women are a bit - well, you know - barely literate. It's an uphill job to get them off the topic of their family life and onto something more... more globally significant, if you know what I mean. I'm afraid the Third World doesn't figure very largely in their world picture and as for the ozone layer... well, I really think I would go stark raving mad if I didn't get over to London once in a while.'

Remembering the purpose of her phone call, Maggie took the bull by the horns. 'Conor often says he feels the same way.'

'Conor? Oh yes, Conor Kavanagh. He was there last night too, wasn't he? Bit of a chauvinist, isn't he, darling? Needs some work done on him, I'd say.'

Maggie gave up. She couldn't see Conor putting up with this sort of thing for very long. Promising to get in touch again, she rang off. But after she had put down the phone, the hysteria that had been bubbling up during her conversation with Prue suddenly ebbed away, leaving her feeling exhausted and lonely. She rested her aching head on her desk.

The next thing she knew there was a sound of banging at the door. Rubbing her eyes, she went to open it. She had been dreaming about Conor.

Two first years stood outside. 'Miss, Miss,' began one of them, a serious looking girl still in the throes of puppy fat.

Her companion nudged her. 'Don't call her Miss.'

'We were wondering if you were going to teach us today - Doctor?'

She felt like bashing their tousled heads together. She looked at her watch.

'Shi... dear me. I was so engrossed in this article I'm writing that I forgot the time. Tell them I'll be along in a minute. We'll be starting on Protestant martyrs today.' Something not only in keeping with her mood, but also nice and difficult. That would teach them to come asking for classes like this and waking up poor lecturers. The girls scuttled away like a pair of bashful crabs. Maggie followed at a more leisurely pace, shaking her head from side to side in an effort to clear away the drowsiness. Sleeping pills are out from now on, she told herself sternly.

She spied Dr McGregor lurking in the doorway of the seminar room. As she drew near, he blinked several times and his sandy hair stood inquisitively on end.

'Oh, they're yours, are they?' he grunted. 'I was wondering who was supposed to be taking them. I have a class next door and they've been creating the most appalling racket.' He glared at her in a manner she couldn't help but find menacing.

Down on her knees and grovel. 'I'm awfully sorry, Dr McGregor. I was unavoidably detained, on a matter of some urgency. It won't happen again.'

'Good,' he retorted. He wriggled his eyebrows in a quite unfriendly fashion and marched back into his office.

She stepped into the windowless seminar room which closely resembled a solitary confinement cell in a Victorian prison. Ten eager first year faces turned expectantly towards her. A picture of Conor floated into her mind. Not only that, but the floor seemed to be rising to meet her. She clutched the back of a chair.

'I... I'm afraid I'm not feeling too well today,' she quavered. 'We'll have to cancel the seminar. I'll make it up some other time.' She turned and fled, hoping desperately that the gathering up of books and the scraping of chairs would not be heard by McGregor next door.

Back in the safety of her office, she decided to cancel the rest of the day and phone Maureen.

'Will you be in if I come round this afternoon?'

'In?' said Maureen, 'I'm always in. I'd love to see you.'

On her way out of the Arts Building, she stumbled over Seamus dawdling in the corridor.

'You haven't seen Fionnuala have you, Dr James? We were supposed to meet to discuss that paper you set us.'

Maggie shook her head, noting the spot on his nose and the blobs of cottonwool hanging from his chin. Oh Seamus, she thought, I hope you're not going to turn out to be one of life's losers. I need your good marks to slap before the Promotions Committee. You mustn't let me down.

As she drove out of the car park, she thought she caught a glimpse of Conor in her rear-view mirror. It couldn't be. What would he be doing here in the middle of the day? She was seeing him everywhere at the moment. Get a grip on yourself, my girl. She took off her sunglasses - they were giving her a headache - and headed in the direction of Rathgar and Maureen.

Walking up Maureen's garden path, she heard ominous sounds coming from within - like a cross between eight whistling kettles going off simultaneously and a very large cat whose tail has just been trodden on by a punk in hobnailed boots. The high-pitched cacophony got louder and louder till the door opened, revealing Maureen with a pink bundle in her arms. It was the bundle which was causing all the noise.

'Thank God you've come!' shouted Maureen. 'I've been dying for an excuse to have a drink.'

She led the way into the front room which had degenerated in recent months from an elegant reception room with low glass tables and Kilkenny design pottery into something closely resembling Lansdowne Road after a match. 'Baby-proof' was how Maureen described it. An assortment of woolly toys lay scattered about a huge pink rug in the middle of the room. In one corner stood a navy-blue, corduroy baby buggy. In another was a giant box of Pampers.

Maureen held out the bundle to be admired. Maggie peeked dutifully at the red, wizened face, the naked gums, the nearly bald head. 'Sweet!' she shouted. 'She's grown, hasn't she?' she added, more doubtfully.

Maureen nodded proudly. 'Art calls her monkey face. I worry that it will have a bad effect on her in later life - you know what Freud says, these first few months mark us for life.'

'Oh, Freud.' Maggie paused and frowned. 'Have you ever envied men, Maureen?'

Maureen looked blank. 'Envied them what?'

'Well, you know... penises.'

Maureen gave a snort. 'Never! Ugly little things, aren't they? Dangling down like that...'

'But fun,' added Maggie.

'Oh yes, fun - but then look what you end up with.'

They stared down at the bundle in Maureen's arms.

The howls were now approaching the stage of a full-scale air-raid warning. Maureen sat down, unbuttoned her shirt and pointed to the kitchen, mouthing 'wine'. She positioned Amber at her left breast. A hush descended on the room, the house and, Maggie imagined, several streets in the vicinity. She went into the kitchen and located a bottle of wine in the vegetable rack (since she had become a mother, Maureen had taken to putting things in very odd places). The corkscrew was one of those which kicks its legs up in the air like a Russian gymnast and the cork came out with a satisfying pop.

'Bliss,' said Maureen, taking the glass of wine. 'I don't know how I would have survived without this stuff. Amber's got seven month colic. She screams from two till six every day. You could set your watch by her - in fact Art does. Arrives home on the dot at ten past six every day. Sod.'

Maggie reflected that she would have expected nothing less from Art. However, the concept of 'the blood' being sacred in Ireland, she thought it wise to refrain from comment.

Amber settled herself comfortably on her mother's lap, leaking milk from the corners of her mouth. 'Amber has a problem with food fall-out,' remarked Maureen, mopping up with a wad of tissues taken from the box on the table where the posh purple Stoneware Jackson lamp used to stand. 'How are you anyway, Maggie? You look a bit under the weather, if

70

you don't mind me saying so. How's Trinity - and Conor?'

Maggie ticked the answers off on her fingers. 'Me, lousy. Trinity, deciding whether to keep me on or not. Conor, has asked for time off.'

'Off? Off what?'

'Me.'

'What for?'

'The usual, Maureen.'

'God, the things men think they can get away with.' She looked severely at Maggie over the top of Amber's bald head. 'I hope you aren't going to let him get away with it?'

'No. I told him he had to choose and he has - her.'

'Who is it?'

'What?'

'Who has Conor gone off with?'

'Well, there are a number of suspects...'

'My God, Maggie, you're the only woman I know who wouldn't have the name, address, date of birth and weight of the other woman by now. That's what comes of working with people who can't tell their arse from their elbow,' she said firmly. Before being overtaken by motherhood, Maureen had taught at a large comprehensive - a job which had contributed to her no-nonsense approach to life.

'Don't you start on my work environment. I've heard enough about that for one day.' retorted Maggie. She told Maureen about the phone call to Prue. 'You see, I have been trying.' She outlined the current list of candidates for the post of *other woman*.

'Hum.' Maureen considered for a minute. 'Yes, she's married all right - probably has children too.'

'What! Why?'

'Maggie, where are your brains? Because he can't see her very often. That must mean kids. It's easy enough to find an excuse to escape a husband. I'm not speaking from experience, you understand...'

'Go on.'

'...But to leave kids requires organisation. And babysitters are a terrible price.'

Amber signaled her agreement with a burp.

'Oh.' Maggie thought about this. It seemed logical enough. 'Ironic, isn't it? I mean Conor always used to say that children should be strangled at birth. And now he's gone off with a woman who has children...' She slumped in her chair. There he was with a ready-made family, without having had to make the slightest effort. It was so unfair.

'Men!' snorted Maureen. 'They never know their own mind. Hey, come on, Maggie, don't cry.' She laid Amber down on the rug among her woolly toys and came over to pat her friend on the shoulder. 'Come on, love, you'll find someone else.'

'I'm not crying really,' said Maggie, despite evidence to the contrary and in between sobs. 'It's the shock of Conor finally leaving like this and the wine and the sleeping pills and - oh, I don't know - I wanted a child. I feel as if the two and a half years I spent with Conor have just gone down the drain. I'm not getting any younger.'

Maureen squeezed her shoulder. 'You're hardly at the menopause yet.'

'Don't *joke* about it!'

'Sorry. You know, I've always thought you were happy working. I've admired the way you kept on with your career, insisted on your independence...'

'A bit like a man, you mean?'

'Maybe. A bit. No, the thing is that I've never seen you as the broody sort. I mean some women work for a few years, like me, and then give it all up for babies and housework. That's not likely to happen to you.'

'Why not?' wailed Maggie. 'What's wrong with me?'

'There's nothing wrong with you. You're different, that's all.'

'But I'm not different! I'm not a separatist like Lallie! And I do want a child. I want both. Child and career.' She paused. 'Well, there's only one thing for it. If I can't conceive a child in a steady relationship, I'll have it on my own.'

Maureen sat down again.

'You're crazy,' she said, solemnly. 'Who'd hold the baby while you had a bath? Who would change the nappies if you got ill? Have you read the statistics on kids from single-parent families...?'

'I wonder whether Gabriel got such a hard time from Mary?' Maggie said, wiping her eyes and pulling a face.

'What?'

'The Annunciation. Anyway, it's not so crazy. Plenty of women in America...'

'Oh, America.' Maureen sniffed.

'And Trinity has a crèche and there'd always be students to babysit.'

Maureen groaned. 'Maggie, this is Ireland, remember? The land of the nuclear family. It doesn't accept people like you.'

'No and it never will until individuals take matters into their own hands and show, by their lives, that it's possible to live in different ways from the Catholic majority and still belong.' Lallie would be proud of me she thought.

Maureen looked at her sternly. 'I hope you're not intending to have a child in order to make a political point?'

'There would be easier ways of doing that, Maureen. No, you must know what it's like. You feel the time is right when you catch yourself gazing with envy at every pregnant woman on the street and scanning the birth columns to get a sort of masochistic thrill from seeing how many people you know of your own age have already started a family.'

'Yes, it gets to everyone in the end.' She sighed. 'But wouldn't you think of going back to London where it's less likely to be called rude names?'

'No. I have my job here. At least, I hope I will have. And Ireland's going to be an exciting country to live in for the next few years, with half the population under twenty-five. That must produce something new. England has gone stale, bland, boring. I don't want my child brought up in a society dominated by Thatcherism, monetarism and class warfare. I want it to have some imagination... and a sense of humour.'

Maureen looked at her. 'Jaysus, you are serious. You're crazier than I thought.'

'Thanks, I'll take that as a compliment.'

Amber chose that moment to recommence her imitation of eight whistling kettles coming to the boil. By dangling various plastic keys, balls and furry animals in front of her, they eventually got her to switch off.

'See what you're in for?' Maureen glowered. 'How will your mother take it?' she asked curiously. 'My mother didn't speak to me for six months when she found out I was living with Art. She only came round when the wedding date was fixed.'

'My mother?' said Maggie, rather blankly. 'Um, well... it's a great thing to put a sea between yourself and the family. At least with me across the water, she's less likely to get stick from the neighbours. She can always say I have a husband in the Lebanon, or designing shopping centres in Saudi Arabia, or recruiting for Hari Krishna; they'd never know.' She paused. She could do better than this. 'The thing that would worry her most is the fact that a child might set my career back a few years. She's always been keen on proving that I'm as good as a son. Dad, on the other hand, is dying for me to get settled down and produce a grandchild.'

'Typical,' sighed Maureen who found this account of the likely reactions of Maggie's parents entirely plausible. 'Why are parents always so keen on their children passing life's landmarks exactly on time? It's such a menace. I used to catch them - my parents and Art's - looking at me as if they were counting the number of child-bearing years I had left. Every time I got promoted, they would say, their eyes flickering delicately over my stomach, "Oh, you're carrying on working then?" When Art got promoted, they brought out the champagne. If they hadn't put on so much pressure, I might have tried to continue at the school after Amber's birth... I made mutterings recently about finding some teaching two mornings a week. My mother sat me down and gave me a fifteen-minute lecture on latch key children. Sometimes I think my womb is the only bit of me they're interested in; it seems to have become family property since I married Art. Already they're on to the dangers of being an only child. The health visitor told me I should join a painting class... to give me a sense of achievement, she said.'

'Why don't you?'

Maureen groaned, 'I'm not sure that drawing wobbly flower pots and square apples would do a ton for my ego.'

They laughed. Maureen poured out the rest of the wine. 'This child is going to suffer from chronic alcoholism before she's very much older,' she remarked. 'You wouldn't mind taking the empty bottle away with you, would you, Maggie? Art disapproves of afternoon drinking.' She sat back in the chair and folded her arms. 'Well, since it sounds as though your mind is made up, I can see I'm going to have to think of a suitable man for you. If I know you, you'll go and choose someone really peculiar.'

'He's certainly got to be extraordinary in some way,' said Maggie, firmly.

'See what I mean?' Maureen glanced at her. 'Will you let him in on the act, so to speak?'

'Depends on the man, I suppose.'

'Better not to. Could be messy. Better no father than one who comes and goes.'

'Ah ha! So there are some advantages to being a single parent?'

'Only in very extreme circumstances,' Maureen replied grimly.

'Well, I'd better get going before rush hour starts,' said Maggie, meaning, before Art arrived.

They went into the hall. Maureen patted her arm. 'Look after yourself, kid. And start socialising. Invite a man to dinner. Let them know you're available again.'

Maggie made a face. 'I don't know any men apart from the ones I work with... and Conor's friends... and they're out. Maybe I'll ask Julian for a drink.'

'Julian Fordham? Don't let him be the father; the child would be born with a book of statistics in its hand.'

Maggie laughed. 'Quoting the percentage of children born to single parents who grow up to become tax dodgers, shoplifters, Mafia bosses, etc.' She gave Maureen a peck on the cheek, took the empty wine bottle from her and started off down the garden path.

'Keep away from babycare books,' Maureen yelled after her. 'They seriously damage your peace of mind.'

On her way home, Maggie stopped at the local supermarket for a tin of soup and a half bottle of whiskey. There were no messages waiting for her; Conor had not phoned. Later in the evening, she trailed a bag of washing round the corner to the laundrette (she supposed that now there was *another woman*, Conor's machine was out of bounds). Whilst she waited for her clothes to dry, she drew up a provisional list of the qualities she would look for in the father of her child. Tall. Irish. She crossed out tall. A contradiction in terms. She couldn't be that lucky twice. She started again. Irish. Witty. Reasonably attractive. HIV-negative. Very intelligent. Some small eccentricities. Imaginative. Sensitive. Warm-hearted... 'And where,' asked her mother, 'do you think you're going to find a man like that?' Maggie crumpled up the list and threw it into the rubbish bin. Perhaps she would put an ad in *In Dublin*. £30 offered for suitable sperm. Candidates selected by interview. Only those with the highest standards of hygiene and intelligence need apply. Free meal for successful applicant. She took the washing out of the dryer and went back to the flat.

She poured herself a glass of whiskey, christening

Conor's birthday present in the process (how appropriate, she thought, that he had bought only one glass). She plugged in the iron. Perhaps Maureen was right, perhaps she was being foolish. What if the child turned out to be handicapped, for instance, how would she cope with that on her own? She untangled the sleeves of a shirt and laid it out on the kitchen table which, since Nolan had been too mean to provide an ironing board, was where she did all her ironing.

There were other things to be considered. How would her friends react? Would they be embarrassed, would they stop inviting her to parties? Would Trinity view her differently because she was a single parent - as someone flighty and irresponsible and not to be trusted? And what about people like Charlotte and Giles? She tunnelled the nose of the iron rather viciously up the sleeve. No, Charlotte and Giles would react with total indifference to anything she did in that line, provided of course that she didn't bring the child with her when she visited. They (especially Giles) were always going on about what a drag children were. Well, it's easily solved, she thought, I simply won't visit them any more. It must be over a year since I last saw them anyway. She finished the whiskey and plonked another shirt on the table.

There would be sleepless nights to be endured, regular meals to be prepared, a whole new way of life to get used to. She would never be able to go out without making intricate and elaborate arrangements for sitters. Later on, there would be the business of ferrying the child to and from school every day (boarding school was out of the question; she wasn't going through all that just to hand her child over to somebody else). There would be ballet classes, riding lessons and whatever else kind of lessons it was thought necessary for children to participate in nowadays. Was she ready, she wondered, for the changes a child would bring? More important, would she be able to give it a fulfilling and happy life? It seemed almost too much to ask of one person on her own. Then she thought of all the love hoarded up inside her over the years, which no one had ever seemed to want, and she knew it would be all right.

Chapter Four

It was her interview. Dressed in a slinky black dress slashed to the thigh, Maggie flung open the door. Ten pairs of eyes (they were bound to be all male - Trinity wouldn't let a woman do anything as serious as sit on a committee) turned towards her, spellbound. The Junior Promotions Committee fell over itself in its efforts to find her a chair, straighten its tie, take its finger out of its nose.

She smiled graciously, to put them at their ease.

'Now Dr James, in your case this interview is, as you will have guessed, a mere formality.' The Provost of Trinity beamed at her. 'No institution could afford to lose a woman with your assets... er, credentials.'

Alternative scenario. She entered briskly, hair drawn back in a bun, straight tweed skirt, Ron's glasses perched on her nose.

'Dr James, I see from your cv that you are well on your way to becoming a scholar of international reputation. Just the sort of person this university needs. We were wondering whether you would find time in your busy schedule to do us the honour of giving a public lecture on a topic of your choice?'

Scenario number three. She slouched in dressed in jeans, T-shirt and Prue's earrings.

'Dr James, your radical approach and ability to interact with your students have been much appreciated over the past three years. The university needs a breath of fresh air. We realise that we have sometimes been slow to move with the times.' That couldn't be Dr McGregor, surely? 'We look to people like you to point the way forward.'

Fourth scenario (and most probable). She sat there as they pulled her three academic articles to pieces.

'We note that you adopt a populist approach to your subject. Have you considered taking up journalism?'

'There have been complaints from the students. They feel that you don't take them altogether seriously.'

'Your absence from Faculty meetings has been observed with alarm.'

'Tell me, Dr James, what do you perceive to be your role here?'

It didn't bear thinking about. She rang Conor. There was no reply. She couldn't face the thought of another evening in and anyway, there was nothing left to iron. She rang Julian on the internal phone.

'Hello Julian. Maggie James here.' She took a deep breath. She wasn't used to doing this. 'I was wondering how you would feel about a drink tonight after work?' She scribbled furiously on her blotting pad.

'Tonight?' He sounded mildly surprised.

Her courage faltered. 'You don't have to. It doesn't matter. It was only a...'

'No, that's OK. What time?'

'About eight?'

'Fine. Where?'

'Oh, anywhere.'

'The Bailey?'

'Right.'

She put down the receiver. Amazing, she thought. It's actually quite easy. She did a dance around her desk and went to collect her post. In the office she bumped into Fergus. She looked at her watch. It was eleven o'clock.

'Hello, Fergus. This is a surprise. What are you doing in so early? You're not ill, are you?'

'Life is on the upturn,' he said smugly. 'Now that Anna has moved in and I don't have to spend the afternoons in bed like the unemployed, I'm getting my career restarted. Have you remembered the sheets by the way?'

'Yes.' They walked back to her office. 'How is Anna?'

'Fine... apart from lack of sleep and a husband who sobs down the phone.'

She handed him the sheets. 'Go gently on them. They're my best pair.'

'Thanks, Maggie, you're a pal.'

'Fergus, if you say that once more, I'll scream.'

He looked puzzled. 'Why, what's wrong?'

'Sometimes I get the feeling that you don't see me as a woman at all.'

'Of course you're a woman. What else would you be? This isn't like you, Maggie. Aren't you feeling well?'

'I'm fine,' she replied, through gritted teeth. 'Just try to remember I'm a woman, that's all.'

'Sure.' He grinned. 'Who else but a woman would have clean sheets to give me?'

'Fergus!' She threw a pencil sharpener at him, but he was out of the door too fast.

On the way to her date with Julian, she was overcome by panic. After all she hardly knew the man - had just passed the time of day with him in the corridor and at Faculty meetings. What shall we find to talk about? she wondered. Hell's bells, perhaps he thinks I do this all the time, asking men for dates. Not a date, a drink, she corrected herself - and no talk of babies. Yet. She turned the corner and was about to flee but Julian was already there, sitting on the pavement outside the Bailey. Dressed in baggy cream trousers and a tweed jacket, he looked like something out of an old Fifties photograph.

'Bit previous.' He grinned, the lock of hair flopping over into his eyes as he looked up. 'I thought I might get a table but as you see, they're all taken.' He waved a large hand about, narrowly missing the groin of a man standing behind him. 'So we'll have to squat here like a couple of tramps. Unless you'd rather sit inside?'

'Here's fine.' She wished he wouldn't shout so in that upper-class English voice of his. Already people were staring. Nervously she bit a nail.

'Good. Plonk yourself down then and bag that bit of kerb whilst I get the drinks. What can I fetch you?'

'A glass of wine, please,' she murmured, hoping that he would take the hint and lower his voice too, but at the same time relieved, in a cowardly sort of way, that he seemed to have everything organised.

He went inside to the bar and Maggie sat down on the pavement. There was a vaguely blue tinge to the sky. It hadn't rained for at least three hours and the scattered tables and umbrellas showed that this corner of Dublin at least, was making a brave attempt to emulate the South of France, even down to small details like the authentic sewer smell coming up through the drain on her right.

She wondered whether Julian had a girlfriend - or boyfriend, she thought, remembering that night at Moira's do. Yes, perhaps he was gay. That wouldn't get her very far. Serve her right, Maureen would say. And even if he wasn't strictly speaking gay, what if he had some nasty disease, what if he had Aids? That terrible picture of sleeping with all the other person's lovers -

one would need several king-size beds to accommodate the whole of Julian's past, she imagined. He was an attractive man. And what about using a condom? Nowadays they said it was really stupid not to. But then that would defeat the whole purpose. Oh God, she groaned, her head in her hands. This is all far too complicated.

'What's the matter? Overcome by the drainage?' He had arrived back with a bottle and two glasses. 'Did you know that twenty per cent of the Irish nation now makes its own wine?' He sat down on the pavement beside her.

'I wouldn't be at all surprised. Elderflower wine, carrot wine, parsnip wine - if it grows, ferment it,' she gabbled, a trifle hysterically. 'Do you ever wonder, Julian, what you, an Englishman, are doing in this country?'

'Frequently.' He poured her some wine. 'Cheers. The proper time to be here for people like us was a hundred years ago. We'd have lived off the sweat of the peasants, ridden to horse and hounds, gone to balls in big country houses, had servants to draw the water for our bath and bring us cocoa in bed...' He closed his eyes in contemplation. 'All totally immoral. But fun.'

'Whereas now, we're blamed for seven hundred years of oppression, genocide through starvation, the destruction of forests...'

'Exactly.' He opened his eyes. 'In Newcastle, we lived in a terrace house with an outside lavatory but because I'm a lecturer at Trinity, I'm treated like a West Brit. I've never even seen a bloody foxhunt.'

'I know. Sometimes I feel as if I personally fought in Cromwell's army.' She swilled the wine round in the bottom of her glass, drank it and held out her glass for more. 'I didn't realise you were a Geordie, Julian. You don't have a Northern accent.'

'Lost it at Sussex. Had to get rid of it when I went South to university. You Southerners are full of prejudices.'

'Oh,' she said, looking at him with wide open eyes, 'you mean you don't all drink tea off saucers and eat pease pudding three times a day?'

'Watch it.' He poked her in the ribs.

It's all right, she thought. It'll be all right. We'll treat the subject, if it comes up, as a joke.

There was a loud crash to their left.

'*Merde!*' Norman stood in the road, a pint of Smithwicks swilling over his open-toed sandals.

'Hello, Norman.'

'Oh, hello, Maggie. Hello, Julian. Excuse the French.' He shook his feet and wrung out the bottoms of his jeans. 'Which silly turd left a glass in the middle of the road?' He looked down at his sodden jeans. His eyes filled with tears. 'Why does everything happen to me?' He walked, rather wetly, into the pub.

'Why was Norman crying?' murmured Julian.

'You noticed too. I wonder what it means?'

'Of course, if you're American, it's an entirely different matter.'

'What is?' asked Maggie, whose mind had been running on Norman's tears.

'In Ireland, if you're American, you're accepted. Take Bridget O'Doherty, for instance...'

'She's Canadian.'

'Well, still foreign. Yet she feels totally at home here...'

'She married an Irishman.'

'Does that make any difference?'

'I think it does,' replied Maggie, wistfully. 'Putting down roots and all that.'

'Well, as to that,' Julian emptied the last of the wine into their glasses and tipped the dregs into the gutter, 'she's gone and pulled them up again.'

'Oh?'

'She's left her husband.' He inspected the label on the bottle. 'This wine is not half bad, incidentally.'

'Left her husband?' Maggie prompted.

'Yes. Pity really. Now there's my definition of a grown up.'

'Who?'

'Bridget's husband. He's managing director of an international company, that is to say, unlike you and me, he works in the real world, types his letters into his laptop computer with a G and T at his elbow, whilst flying Concorde.'

She laughed. 'If that's your definition, I'll never be grown up in this lifetime.'

'Me neither, not on a lecturer's salary.'

'They'd been together quite a while, hadn't they?'

'Ten years.'

'Wow! It must be pretty traumatic to split up after all that time.' To Maggie, whose lengthiest relationship had been with Conor, anything over three years seemed an awe-inspiring amount of time to spend with the same person.

Julian shrugged. 'The writing's been on the wall for some months now, apparently. It's hard on the kid, though.'

The wine glass paused on its way to Maggie's mouth. 'They have a child?'

'A girl of about four, I believe.'

Maggie thought hard. 'Did this happen recently,

Julian?'

'A few days ago, I think. Why?'

'Nothing, nothing. It just occurred to me that... It doesn't matter.' She finished her wine. Suddenly the thought of her empty flat seemed quite unappealing. Do I dare? she wondered.

'Are you um... hungry? I could - you know - cook you something at my place. Nothing elaborate, mind.'
He grinned. 'I never refuse the offer of a free meal. I'll pick up some wine.'

She swallowed. It was all turning out to be far simpler than she had imagined. She gave him instructions on how to get to her flat. 'You can phone from there, if you like.'

'Phone? Who?'

She flushed. 'Well, I thought perhaps...'

He laughed. 'There's no one expecting me, if that's what you mean. I live alone. It's the only way to ensure I'm always at my desk by seven.'

'I suppose you've hit thirty too,' Maggie commented, as they walked back to their cars. 'Why are men of thirty so obsessed with their careers?'

'Thirty is the horror age for men,' he said, seriously. 'Between thirty and forty they've got to succeed or they've had it.' She yawned, extensively. 'It's the same with women,' he added. 'Only in their case, it's usually babies.'

'I see.' She got into her car.

She bought avocados and tuna from the corner shop and some pork steak, mushrooms and yoghurt to eat with rice, which was one thing she did have in the flat. She did a whirlwind tidy up, sweeping off the books and journals that lay scattered across the table in the living room and heaping them into neat piles in the corner. She carried a mountain of unmarked essays into the bedroom and shoved them under the bed (Julian had always seemed to her like a man who would mark his essays on time). She closed the bedroom door, which usually stood open, then thought that looked too tight-arsed and suspicious, so compromised and left it slightly ajar. This is madness, she told herself. Act like a normal human being; he's only here for dinner. Since living with Conor, she had got out of the way of the single life; she was no longer sure how things were done. Thinking of Conor led her on to Bridget. Bridget, Bridget, she thought, you are beginning to look like the enemy. She stuck her knife ruthlessly into an avocado and slit it open just as the doorbell rang.

Julian was standing on the steps, a bottle of wine under each arm. He pointed silently downwards in the direction of the basement and mouthed, 'Landlord.'

'Is he peeping again? It's all right,' she whispered. 'You can stop shuffling around like a Russian spy. It's only after midnight that the situation changes. Conor calls it the anti-heterosexual rule.' She scanned his face carefully for clues. But if Julian was gay, the expression on his face gave nothing away.

Whilst she mixed the tuna and mayonnaise and filled the avocados, he opened one of the bottles he had brought.

'Mmm. Very good. Definitely not elderflower,' she said, tasting it.

'I should think not. I know my wines.'

She prepared the yoghurt and mushroom sauce, squeezed lemon juice over the tuna mixture and placed the avocados on the table. They sat down to eat.

Now that the two of them were alone, she felt an

attack of shyness coming on. To fight it off, she said hurriedly, choosing the only subject she was certain would interest him, 'What are you working on at the moment, Julian?'

'Attitudes to sex - what's the matter?'

'Nothing. Go on.'

'How they're coloured by one's first sexual encounter. I'm giving a paper at a conference in Birmingham in a few weeks' time. I might do a little research on you when you've drunk some more wine.' She got up nervously to give the sauce a stir. 'Talking of such matters, how are things with Conor? I ran into him in college yesterday.'

So it *was* him she had seen. She finished frying the pork steak, poured the sauce over it and dished it out onto two plates. 'Where?'

'Checking up, eh? I can't remember exactly. Somewhere in the Arts Building. Third floor, I think.'

She sat down. The art history department was on the third floor. Bridget again. She looked thoughtful.

'You're looking thoughtful,' said Julian, his mouth full of pork steak. 'What's up?'

'He's left me.'

He swallowed. 'Oh dear. Still... a journalist...'

'The trouble with you, Julian, is that you're a terrible snob.'

He grinned. 'Working-class insecurity. I admit it. At home we had flying ducks over the mantelpiece, lino in the hall and a front room where the furniture was kept in covers and never used except when we had guests. We ate dinner at lunchtime and high tea at dinner. I've a lot to live down. That's why I adore being in Ireland. None of that matters over here.'

'One needs roots, don't you think?' she said, putting

out some biscuits and cheese.

'Why?'

'Well, if something happened, a crisis or something...' It seemed to her so obvious why that she found it difficult to put into words.

'I've good friends, they'd see me through. I like being rootless. I found family life rather stifling, to tell you the truth.'

Oh dear, she thought.

'Tell you what though, I'm a snob about cheese.' He tapped the Brie with his knife. 'This one looks set in its ways.'

'I bought it yesterday. It hasn't had time to run away yet.'

'Tut tut. Cheese should be five days old before you serve it - at least to guests as discerning as myself.'

'Huh! I bet you didn't learn that in Newcastle.'

'No indeed, my dear. Up there, we had cheese once a year - on Christmas Day with our cake.'

'With cake? Yeuck!'

'It's very good. You should try it. A nice slice of Wensleydale with the mince pies. Goes down a treat.'

'I'll make the coffee. No Wensleydale, I'm afraid. What about a whiskey?'

'A small one. Have to keep a clear head.'

'For the office?'

'Exactly.'

She felt she was getting the hang of conversation with Julian.

He got up from the table, settled his bulky body into the outsize bean bag that took the place of a sofa and stretched out. Maggie sat opposite him in the only armchair Nolan had deemed it necessary to provide.

'Right then,' he said, 'tell me about your first sexual

encounter.'

'Well, I...'

'Don't be coy. This is all in the interests of science, you realise.'

'Golly! Well... er...' Fortunately or unfortunately, the wine had begun to go to her head. She was beginning to feel quite splendid. This had the effect of loosening her tongue. 'Let's see. London, late seventies. It wasn't exactly planned. It was his first time too. At least he said it was and I believed him. We'd spent a lot of afternoons lying together naked on the bed in his hall of residence, getting used to the idea, I suppose. All of a sudden, we decided to have it over with. Virginity was beginning to weigh heavily on both of us. We wanted to get on with the rest of life. He went down to buy contraceptives from the slot machine in the men's toilet. Afterwards (it was fairly quick, as you might imagine), I lay back listening to Neil Young, you know, the one with church bells, a maid and a man, and I was thinking how kind of symbolic it was when he said, "I feel as if I've just scored a goal for the first team." He played for the university, so I guess it was some sort of a compliment to be ranked with football in his life. I didn't think so at the time, though.'

'Did you come?' he asked, from the floor.

'Jesus, Julian! Are you taking notes on all this? I can't remember. Probably not. Did women come in those days?'

'So basically your first sexual experience was comic? How interesting.' He took out his notebook.

'Comic with tragic undertones. He left me some weeks later. It was only wanting to lose our virginity that had kept us together. Still, I like to think that we started each other off on our sexual adventures. I often wonder how he's made out since.'

Julian paused in his note taking.

'Do you think that the relatively ephemeral nature of this first sexual encounter affected your later relations with men?'

'Put a sock in it, Julian.'

He grinned. 'You weren't afraid of getting pregnant?'

'No, not really. Gosh, it's so hard to remember. Perhaps I was, a little. It was such a disaster then, pregnancy, wasn't it? I remember one girl had to leave in a hurry half way through the course to get married. Others, well...'

'Abortions?'

'Yes.' She wondered why all of a sudden she found it so hard to say that word. How long ago it all seemed, how differently she had felt then.

'But not you?'

'No, thank God, I never had to face that, but I saw what it did to other women...' She fidgeted with her coffee cup and cast him a sidelong glance. 'Well, and what about you? I think I'm entitled to know after telling you all that.'

'Me? I'm going through a celibate phase,' he replied, shutting up his notebook and putting it back in his pocket. Oh dear, she thought. 'I find it's the only way I can get any work done. Anyway, with this Aids business...'

'Julian, can I ask you something?'

His eyes narrowed. 'Sure, fire away.'

'Are you gay?'

'Gay?' For a moment, he looked puzzled. Then he smiled and the lock of hair once more fell over into his eyes, making him look really very attractive, she thought. 'Oh, you mean Moira's party?' He burrowed his large behind into the bean bag. 'That was research again. I'm examining the gay scene in Dublin. Terrible existence those people have, clanking around in chains and doing bizarre things with small animals. That's life in the fast lane,' he added hastily. 'I wouldn't want you to think I'm prejudiced. Some of my best friends are..'

'Quite.' She got up to pour them both another coffee. 'Julian, tell me something - do you find Bridget O'Doherty attractive?' Please say no, she thought. Oh God, please say no and then perhaps I can believe Conor doesn't like her, either.

'Bridget? I've never thought of her in that way. As long as I've known her she's been married - and cutting in on other people isn't my style.' He sighed. 'I suppose if ever I come out of this celibate phase, basically what I'll be looking for is a user-friendly woman.'

'But if you didn't know she was married,' Maggie persisted. 'Would you be attracted to her then?'

He scratched his large nose. 'I don't know, American women are so big and clean - all those white teeth - I'm not sure one could feel romantic about them... but she's a sweet, homely sort of woman.'

'An Irish mother type?'

'Sort of. Very different from you.'

Unaccountably, she felt a stab of pain. 'What, don't you think I'd make a good mother?'

'Oh, I don't know about that. I meant that I've, well, always thought of you as a colleague. I mean you work late. You're not distracted like other women by homes, husbands and babies. You're financially independent, you live on your own...'

'A bit like a man, you mean?'

'I suppose you are, a little. Your life isn't any

different from mine really, is it? We earn the same salary, cook for ourselves... I suppose it's inevitable that the sexes will become more and more alike in the way they live.'

'Surely that's a bad thing? I mean, there must be some differences.'

'Well, I do admit to feeling occasionally, when I get out the hoover, that my masculinity is being eroded in some vital way.' He laughed. 'And then there are still plenty of women content (Lord knows why!) to give up their careers for babies - but that's not likely to happen to you.'

'Why not?'

He shrugged. 'You're just not that sort.'

'I do feel broody sometimes, you know,' she replied stiffly. 'Even me.'

'Of course you do. The old stereotypes are bound to reassert themselves from time to time. The thing is to recognise them for what they are and work out a way to ignore them.'

Maggie was silent.

'I say, you're not offended, are you? I mean, you're an attractive woman.'

'I'm glad you said that.' She grimaced. 'I was beginning to feel I had sprouted a moustache.'

There was a silence. She fiddled with her coffee spoon. Soon he would be gone. It was now or never.

'What about you, Julian, wouldn't you fancy being a father sometime?'

'I did have children once, you know.' He laughed at the expression on her face. 'It's all right, I haven't abandoned them. They were fantasy children.'

This sounded more promising. She smiled encouragement.

'I was going out with this high-powered business woman, Rachel,' he lingered for a moment on the name. 'She had her own PR company. Flew all over the world. We saw each other only at weekends. Children, marriage even, were out of the question as far as she was concerned. So we invented some. Jennifer and Hugh were their names. Six and three, respectively. Jennifer was down for Roedean - the kind of place *you* went to, I imagine...'

'You're wrong,' she said, quickly. 'I went to the Thomas More comprehensive in Mill Hill.'

'Oh? I could have sworn...' For a second, he looked nonplussed. 'I must be losing my touch.' He shrugged. 'Oh, well. Hugh, who was sporty, was to go to Rugby. *Not* my old school.' He paused, obviously enjoying his memories. 'We even went so far as to buy toys for them. Yes, she was special, was Rachel. After her, well...' He gazed down at the carpet and sighed. 'Ties, ties. I don't think I'm ready yet to try again.'

She hesitated. 'But if there were no ties?'

Something in her tone made him glance up. 'What are you saying, Maggie?'

She took a deep breath and said, very quickly, not looking at him, 'I'm thinking of having a child. I mean on my own, as a single parent. I wondered whether...'

'Ah.' There was a silence. She felt herself going redder and redder. 'Look at me, Maggie.' And, as she kept her head averted, he got up off the floor and walked round till he could see the expression on her face. Then she did look up. He was smiling at her, quite gently.

'Sorry.' She screwed up her face. 'Oh God, I feel so embarrassed.'

'It's OK, it's OK,' he said softly, bending over her.

'I'm touched and slightly flattered that you should have thought of me.'

'But?'

'But I couldn't do it.' He straightened up.

'Oh.'

'Sorry, Maggie. It must be something in my puritan Northern upbringing. I couldn't possibly father a child and then walk away.'

'No, of course not.' She willed the floor to open and swallow her up. 'It was a silly idea. Forget it. I don't know what I was thinking of.'

He sat back on his heels and looked at her.

'Perhaps not such a silly idea. You chose the wrong person to ask, that's all.'

'I feel so stupid!' she groaned.

He took her hands. 'Don't, you mustn't.'

'Promise you'll forget what I said, or I don't know how I'll face you ever again.'

'I've forgotten already.'

'Thanks.' She kept her eyes firmly fixed on her lap, feeling that she might burst into tears at any moment.

'Hey, look at me.' Reluctantly, she met his gaze. 'Friends are what I need right now. How about it?'

'Friends. OK.'

'Good. And now we're going to have a good long smooch in the Hollywood tradition. So long,' he added,' as you promise me one thing.'

'What's that?'

'That it won't make you pregnant.'

She smiled.

'That's better.' He brushed his lips against hers, then kissed her lengthily and well. He felt so warm and solid in her arms, so utterly dependable. But it was illusions like that she must guard against, after Conor.

She could not afford to be taken in a second time.

'Mmm,' he murmured. 'Delightful, really delightful. And now I must go. If I stayed, who knows what might happen and my celibacy phase isn't due to end for another seven and a half weeks.' He stood up and put on his jacket. 'Thanks for the meal. I'll cook you one some time.'

'Equality.' She winced.

'Don't knock it. The advantages are all on your side.'

She accompanied him down the stairs to the front door.

'You know,' he said solemnly, 'babies are terrifically exhausting things. If I were you, I should put off having one till you're at least thirty-five and a Fellow.' He waved and was gone.

She shut the door and went back upstairs.

'You can't expect a man to understand,' whispered her mother.

'Do what feels right,' said her father. 'Never mind about fellowships and promotion.'

It feels right to want a baby, Dad. It really does, she thought, staring at the dirty dishes in the sink.

Chapter Five

At five the next morning, Maggie woke up in a cold
sweat. In her dreams, Bridget O'Doherty had
metamorphosed into a raving beauty. Damn, she
thought, how well it all fitted in - the need for secrecy
(gossip spread more easily than margarine at Trinity),
Bridget's furtive glances across the Common Room,
Conor's sudden appearance in the Arts Building. F2 for
feminine intuition, Maggie James, she thought. Come
back for resits in September.

At five in the morning, there was not much else to do
but fantasise ... about pushing Bridget into Blessington
lake, bribing a student to seduce her in the Front
Square, challenging her to a duel on Stephen's Green.

She went back to sleep and dreamt about giving
birth. She was in the delivery room surrounded by
people in white coats. She felt enormous; she was
straining, straining to push out the new life. It wasn't
so much painful as exhilarating and somehow oddly
sexual. She woke at eight, feeling drained and
exhausted, a hollow sensation in the pit of her stomach.
With difficulty, she dragged herself out of bed and into
work.

In the office, she had a phone call from an obscenely
exuberant Fergus. To prick his bubble a little and
because she felt like complaining to someone, Maggie
told him of her suspicions about Bridget and Conor.

'Oh, I meant to tell you,' he said cheerfully. 'I saw
them walking down Grafton Street together yesterday

afternoon.'

'Jeepers, Fergus, you might have told me sooner. How walking?'

'Well you know, one foot in front of the other, arms swinging. Pretty normal for a couple of bipeds.'

'Fergus! Were they holding hands, did their eyes sparkle, were their heads touching, that sort of thing?'

'Oh no. Nothing like that.'

Now, a woman, she thought, would have been able to give all the details. She rang Maureen.

'I think I've found out who the other woman is.' She outlined her reasons.

'Sounds like Bridget all right,' agreed Maureen. 'What are you going to do about it?'

'Blow their cover for a start.'

'Quite right. And give Conor a kick in the balls from me.'

'Thanks, Maureen. You're a good friend.'

'I'm in the middle of making a list of nice fathers for you. I've... Oh hell, got to go, Amber's trying to eat the coal. I'll give you a ring tomorrow.'

'OK.' She hesitated. She had no wish to become the talk of Dublin. 'Maureen... um... you haven't told Art, have you?'

'Not at all. What do you take me for?'

'Sorry.'

'I should think so. 'Bye.'

She gathered up her notes for a lecture on sixteenth-century medical theory. Was it morally right, she wondered, to explain to these bright first year girls, with their careers in front of them, the old theories about the womb having a life of its own and an independent yearning for procreation? It seemed cruel to disillusion them so early on in life, to tell them that the mothering instinct couldn't be fought, that even if they rose to be company directors, it would get them in the end. On the other hand, it seemed wrong to play it down as had been the fashion when she was growing up and the emphasis had been, not on motherhood, but on new and more efficient methods of contraception. The media, her teachers, her parents had constantly warned of the horrors of an unwanted pregnancy, but never once mentioned the misery of childlessness. It was an insoluble problem. Perhaps she would just give them the page reference.

Coming out of the lecture room an hour later, she noticed old Professor Mayhew wandering around with a grubby piece of paper in his hand. Mayhew had gone senile a while back and been awarded a personal chair. He was muttering to himself. As she walked past, he thrust the piece of paper in front of her face.

'I found this on the floor,' he grunted, his small, moist eyes glittering with rage. 'It shouldn't be on the floor. Piggott-Smith's my friend. Put it back at once.'

'Certainly, Professor.' (It was best to play safe. They might have forgotten to remove Mayhew from the Junior Promotions Committee). She decanted her books onto the floor and dashed to a nearby notice board to pin up what she now saw was an announcement of a forthcoming presentation to Professor Piggott-Smith, formerly Professor of history, of a book of essays in his honour. There had been some sense (not a lot) in Mayhew's comments.

'There, that's better, isn't it?' she said, in her head-nurse-of-a-psychiatric-ward voice.

Mayhew pressed his fat little body up against hers. She wondered when he had last had a bath.

'It's my birthday today, you know,' he said, with a

hint of menace.

'Is it? That's nice,' stammered Maggie.

'Well, you might wish me happy birthday.'

'Of course. Sorry. Many happy returns.'

She was wondering whether she should ask him how old he was and what he was doing to celebrate when he suddenly turned and began muttering his way back down the corridor. In the three years she had been at Trinity, Mayhew had never once addressed a word to her. Maggie looked forward to another conversation with him in 1992.

The phone was ringing as she reached her office. Honestly, Fergus, she thought, are hourly bulletins on the state of your love life really necessary?

'It's me,' said Conor.

She sank into the swivel chair and did a half turn. 'Hello, me.'

'Are you free for coffee this afternoon?'

Was she free!

'I think so,' she replied, doing her best to sound as if she was consulting a very full diary.

'Bewleys then, at three.'

She wondered, as she put down the phone, whether she should have pretended to be busy all afternoon. A bit of mystery might do no harm... What was she talking about? She'd lived with Conor for two and a half years. He knew how often she brushed her teeth, how many cups of coffee she drank a day, who her favourite newsreaders were. She had no mystery left at all.

There was a tap at her door.

'*Entrez.*'

It was Norman. 'I say Maggie, are you going to this Piggott-Smith thingie? I've just seen the notice.'

'I pinned it up.' She described her highly condensed conversation with Mayhew.

'That man is a menace. They really ought to lock him up.'

Appropriate sentiments, she thought, from an ex-policeman.

'The thing is, I was hoping to skip the presentation but the secretary's told me that Big White Chief Gardener wants us all to be there. Sodding bore. I thought if you skipped it, so would I. I've an important appointment that afternoon.' He flicked back his hair which seemed to have grown longer in recent weeks.

'I have to be there, Norman, I have to keep my nose clean. I go before the Junior Promotions Committee in a few weeks' time.'

'Oh dear.' He heaved a sigh. 'Life's so complicated, isn't it?'

For a moment she feared he was going to burst into tears again. What is the matter with him, she wondered. A man who looks like the toughest officer on the force shouldn't keep bursting into tears.

Norman recovered himself and wandered around the room, inspecting her books, her Amstrad, picking up postcards, rearranging pencils, very much like a policeman looking for clues, she thought. 'Your plants need watering,' he remarked, unnecessarily. Maggie had two kinds of colleagues, those who hovered uncertainly in the doorway and those who came to stay. Norman was one of the latter. She could never make up her mind which sort she preferred.

He fingered a modern edition of a sixteenth-century medical work. 'What is the structuralist interpretation of this?'

Maggie grimaced at the waste paper bin. 'Must you,

Norman? This office is a structuralist-free zone. Keep your grubby little mind off the sixteenth century.'

'Okay, okay, so you don't want to move with the times.' He picked up the book and began leafing through it. 'What's between you and McGregor?' he asked suddenly.

Maggie lurched forward in her chair. 'What do you mean? What have you heard?'

'Oh, nothing in particular,' he replied, with irritating vagueness. 'I thought I'd let you know - he's been co-opted onto the Junior Promotions Committee.'

'What? Hell's bells!'

'Probably nothing to worry about. As I say, I thought you ought to know, as one friend to another.' He looked up from his book. 'We are friends, aren't we, Maggie?'

'Y... yes,' she said uncertainly.

'Good.' He gazed into the middle distance, fingering his chin. 'You're a woman, you see...'

'Thank God someone's noticed,' she muttered.

'What?'

'Nothing.'

'I don't have many women friends.'

Where was this leading?

'There's your wife,' she pointed out.

'Ah, my wife...' He paused. 'That's different.' He looked back at the book. 'I say, did they have a theory on impotence in the sixteenth century?'

'I'm not sure. I think they mainly treated it as a bit of a joke.'

'Joke?' He frowned. 'Can I borrow this?' He held up a volume on Tiresias.

'Of course.'

'See you then. 'Bye.'

He went out, tripping over a chair on his way and banging his shoulder against the wall. Sometimes she worried that there was a sticky end in store for Norman. These days his body seemed out of his control. And what was all that about being friends? What had he been getting at?

Just after three, she was sitting on the veranda at Bewleys with Conor, watching young people, dressed in whites and yellows and pinks, saunter past in the street below. There was a holiday feel in the air. Up the road, a crowd stood watching a couple of mime artists in black evening clothes, their faces chalked an eerie white. Directly opposite the café, a sweet-faced woman in a beige mackintosh stood forlornly in a doorway with a pile of pamphlets in her hand. Publicity for some Catholic mission or other, judging by the type of people she was attempting to stop - old age pensioners, young women with small children in tow. She was doing badly. The Hari Krishna people had taken all her trade. They stood in the middle of the road, in their long orange robes and dirty plimsolls, handing out leaflets and records and confidently haranguing passers-by. A woman laden down with shopping bags went past, dragging a screaming three-year old. As Maggie watched, the woman stopped and gave the child a wallop across the back of its legs. Several passers-by stared after her in disapproval. If I had a child, thought Maggie, I would never... But she didn't, so what right had she to judge?

She stared at Conor calmly sitting opposite her in his leather jacket and red trousers, eating a bun and drinking Jersey milk. How can he not understand, she thought, gripping the edge of the table. How can he not see that this is tearing me apart?

His words drifted over her. 'Reception... all the big guys will be there... she's going to publish me every month... the publicity will be good for me... keeps my name in circulation.'

She thought of what Fergus had once said: that Conor was a true child of Sixties Ireland when money and economic growth were everything and Dublin copied swinging, capitalist London. His words kept slipping in and out of her consciousness. She found it hard to concentrate. She was thinking that today was Friday and that he might be sleeping with Bridget tonight. And what's more, Bridget was a *mother*. Maggie had a sudden mental picture of herself looking down on both of them sitting there on the balcony at Bewleys, Conor waving his hands about, talking non stop, she with her head on one side, stirring her coffee. She wondered gloomily whether this was what the psychologists called 'the out-of-body' experience.

'Are you all right?'

She shook herself. 'Yes, fine. I'm glad things are going so well for you.' 'Liar,' said her mother. 'What you really want is for him to fail at something and come running back to you.' Well, and I would look after him, she thought, for I understand him, understand the insecurity (and the ambition) that pushes him on. And his need for tenderness.

'Remember when you were unemployed and I was just starting out as a lecturer and we used to make a bottle of wine last all week?' she said.

'It seems like years ago. Another life.'

Every bond she tried to retie, he carefully undid again.

'I know who she is, anyway.' Oh Maggie, this is foolish, she thought.

He looked at her, considering.

'Well, if you do know, I hope you'll be discreet. There are a lot of people involved here.'

'I don't see why I should be in the least discreet. If you can't face up to the consequences of your actions, it's not my fault.' Hell, this wasn't at all the way she had meant it to go.

He looked at his watch. 'I have to get back.'

'That's right, run away.'

'Maggie, I don't want a scene.'

People were already glancing over at them. She contemplated giving them value for money by pushing Conor off the balcony. But where would that get her? They paid their bill, scrupulously dividing up the amount between them, and left.

'Why did you phone me then?' she asked, as they hurried down the stairs and into the street.

'I wanted to see you, that's all. I told you - I'm still fond of you.'

'Thanks a bunch! Just watch out, that's all. Just you watch out!' She was shaking.

'Is that a threat?' He smiled slightly and moved on down Grafton Street, leaving her standing on the pavement feeling faintly ridiculous.

'And tell her to stop staring at me across the Common Room,' she shouted after him.

Oh dear, she thought, I have not come out of this well.

Chapter Six

Conor had phoned. 'Bridget's moving in with me,' he said. 'I have to tell you. She's pregnant. I've always wanted a child.'

'You could have had one from me, me, me!' she cried, her womb aching with emptiness.

'Oh no. You don't want children. You're not that sort of woman. You're going to be a star, like me. A child would only get in your way.'

She woke up with Conor's name on her lips and her face wet with tears. Her jaw felt stiff, her legs tingled as if someone was pulling sharply on her nerve ends. She wrapped the duvet around herself. She was tempted to take a sleeping pill and be numbed for the day - that way nothing would touch her. 'Pull yourself together,' said her mother. 'Sod it,' said her father. 'It's the weekend. Why don't you spend the day in bed?' 'Just because one man lets you down, you go to pieces,' sniffed her mother. He was special. 'You're wasting your time. He'll never come back to you.' Give me a break, you two. She buried her head in her pillow to drown their jangling voices.

Through the pillow, she heard the phone ringing down in the hall. Conor? 'Come back Maggie. All is forgiven. Bridget's turned out to be frigid/lesbian/a nymphomaniac.'

It was Maureen. She could hear Amber shrieking in the background.

'Maggie, listen, I've got it. Fergus.'

She shook her head to clear the cobwebs. 'What are you talking about?'

'Fergus McKenna. The ideal man. Irish (you wanted an Irish child), not totally unattractive, intelligent, even if he does work in that place...'

'Maureen!'

'...An older man so he won't get sentimental...'

'Maureen! Fergus would never understand, he doesn't like children.'

'How do you know?'

'Stands to reason. He was married for eight years. If he'd wanted some he'd have had them by now, wouldn't he? Anyway, he's having this passionate love aff...'

'He only has to do it once, for God's sake; or at most a couple of times if it doesn't work immediately. Art! Please see to your daughter! And if he dislikes children, so much the better. I thought you wanted to bring it up on your own... What are you laughing for?'

'Sorry, it's just so funny! What ever made you think of Fergus? I've never seen him in that light before.'

'Well, you wouldn't want someone you didn't know anything about, would you? You could always get drunk. I'm sure it would be quite painless...'

'Maureen, it wouldn't work. For a start, Fergus thinks I'm a man.'

'What? Amber, stop that!'

'What's she doing?'

'Farting. She gets it from her father.'

'Oh dear. Look, Maureen, I'm really grateful, you know. I promise I'll think it over.' She giggled again. 'Fergus!'

'I was only trying to inject a sense of reality into the whole business,' Maureen replied, somewhat tartly, and rang off.

'Now that you're up,' said her mother, 'why don't you try getting your life sorted out?'

But where can I begin? she wondered, going back upstairs to put on a pair of jeans. There were so many things to be decided. If she lost her job, for instance, there would no longer be anything keeping her here; she could move back to England. But what she had told Maureen was true, she hated how England had become, greedy, selfish, violent. Was Ireland really any better though, she asked herself as she sat at the kitchen table, sipping her coffee. She decided to make a list (her mother was a great believer in lists).

She took out paper and a pencil and wrote down the things she hated most about Ireland - its conspicuous consumerism, its conviction that all the English were imperialists and royalists, its inability to be different from England, the way it cared so little about its national heritage that it allowed office blocks to be built over it, the way it had jettisoned its old values in the name of something called modernism. 'The rise of the Irish middle-class,' Fergus had said once, 'is eroding the difference between Protestant and Catholic in the Republic. Look how many Protestant churches have been shut down in the last few months. Even attendance at mass is falling off. Progress in Ireland will have been a gradual reductive process. We'll soon be secular Europeans devoted entirely to economic growth and consumerism.'

She listed the things she hated most about Conor - his fetish for gadgets (Sony Walkmans, answering machines, word processors, satellite dishes), his worship of all things English or, better still, American, his determination to 'get on', whatever the price.

To preserve the balance, she made another list of the things she hated most about herself - her boyish hips and small breasts, her feeling of being flattered when her male colleagues treated her as one of themselves, the way Irish people made her feel stiff and formal and slightly slow, her inability to offer any viable alternative to Conor's view of life...

'Be more positive,' said her mother.

'Emphasise the qualities that make you different from Conor,' said her father. 'The feminine ones.'

She had a sudden picture of herself pregnant and out of work, living in a damp bedsit somewhere - Nolan would be sure to draw the line at children and what other kind of lodging would a single, unemployed, pregnant woman be able to find in Dublin? Was this what it meant to be a woman? No thanks, Dad, she said, tearing up the lists. I'll stick to my career. It's safer. She heard Prue's voice: 'You're trapped, Maggie, trapped in a male-structured world.' No! she muttered, banging her fist on the table and making the sugar bowl jump. I refuse to believe it. I can control my life. I can have the things I need. It just doesn't seem like it at the moment.

She went shopping in the centre and found herself staring after every woman who passed by with a child, trying to work out how old she must be. Her spirits rose whenever she caught sight of a grey-haired woman with a toddler. It was a sign of hope, that she hadn't, after all, left it too late - though on second thoughts the woman might be an aunt, or even the grandmother (there were girls who looked no more than fifteen pushing buggies). How I have frittered away my time, she thought. Watching all this to-ing and fro-ing on the streets made her feel quite drained.

She sought refuge in Bewleys, choosing exactly the same table she had sat at the previous day with Conor- (One never knew. She might be lucky. A lot of people came into Bewleys on a Saturday).

She ordered a coffee and opened *The Irish Times*. A woman of forty-two had just given birth in the Rotunda - twins conceived by the GIFT method. Maggie loved this kind of story. She had been particularly impressed when a certain well-known film actress had had her first child at the age of forty-five - she still had the cutting somewhere. But these methods, GIFT, IVF, were only available in Ireland to married couples. If it didn't work for her, she wouldn't, as a single woman, be entitled to treatment. Infertility was a word which sent shivers down her spine, conjuring up in her mind a picture of a bleak landscape and dead trees. Sterile, barren. Terrible, dreadful words. Miscarriage was another.

At school, it had been a joke. Whenever they clambered over fences or through barbed wire, they would say to one another, 'Be careful now. You don't want to spoil your chances of a happy motherhood.' But what if she was unable to have children? What if all that contraception had been a waste of time? You couldn't be sure till you tried...

She supposed they were all married now, her classmates, leading grown up lives, worrying about mortgages, dry rot and finding the right prep school. She had been the only one of them with ambition, the only one who had bothered to take her A-levels seriously. And where had it got her? She skimmed along the surface of life, without ties, without responsibilities, without roots. It made her feel dizzy sometimes. She looked around at the other tables, all seemingly occupied by couples and families with small children. (She knew she was being selective. If she looked carefully enough, there were several people who, like herself, were sitting on their own, drinking their coffee and reading the newspaper). But I don't want to be like this, she thought, a shadow. I want to participate.

In the afternoon she went to the cinema. It was an American film about a woman who lost custody of her four-year-old daughter because her lover had unthinkingly allowed the child to touch his penis in the shower. There had been a lot of feminist debate about it. Hard-heartedly, Maggie decided she was unable to summon up much sympathy for the mother. Even if she did only see her daughter one weekend out of four, at least she had a child. She knew what it felt like.

Back in the flat later that evening, she was reading her way through the book on pregnancy and child care she had purchased that afternoon (resolution 3a) and wrapped in brown paper covers, in case anyone should call by unexpectedly and catch her with it, when the phone rang. She ran down to answer it.

'Hello, darling!' screeched Charlotte, following her usual custom of employing two vowels where one would do. 'What are you doing in on a Saturday evening?'

'Resting. Life has been extremely hectic recently. Parties and so on.' Lying to Charlotte was becoming a habit.

'Don't I just know the feeling? Darling, I have a lovely surprise for you. You'll never guess - Giles and I are coming to visit you.'

'Visit me?' Did Charlotte really say that? No, she must have misheard.

'Yes, visit you, darling. Isn't it marvellous?'

'Here in Dublin?'

'Well that's where you are, aren't you, darling?'

There was a silence whilst Maggie digested this news.

'Why?' she said, eventually. 'You've never visited me here before.' Oh shit, she thought.

'Darling! You've never invited us.'

'That's true,' she responded, instantly and meaningfully.

But Charlotte was not easily put off. 'We're leaving Antibes for California in a few days' time so we thought it would be splendid fun to call in and see you on the way.'

'It's not on the way. Why don't you fly direct? Nice to San Francisco. I'm sure there must be a service. I'll make enquiries for you.'

'No good, darling. You see, after visiting you, we want to motor on and spend some time with Gloria and Charles in their dear little house in Connemara. We plan to fly on to California from Shannon. Giles dug out a terrific agent in Antibes who has arranged it all for us. Rather a dashing young man.' She paused. 'When I say house, I mean castle, because that's really more or less what Gloria's place is.'

It would be, thought Maggie. 'Er... how long were you planning to stay?'

Charlotte chuckled, the deep, throaty, sexy chuckle she had perfected over the years. 'You always were so pedantic, my sweet. Two or three days, as the mood takes us. You know Giles, he likes to keep things loose, act...'

'Spontaneously. Yes, I know.' She made a rude face down the phone. 'Well, you can't stay here.'

'Oh, what a disappointment! Why not?'

'Because, because...' She groped desperately for a reason that would be acceptable to Charlotte. 'Because I'm having the interior decorators in.'

'Oh darling, you should have told me. I know the perfect little person. She did wonders on the house in Kensington.'

'Um. So I'll book you into the Shelbourne, shall I?'

'That quaint little place that's advertised in all the brochures? That will be fun! Get us a large suite, would you, darling? You know what Giles is like.'

'Yes, I do.' There was a pause. 'Well, hadn't we better hang up now? This call must be costing you a fortune.'

'You are a sweety. You never change, do you? Always so practical. All my love.' She rang off.

'Who was that?' asked her mother, curiously.

Maggie shrugged. 'Oh, just someone called Charlotte.'

The weekend dragged itself out uneventfully after Charlotte's phone call. Driving into work on Monday morning, she felt her hands grow clammy at the thought that she might accidentally bump into Bridget. That woman had jolly well better keep a low profile around college from now on, she told herself.

Crossing the Front Square, she noticed Fergus's wife, Gráinne, in conversation with someone who, from Fergus's description, could only be Anna's husband. She feared it boded no good for Fergus. In the corridor, she passed Julian who contrived somehow to wink and smirk at her at the same time. 'I've forgotten all about it,' he said, in a low, conspiratorial whisper. She blushed, nodded and hastily moved on. Outside her door, in the place where her name was supposed to be, someone had stuck a playing card - the joker. She removed it quickly. She had a sneaking suspicion that someone in Trinity had it in for her. Not a member of the Junior Promotions Committee, she hoped.

She glanced at her watch. Ten minutes to go before the seminar with Seamus, Fionnuala and Niall. She decided to give herself a treat. She dialled Bridget's number on the internal phone.

'Bridget O'Doherty. Art history department.'

'I am a reporter from ze Paree-Match magazine. Peraps you 'ave 'eard of eet, no? I'm investigating ze role of working weemen in Irlande. Eez eet true that seengle weemen 'ave to submeet to a 'ow you say eet, virginitee test een horder to be hemployed in Irlande?'

'Who is this? What on earth are you talking about?'

Maggie put the phone down and grinned.

A tap on the door and Fionnuala tripped in, wearing a flowing navy and red striped Laura Ashley dress with billowing sleeves and accessories to match. Maggie crossed her legs to hide the tear in her jeans. Seamus followed, still in sports jacket and tie, but with eyelids looking suspiciously droopy. Maggie sighed. Niall trailed behind, without his usual relaxed smile, looking in fact quite pasty faced. The dark shadows under his eyes made her suspect a bad trip. He sat down and took out his cigarette papers. She resolved to draw the line at pot, if the question ever arose. For one thing, Fionnuala would never allow it.

Fionnuala pulled out a very large plastic file with a design copied from Brighton Pavilion on the covers. She laid it open on her lap. There looked to be an ominous amount of paperwork in it. I wish she'd give up thinking for herself, thought Maggie wearily. She nodded at her to begin.

'We divided the topic into two parts,' explained

115

Fionnuala, 'so that we could work on it separately.'

Oh Seamus, thought Maggie, you're hopeless.

'In order to reconcile Protestants and Catholics,' began Fionnuala, in the well-bred tones her years at Alex's had taught her, 'the Frenchman, Sebastian Castellion, proposed reducing the number of essential Christian doctrines, omitting what seemed to him non-essentials like predestination, the nature of the after-life, etc. He argued that it would be sufficient if Christians were to agree on such basics as the resurrection. Others, for example, Calvin, argued that this would result in the watering down and eventual disintegration of religious belief, leading in turn to the collapse of society...'

'Like the amendment debate on abortion,' growled Niall.

'I beg your pardon?' said Fionnuala, momentarily disconcerted.

'Like the amendment debate a few years ago. Those were precisely the arguments put forward by the so-called Pro-Life group. Give in to the Prods and the secularists over abortion, they said, and the fabric of Irish society will disintegrate. So much for twentieth-century tolerance,' Niall continued, with a display of passion unusual for him. 'In this country we don't seem to have advanced much since the sixteenth century!'

He glanced intensely round the room at them all. It was the first time Maggie had seem him so roused. He generally went through her seminars slumped in his chair, enveloped in a cloud of cigarette smoke.

'An interesting, though tangential, point, I feel,' remarked Fionnuala, recovering herself.

Good heavens, thought Maggie, she must have been attending McGregor's classes. She tore herself away from totting up the cost of Fionnuala's outfit, including accessories, and took control of the seminar. She felt too dispirited to work out any more manoeuvres on Seamus' behalf. From now on, he would have to fend for himself.

When they had left, she picked up the receiver again.

'Bridget O'Doherty. Art history department,' said the voice on the other end.

'Good morning. I'm from the Women's Health Clinic. We're doing a survey on the number of women in Ireland who have contracted venereal disease during the past five years. All information received will be treated in the utmost confidence, naturally. Could you tell me...?'

'Certainly not.' The phone went dead.

Maggie tapped her pen on the desk. She felt curiously dissatisfied with this exchange. She must be losing her touch.

Later in the day she climbed the stairs to the Common Room where the presentation for Professor Piggott-Smith was being held. The first thing that met her line of vision was the square Ulster jaw of Dr McGregor. They nodded grimly at each other, in the manner of old foes. Maggie took a small sherry from the tray of small sherries Seamus was handing round.

'How much are they paying you for this, Seamus?'

'Two pounds an hour, Dr James.'

'Gross exploitation.'

He grinned. 'That's what Lallie said. She's bringing it up at the next Faculty meeting. Still, every little bit counts. It's all going towards my Fionnuala fund, you see.' He winked and passed on. She began to feel more hopeful about him.

The room was full of people she didn't know. Former

students of Professor Piggott-Smith who had distinguished themselves in some way had been invited - civil servants, headmasters, one or two people in the media. It was with relief that she caught sight of Fergus. He was looking very Cheshire cattish.

'Hello, Fergus. Fancy meeting you in college in the middle of the afternoon.'

'Sarcasm cannot touch me, Maggie,' he replied, knocking back the sherry as if it was beer.

'The world is expecting great things from you, Fergus, now that you have returned to an eight-hour day.'

He nodded smugly. 'This is what love does for you.'

She made sick noises into her glass.

'Oh, there are problems,' he said, making an effort to sound gloomy. 'Anna misses the children. She worries I'll leave her. "If you left Gráinne, you could leave me," she says. And of course ould eyes filling is still sobbing down the phone every day. She cries over him sometimes...'

'I think I saw him this morning, with Gráinne, as a matter of fact.'

'Um.' He fingered his beard nervously. 'Plotting, eh?'

'Don't you have any contact with her at all?'

'No. Gráinne's acting aloof and stern at the moment. A proud woman. She'll never forgive me.' He shook his head. 'I say, does anything strike you as odd about Norman?'

'Oh, so he's turned up after all? The Professor must have got out the three-line whip.'

'Whips! Precisely. I saw our Norman in the company of some very peculiar looking people recently.'

'Probably a crowd of ex-cons.'

'What?'

'I've always thought of Norman as an ex-policeman,' she explained.

'Oh? How odd of you.'

'Yes, I am odd.'

'Anyway, you're wrong. He was a kindergarten teacher.'

'Oh.'

'So much for female intuition.'

'But according to you I'm not a woman,' she reminded him.

'No, that's right.' He grinned.

She nudged him sharply.

'In what way were these people peculiar?'

'Oh you know - just peculiar.'

Maggie sometimes thought Fergus's powers of description were not all they might be. She looked across the room to where Norman was standing in conversation with a member of the German department.

'Well, he has become a nicer person recently, softer, less sarcastic.'

'Exactly. He's in a muddle if you ask me.'

'Nonsense. You would say that. There's nothing wrong with a man showing his feelings now and then.'

'Maybe not. It's just not Norman, that's all. He asked me to analyse his personality the other day. There are rumours his wife has left him,' he added darkly.

'Goodness, doesn't anyone stay together any more?' she exclaimed.

A smell of Chanel wafted past her nostrils. Lallie drifted by. Beside the drinks table, Mayhew, his gown spattered with food and his tie far from the perpendicular, was happily conversing with himself.

'Which one is Piggott-Smith?' she asked.

Fergus pointed to a shrunken little man with a face like a skeleton and skin the colour and texture of walnut shells. He was wearing a shabby raincoat several sizes too large for him and could easily have been mistaken on a dark night for a tramp or a flasher.

'Not so much wheeled out of retirement,' whispered Maggie, 'as raised from the dead.'

'My, you are coming along.' Fergus grinned. 'You'll be as sharp as an Irishwoman soon. Well, I'd better go and speak to Piggott-Smith. I used to be a student of his, you know, about a hundred years ago.'

She stood in the corner and wondered where Conor was at that moment and what he was doing.

'Hey, you're supposed to be socialising, not staring into space.'

She turned round to find a tall, fair-haired man of about sixty. He was wearing a pair of light trousers, a blue shirt and a rather weary expression. He was also, she observed, unshaven. This didn't have the effect of making him seem unattractive, however. Rather the opposite. He held up a wine glass in invitation. As Seamus passed by again with a tray of wine, he deftly scooped up a glass.

'Here. You look as if you could do with this. Sherry never did anyone any good.' He handed her the glass. 'Cheers. I see they haven't reconstructed Piggott-Smith. Nor Mayhew, for that matter, a real departure from the evolutionary mainstream. Why are you here, amongst the dead?'

'I lecture in the history department.' She noticed his very piercing blue eyes, not unfriendly, not unattractive, either.

He raised an eyebrow. 'You're not Irish, are you? How do you like our country?'

'I like it. It doesn't like me much, being English.' She smiled.

'Stop encouraging him,' whispered her mother.

'Some of we Irish think we've treated you English rather badly,' he said, paraphrasing Haynes. 'Do you like Joyce? I expect you do. The English are terrified they're going to miss the next James Joyce so they fall over themselves to praise any ould drivel that comes out of Ireland. Guilt, you see. Does wonders for my book sales over there. My name is Patrick by the way.' He took her hand. A firm, crisp handshake. 'I was taught by Piggott-Smith in the days when it was a mortal sin for a Catholic like myself to come here. I hardly ever visit the place nowadays. I find a few more brain cells drop off each time I come back.'

'Get rid of him,' ordered her mother. 'He's clearly drunk.'

She withdrew her hand. 'My name is Maggie James,' she said stiffly.

'Indeed? I've heard about you then,' he replied, with a smile.

'Oh? From whom?' she asked, slightly alarmed, at the same time noticing, rather unwillingly, that his smile made him look years younger.

'From Stephen McGregor.'

An uncomfortable sensation slid down her back. What has McGregor been saying about me, she wondered. 'Don't ask,' said her mother. 'You'll only get involved.'

'What has he been saying about me?'

Patrick seemed to hesitate. 'He...' He was interrupted by someone banging on the table for silence. 'Look,' he said hurriedly, 'why don't you come and visit me and we can continue this conversation in peace? Tomorrow

121

evening, what about it? Rathmines. Here's my address.'
He took a card from his trouser pocket and handed it
to her.

'But...'

'But, but, but. About nine?'

'Silence, please!' Professor Gardener stood at the top
of the room looking like a shy rugby player. His lips
were pursed, his head was thrown back and his hands
were folded neatly in front of his genitals. Beside him,
and several feet shorter, stood Piggott-Smith.

Professor Gardener coughed. 'Er... er. I welcome you
here today to celebrate the publication of this er...
volume of essays to which several of you in this room,
including myself,' eyes modestly lowered, 'have
contributed in honour of Professor Piggott-Smith. The
Professor is by way of being something of a legend in
his own lifetime...'

'I'm fond of a good cliché myself,' whispered Patrick
in her left ear.

'...his reputation for maintaining high standards and
requiring that his students adopt a similarly
professional attitude to scholarship has made him er...
well, legendary. Whilst at Trinity, he acquired international renown as a specialist in the late medieval wool
industry. Some of the essays in this volume indeed
touch upon this subject. We hope Professor Piggott-
Smith will enjoy them, approve of them and - and so
on and so forth.'

Beaming, Professor Gardener handed over the
volume.

'Is that your Head of department?' said Patrick. 'I see
what McGregor means. The throbbing intellect within
is cunningly disguised.'

'Oh, he's not that bad,' murmured Maggie. 'Not as

bad as McGregor, anyway,' she added pointedly.

'Come and see me tomorrow evening, Miss, for a different view on the matter.'

She was about to reply when someone turned round and said 'Ssh!' to them. Piggott-Smith shuffled forward. His voice was surprisingly sprightly for one of such sepulchral appearance.

'I don't want to keep you folks longer than necessary, but I would like to say how honoured and touched I am by this volume of essays. Looking round, I am flattered to see so many of my old students here,' (his gaze lingered on Patrick) 'but I also see a lot of young faces amongst you today and I think therefore it might interest you to hear what life was like when I was a student at Trinity, around 1920, and subsequently as a lecturer.'

'Is he serious? Jaysus, Mary Mother o' God and all the saints preserve us, as the Catholics would say. We'll be here for weeks,' groaned Fergus behind her.

'Those were the days when bus rides cost a penny.' Piggott-Smith held up a bus ticket as evidence. 'And Bewley's buns cost a farthing.' He held up a receipt. 'In 1921, I joined Players and acted minor roles in several plays. I have a review of one of them here.' He took out a faded cutting from *The Irish Times*. '"Mr Piggott-Smith acted with enthusiasm..."'

Patrick poked her arm. 'History as fiction. Never trust anyone's account of their own life. See you tomorrow at eight.'

His footsteps clattered noisily down the stairs. As they faded out, Piggott-Smith resumed '"...with enthusiasm and gusto". That was the end of my acting career.'

There was a general ripple of disbelieving laughter.

'Jaysus, don't encourage the bugger,' moaned Fergus.

They were treated to details of Piggott-Smith's class marks, his graduation ceremony, holiday jobs. The years rolled by, 1926, 1929, 1930. She could hear Fergus ticking them off on his fingers. Only another half century to go. Suddenly and arbitrarily, he came to a halt in 1941. 'Well I guess I don't want to bore you folks, so I'll stop there.'

Looking heartily relieved, Professor Gardener led the clapping.

'So you've made the acquaintance of Patrick Brophy,' said Fergus under cover of the applause.

Maggie looked down at the card in her hand. Patrick Brophy! Six good novels and twice runner-up for the Booker Prize. She was impressed.

'You don't want to get involved with him,' said Fergus, as they walked back down the stairs. 'He is reputed to be extremely odd.'

'Now, Fergus,' she laughed. 'Is it likely? He must be sixty if he's a day. Besides, I can't stand artists.'

On her way home, she stopped at the Shelbourne to book a suite for Charlotte and Giles. She was pleased to learn that the only one available was the most expensive in the hotel. Serves them right, she thought, for landing on me like this.

When she got home, Conor rang.

'It's me. Listen, it's all right now, Maggie,' (for a second, her heart stood still in hope), 'everything's out in the open - about Bridget and me.'

'Oh?'

'Yes. I had a few jars last night with her husband. We swapped football stories. It went well.'

'You don't know any football stories.'

'I made them up. Look, why don't you come round

later? We could go for a pint.'

And talk about old times? She felt a sudden wave of exhaustion come over her. 'Thanks, Conor, but I think I'll have an early night.' She had been finding recently that sleep was a remarkably good alternative to life; at least there were no surprises.

'OK.' He didn't sound as devastated as she had hoped. 'You all right? You sound a bit down.'

'Down? Heavens, no,' she said quickly. 'Too much of the good life. Speaking of which, Charlotte rang the other day.'

'Wow! You know, I'd really like to get to meet her. Where is she now?'

'Swanning around in Antibes with Giles.'

'You're going to have to do something about those two. It's childish the way you go on.'

'I know, I know, but I've been so busy lately having such a good time.' She particularly wanted to emphasise this. Pity was off the agenda as far as she was concerned.

'I see. Anyone I know?' Was there an edge in his voice?

'No.'

'Good. Keep it clean.'

He rang off. Ten minutes later, he rang again.

'I've been talking to Bridget. You must stop making these obscene telephone calls.'

'Oh, she guessed.'

'She didn't, I did. Really, Maggie, it's time you grew up.'

Babies make you grow up, she thought as she stood forlornly in the cold hallway.

Chapter Seven

'Hi,' said Julian the next morning, hastily repressing the smirk which had become his usual greeting to her. 'I see your department is one less today.'

She stared at him, experiencing a sudden rush of panic. 'What do you mean?'

'Ron's left. The balding Ron. Or rather, he's been sacked.'

'Sacked?' Someone was tipping ice-cold water down her spine. 'They can't do that,' she gabbled wildly. 'He's a Fellow, he's got tenure. They can't fire him.'

Julian shrugged. 'He cleared out his office yesterday evening. I was working late, heard this noise and went to investigate. It was Ron, snivelling over his cardboard boxes. He was in bits, poor chap.'

'I bet he was. Why are they chucking him out?'

'Didn't say, but you know what the rules are,' he replied, with what she thought was an unbecoming glint in his eye, 'Fellows can't be fired except for gross moral turpitude or fiddling the accounts.'

'Neither of those sounds like Ron.'

'I agree, but with all the cutbacks, the Board is coming down like a ton of bricks on anyone who doesn't toe the line.'

If they can fire a Fellow with such ease, she reflected, what might they do to a very junior lecturer? She whipped round to Fergus's office, normally a place she avoided. It was dark and cluttered and smelled distinctly of cheese and sour milk. He was bending over his Apple Macintosh.

'It's amazing the hours you keep,' she commented. She paused. 'Er... what's that noise? It sounds like...'

'Someone throwing up, yes I know.' He sighed. 'The dratted thing has a virus. Look.'

She came nearer and saw on the screen a little picture of a very sad face with its tongue hanging out.

'Some joker deliberately put this virus into the system. I shall have to get the thing vaccinated. That'll teach me to lend out my disks.' He pressed a button and swivelled round on his chair to face her. 'Never be promiscuous with your disks, Maggie.'

'No, Fergus, I won't,' she said primly, then sniggered as the computer vomited again. 'It's like morning sickness, I suppose, except that in the case of your computer it seems likely to last all day....' She tailed away. He wasn't laughing.

'Just when I was beginning to make up for lost time on the work front.' He glowered. 'Well, did you want something?'

'To ask you about Ron.' She recounted what Julian had told her.

'It's true, I'm afraid - though as to why he was fired, I haven't a clue.' He looked at her. 'Why are you so worked up? Are you after his office or something? If so, prepare yourself for a fight, it's the only one in the building with any sort of a view. I was thinking of putting in for it myself.'

She thought these remarks in astonishingly poor taste. What was it with men and offices? The bigger the better, they seemed to think. A classic phallic symbol.

'It's not offices I'm worried about right now. It's my job. If they can do that to Ron who's been here, what - fifteen years? - they won't think twice about removing a junior lecturer like myself.'

'Keep calm,' advised Fergus, with all the insouciance of someone who has a job for life. 'Oh, sod it,' he added, as the computer vomited again.

'Calm! Calm!' She felt like lifting herself up by the hair in despair, like some character out of Dickens. And she was sure those were shoulder pads in his jacket. To impress Anna, she supposed. The creep. 'Yesterday, Patrick Brophy told me he'd heard of me through McGregor. What do you think McGregor can have been saying about me, Fergus?'

I could find out, she thought. 'I should put any idea about visiting that Brophy person right out of your head,' said her mother sharply. Of course, mother. She fingered a disk on Fergus's desk. 'When you said odd, Fergus, what exactly did you mean?'

'Oh, you know - alcohol, women, the usual sort of thing.'

'You're definitely not going,' said her mother. It might be useful, though, to find out what McGregor was saying about her behind her back, purely for professional reasons, naturally. [His eyes had been nice, too.]. Her mother gave her a warning look.

'I shouldn't worry about McGregor if I were you,' said Fergus. 'No one takes any notice of him. He's a race apart. I may be Protestant myself, but I've no time for the Ulster variety. They seem like foreigners to me. They don't like the Republic and they don't even much like the British any more. What they're angling for is their own separate parliament, and who's going to give them that? I look at a man like McGregor now,' he continued, really warming to his favourite theme, 'and I feel just as alienated from him as I do from the English - oh, sorry.'

'It's all right, Fergus,' she said dryly. 'Any time.'

Her next call was on Lallie. She was sitting with her feet up on her desk, reading the *Marxist Feminist Review*. Her office smelled of Chanel No.5 and was decorated with posters of cats.

'Did you know they've fired Ron?'

'Y-yes.' Lallie put down the review, took her feet off her desk and looked about as uncomfortable as Maggie had ever seen her look.

Maggie stared at her. 'Well, what is the union going to do about it?'

'Um ... in this case, we've decided not to take any action.'

'Why not?' said Maggie, indignantly. 'That's what you're here for, isn't it? To protect employees from management's silly decisions?'

'In theory, yes, but in this case - well, there are special circumstances.'

'What circumstances?'

Lallie spread out her hands. 'I'm sorry, Maggie, I'm afraid I can't tell you. I'd be breaking a confidence.' She leant over her desk. 'But since it's you, I'll give you a clue. There have been a number of incidents,' she whispered, 'culminating yesterday in what he did with the lemon soufflé.'

Maggie frowned. 'I see.' To tell the truth, she found Lallie's clue most unhelpful, but thought that to say so might display a lack of sophistication.

'Don't worry.' Lallie smiled. 'You're in quite a different position from Ron.'

A double entendre? And anyway was she in a different position? Or, when it came to the crunch, would the union abandon her too? Treachery, treachery everywhere, she muttered, going back to her office.

About seven o'clock that evening, she called round to Conor's house. There was no reply. She prowled about in the garden. The roses she had pruned last year were beginning to bloom. She had done a good job on them. She noticed that the rubbish had already been put out in plastic bags for collection the following morning. He was not intending to be in, then, that night. One of the bags had split open. Orange peel, coke cans and potato skins were strewn over the path and - what was that? Two used condoms. She left a note. 'Called round to see you. Roses doing well. Clear up your rubbish, this is a Catholic country.'

Getting back into her car, she noticed two teenagers in a tight clinch up against the side of Maeve's house. Adolescents, she had observed, kissed and copulated more openly in Ireland than they did in England, in parks, in fields, at bus stops, up against walls. God, she thought, life's sordid. She felt, suddenly, middle-aged and weary. She glanced down at the address on the seat, put the car into gear and drove in the direction of Rathmines. 'I'm furthering my career,' she told her mother.

She parked the car in a street of red-brick houses and got out, clutching the packet of cigarettes she had bought along the way. She walked up the tiny garden path and listened outside the door for a moment. There were no sounds from within. Well, he was a famous writer, why should he wait in just for her? She knocked softly and then stood back, trying to look as if she hadn't knocked at all. She would say she had been passing by and had called on the off-chance. 'A likely story,' sniffed her mother.

Then the door opened and he was standing there

smiling, still unshaven, still dressed in the light trousers and blue shirt, a glass of whiskey in his hand.

'Hello.'

'Is this right? Am I supposed to be here?'

'Of course. Come in.' He stood back to let her past, then showed her into a large, old-fashioned room furnished with bookcases with glass doors, family portraits and a horsehair sofa. In one corner stood a wooden table covered with papers and books. In another, a lamp with heavy silk tassles, a Victorian parlour lamp of the kind that Maggie had seen only in films set in brothels. The carpet, which was brown, was covered with letters, envelopes, scraps of paper.

'Sit down. Have a whiskey.'

She picked her way through the letters and sat down in a sagging armchair. From the kitchen, she heard the sound of a cap being unscrewed, a fridge door opening, the clink of ice in a glass, a tap running. She lit a cigarette and glanced down at the letters. Dear Patrick. Dear Mr Brophy. Brophy, how are you, old sod? One envelope was addressed simply Patrick Brophy, Ireland.

He put a glass into her hand and sat down in the armchair opposite, stretching out his long legs in front of him. 'Well,' he said, looking at her quizzically.

'Well,' she countered, noticing again how blue his eyes were.

'I didn't think you'd come.'

'Why not?'

'I thought you'd forget. No. I thought you'd remember to forget.'

'I nearly did.'

He smiled wryly. 'It took a certain amount of courage to come here.'

She drew on her cigarette. 'What has McGregor been saying about me and how do you know him?'

He grinned. 'Nervous, eh? To answer your second question, I used to give the odd class some years back, long before your time. Left - students rot the brain.' He was silent for a moment. 'To answer your first - McGregor thinks women are a liability. Something to do with their wombs.'

'Lallie's been around a long time.'

'Lesbian. Doesn't count.'

'Goodness, you do know a lot.'

'That's Dublin. Someone pisses in Stephen's Green and it's written up in the Sunday papers, with the name of his great aunt. Couldn't stand it myself.'

'You don't live here then?' She looked around. There was an old photograph of him on the mantelpiece, with his arm round a rather stern looking woman with blonde hair.

'My brother's place. I'm caretaking for a fortnight while he's off on holiday. It suited me anyway - I had to come up to Dublin for... business. I thought I'd probably meet someone new.'

'Why?' she asked, startled.

'Just a feeling. I sometimes get feelings... about the future. Don't you?'

She shook her head.

'No, I don't suppose you would, working in that place.' He looked across at her. 'You all right? You seem on edge. Relax.'

'I am relaxed.' She gulped down a mouthful of whiskey and clutched the arm of her chair. Conversation with Patrick seemed to take unpredictable turns. He unnerved her slightly. 'I am relaxed. Why don't you answer your letters?'

He frowned down at the floor.

'Do you think I should? Every morning, there are at least five more.' He leant down rather stiffly and picked one up. 'This is a good one. Let me read it to you.' He placed his glass on the small table beside him and, rather to her disappointment, put on a pair of spectacles. '"Dear Mr Brophy, I have just finished your novel. I was lying in bed, with your book between the sunlight and my eyes. You made me feel like laughing and crying and then laughing again. How do you do it, you bastard?" A pensioner from Wexford.' He looked sad. 'He writes every month. He's lonely. But if he can complain, he's all right.' He nodded, as if to reassure himself. 'I can't answer all of them.' He threw down the letter and sighed, heavily. Then looked at her again. 'You OK? Relax.'

'I am rel...'

'I wrote a couple of pages today. Want to hear them?'

She nodded. He took a dirty notebook out of his trouser pocket and read her a rather strange piece about Job. 'What do you think of it?' he asked, taking off his spectacles.

'I like it,' she said doubtfully. What did he expect her to say?

'Ah, you're not being honest,' he said. 'You come from England. I suppose you don't believe in all this?'

'The Bible? Certainly not,' she replied indignantly. 'It's full of people of bad faith, thinking they have no free will, thinking their lives are determined for them by some kind of divine providence.'

He raised an eyebrow. 'You think we're free agents?'

'History is created by men and women, by their actions. Why bring God into it?'

He shook his head. 'Very soon this country will be

133

full of people like you.' He fell silent. Maggie was relieved. She had begun to find the conversation in rather poor taste. 'I meant to write a story about Job. So many things to do,' he murmured. He put the notebook back in his pocket and looked at his empty glass. 'Want another?'

'Not yet,' she replied primly.

He untangled his long legs and shambled off into the kitchen. She lit another cigarette and wondered whether he really didn't believe in free will and why this conversation with him was turning out so differently from her conversations with other people. When she looked up, he was standing in the doorway watching.

'You'll kill yourself with those things.' He pointed to the cigarette.

'It's better than alcohol.'

He frowned.

She blushed and fingered her glass. Yes, that was impertinent. It was none of her business. He sat down again. 'Why did you invite me here tonight?' she asked, suddenly uncomfortable.

He ran his fingers through his fair, slightly receding hair. 'I can feel when someone is in pain,' he murmured.

'Me? I'm not in pain,' she replied angrily.

There was a silence. 'You're not used to being honest, are you?' he said. 'I saw you standing miserably in the corner. What is it? Husband trouble? Work?'

'I'm not married.'

He glanced at her. 'Not married, eh? Do you have a lover?'

'No... yes... I don't know.'

'Don't know? Hard not to know about a thing like

that, I should have thought.'

'All right, I'll tell you. I did have a lover till last week. Somebody pinched him.'

'Tut, tut, very careless of you to let that happen. Anyone I know?'

'Bridget O'Doherty.'

'I know. Sweet girl. American teeth. What does he do, your ex?'

'He's a journalist.'

'Poor sod.' He sank back into the armchair. For a moment she thought he had fallen asleep. Then he looked across at her. 'So you fell for a journalist, eh? Have you no sense of style?'

'Excuse me. I do lecture in the...'

'History department. All right, all right. I suppose you're planning your revenge?'

She started.

'Do you believe in magic?' he asked suddenly.

'Of course not.'

'Why of course? This country is full of magic - wishing wells, Celtic crosses, burial mounds, singing walls - all that power waiting to be tapped. And here you are, measuring reality, plotting revenge. That's for weak, ignorant people. You should show you're above all that.'

'But I'm not.'

'Well,' he said, 'that's honest at least.' He leaned back and closed his eyes.

Maggie began to feel perplexed. She smoked her cigarette down to the filter and stubbed it out regretfully. She glanced across at him, noting the way his hair curled gently at the nape of his neck. He looked considerably more than sixty with his eyes shut. There were deep lines around his mouth and nose, but it was an attractive face nevertheless, a face full of experience. 'What kind of experience?' asked her mother. Shut up and let me find out.

'Are you married?'

He opened one eye and nodded in the direction of the mantelpiece. 'Was. Don't you read the gossip columns? My ex-wife's in Australia. She would have gone further if there had been any place further to go.'

'Why did you say this country will soon be full of people like me?'

He sat up. 'Because this country's convinced that the *normal* way of doing things is the English way - the South East English way, to be precise. I did think, once, that Ireland had a chance to be a different sort of country from the rest of Europe, but economics dictates the way people live here, just like everywhere else. Unity if it ever comes to Ireland will come for economic reasons, not political ones.'

'Why hasn't Ireland become different then?'

'Lack of confidence in itself, I suppose. I can't believe a country is truly independent if it's always looking over its shoulder at what its neighbour is doing. It's a child that can't grow up.' He stared very hard at her.

It's as if he can read my mind, she thought.

'That's not my problem,' she said snappishly.

'Did I say it was?'

'I told you you'd have trouble,' said her mother. 'He's too clever by half.'

She nudged the conversation back to politics.

'So what do you want? De Valera?'

'Comely maidens dancing at the crossroads? Certainly not.' He looked into his glass. 'If we're going to talk about Ireland, we'd better both have another whiskey.'

This time, he brought the bottle back with him.

'You know, if only this country would stop seeing itself through other people's eyes, it could be really distinctive, instead of the derivative society it is now.' He paused. 'Do you know what I had to struggle hardest against when I became known as a novelist in England? The temptation to live up to the stock image of the "Irish Writer" - irresponsible, witty, poetic, drunk. I tried to be something else. I can't say I've succeeded, especially with the last. It's difficult not to be governed by other people's expectations. And it's the same with Ireland. As long as we borrow other countries' judgements of ourselves, we'll always be second rate - politically, economically and all the rest of it. But if our values are something else, more spiritual and literary, more "feminine" and caring, then we might take a higher estimate of ourselves. But these are precisely the values that are slipping away from us... That's what I meant when I said that the country will soon be full of people like you.' He grinned at her. 'Sorry for the lecture, but you did ask.'

She flicked a finger against her glass. 'I'm not quite so wedded to the materialistic society as you seem to think.' She was silent for a moment. 'On the other hand, I certainly don't believe in what you call magic... and organised religion just leaves me cold.'

'Me too. An extremely lapsed Catholic.'

She rubbed her forehead. 'So where does God come in?'

'I've settled for a religion without a Church. Many people would call it no religion at all.' There was a silence. 'So tell me about yourself. Have you family?'

'Not a great deal by Irish standards. I'm an only child. My parents live in London.'

137

'Fond of them?'

'Oh yes. They're perfectly ordinary, sweet, caring people.'

'Proud of you, I should imagine?'

'Very. They sacrificed quite a bit for my education. They're not particularly well off. My father was an accounts clerk before his retirement.'

'Mmm.' He looked at her thoughtfully. 'There's something here that doesn't quite ring true.'

'Are you doubting my family history?' she asked, taken aback.

He moved restlessly in his chair. 'Oh, history - one can make it mean almost anything, depending on the questions one asks. There's been too much dwelling on history in this country. That's its problem. Its heart has not been large enough to reach out and forgive.'

'Why forgive?' asked Maggie sharply.

'Because through forgiveness comes healing and ... peace.' He paused. 'Or perhaps not forgiveness. Perhaps that's too much to ask. Just the grace to look inwards and see treasures that its colonisers did not begin to appreciate - delicacy, quickness of spirit, subtlety, unique music and language ... Meanwhile all this history just leaves Ireland floundering.' He glanced across at her. 'Well, it's none of my business.'

'Ireland?'

'No, you. How you understand your past.'

'No, it isn't,' she agreed. 'None of your business.'

'Only - ' He hesitated.

'Only what?'

'It's a terrible thing to let the past weigh on the present.'

'Sometimes one cannot help that,' she replied. She looked at her watch. 'Gosh! Is that the time? I must

138

dash.' She stood up.

'Conversation getting too personal, eh?' He grinned.

'Not at all,' she said briskly. 'You asked for that,' said her mother. 'I told you how it would be. There is such a thing as being too clever, you know.'

He got to his feet. For a moment they stood looking at one another. She noticed bitterly how absurdly intelligent he looked. Such a man could never be for her.

'Look,' he said, 'I'm here for another week. Let's meet for a coffee before I disappear.'

She hesitated. 'You're asking for trouble,' her mother warned. 'This man will find out too much about you. Get out now while the going's good.' She nodded. 'OK.'

He showed her to the door. His hand on the latch, he leant forward. For one moment she thought he was going to do something quite dreadful like kiss her, but instead he said, 'Miracles - they're the force by which we're nourished and sustained. It doesn't do to underestimate them, you know.'

Walking back down the garden path, she felt a moment's regret that he hadn't tried to kiss her. But after all, she thought, getting into her car, what would be the point? He's old, he's eccentric, he doesn't even live in Dublin...

Chapter Eight

The next day, two things happened. Charlotte and Giles arrived and someone moved into the flat downstairs. Nolan was cock a hoop. 'You'll like him,' he assured her. 'He's a respectable looking boy. Shoes so polished you could eat your dinner off them, so you could.'

They were too. Paul Maloney was his name. He was hanging about in the hall, supervising removal men, when she hurried past on her way to the airport to meet Charlotte and Giles. They introduced themselves, he informing her, in a manner which suggested she would find this of intense interest, that he worked for a firm of accountants.

'Been with them three months and they haven't sacked me yet. Touch wood.' His fingers brushed the top of the banister.

'My father was an accountant,' she said distractedly, looking at her watch and realising that it was later than she had thought.

'Really?' His eyes gleamed. 'Mr Nolan was telling me we would find things in common. Which firm?'

'Oh, it was in England,' she replied hastily. She ran her eyes over his glossy black hair, his thin, pinched, rather spotty face, the navy double breasted jacket with shiny gold buttons, the impeccably pressed trousers, white socks and, at the end of it all, the gleaming black shoes, and thought that he dressed like no one else she knew. 'Anyway, he's retired now. Look, I'm awfully sorry, I must da ...'

He laid a detaining hand on her arm. 'And what do you do, Maggie?'

'I work at Trinity.'

'The university? You a secretary or something?'

'No. A lecturer,' she replied briskly.

'My!' He gazed at her with awe. 'You must be clever.'

'Not particularly. Look, I really must go. I'm meeting some people at the airport.'

'The airport?' His face took on an expression of acute distress. 'Oh, I hope the plane won't be too delayed.'

'No. Why should it be?'

'They generally are these days. Dreadful business air travel. But then if one goes by car there're always breakdowns to contend with, and coaches are no good because the driver's bound to be drunk, and the trains, well, one can never be sure that the signals will be working properly... or if it's not the signals, it could be that they've forgotten to switch the points.'

'Indeed,' she replied, a little alarmed, for he seemed to be working himself up into quite a state.

'Where are your friends coming from?'

Maggie had never classed Charlotte and Giles as friends but she hadn't time to argue. 'France.'

'Ha ha, you see,' he said, with a little air of satisfaction. 'I once waited five hours for a plane to arrive from France. They had had to make an emergency landing at Dieppe. All the passengers had been struck down by vomiting and diarrhoea... the cabin crew couldn't cope.' He leaned forward and said in a low, confidential voice, as if handing out classified information, 'Those airplane meals are a breeding ground for listeria, you know. Never touch them myself. Always take a packed lunch on board.'

141

'I see. Well, let's look on the bright side, shall we? Perhaps the plane won't be delayed and perhaps Charlotte and Giles won't get sick.' She made a move to get past him, but he kept his hand on her arm.

'Might I float the suggestion that we have a drink together sometime?'

'Sure.' She was perfectly prepared to be neighbourly.

'And you can let me in on all the snags of living in this place.'

Maggie stared at him. 'There aren't any snags. What you see is what you get.' She had picked up this term from Conor. 'It lacks style, I know, but it's quiet and reasonably clean for the price. What particular snags were you thinking of?'

He wagged a finger at her, at the same time, to her relief, releasing her arm. 'I know you're just trying to cheer me up on my first day, but I've moved around this city enough to know that every rented apartment has its drawbacks. It's best to be realistic. What is it here? The roof? Water pressure? Neighbours' dogs?'

'Perhaps I shouldn't disillusion you on your first day.' She flashed him a smile and walked out of the front door.

'Safe journey!' he called after her. 'Fingers crossed that you don't get a puncture.'

If this meeting was vaguely unsatisfactory, the one with Charlotte and Giles was even more so. For a start, they were excruciatingly embarrassing people to meet at an airport. Charlotte rushed up to Maggie, screeching loudly and flapping her arms in a manner calculated to attract the maximum amount of attention to herself. She hasn't changed a bit, thought Maggie, submitting to a peck on the cheek. Giles plodded behind, laden down with masses of Louis Vuitton

142

luggage. He kissed her, almost absent-mindedly, and plonked the cases on the floor.

'We couldn't find a trolley,' explained Charlotte, gazing around her, quite oblivious to people's stares. 'And where have all the porters got to?'

'There aren't any,' muttered Maggie.

'No porters? Darling, how odd. I thought this was a Catholic country.' Her upper-class English tones carried far and wide across the airport. 'Aren't Catholics supposed to be hot on things like service? I don't suppose you have much trouble finding domestics over here, do you?'

'Shut up, Charlotte,' hissed Maggie, conscious, as Charlotte was not, that people were staring.

'Who are these two?' whispered her mother. 'And why are they dressed in such extraordinary clothes?'

Personally, Maggie thought their clothes quite tame compared with some of the outfits she had seen them in in the past. Charlotte was dressed in a bright red, ruched miniskirt with matching bright red tights and a skimpy black T-shirt which fell off the left shoulder to reveal a pink bra strap. Maggie supposed that was deliberate. Everything Charlotte did was always carefully organised for maximum effect. Her hair, which had been ash-blonde the last time Maggie had seen her, had now turned into a Duchess-of-York-ginger colour. Giles' hair, which also changed colour periodically, was hidden beneath a black felt hat pulled down low over his forehead. He was wearing loose yellow trousers, a pink T-shirt and a yellow and green striped jacket. In one ear was a diamond stud. Both of them wore self-reflecting sunglasses. They must have got to the stage of having to worry about wrinkles, thought Maggie, nastily. They were considerably older than herself.

'I'll see if I can dig up a trolley,' she said.

'Breezy,' responded Giles, sitting down on one of the Louis Vuitton suitcases and taking out a packet of cigarette papers.

'Not here,' warned Maggie. 'The place is stuffed with security men.'

He waved a paper at her. 'Don't worry, hon. Nothing but the purest tobacco.'

'You are a sweetie,' said Charlotte, generously giving her another peck on the cheek. 'You never change, do you? So dependable.'

Maggie frowned. 'Let's find my car, shall we?'

They rounded up Giles who had been chatting to a party of teenagers about to depart on a school trip, and made their way to the exit. When they got to Maggie's car, they discovered that the cases wouldn't all fit into her boot and had to seek out a taxi to take the rest of the luggage to the hotel.

'You climb in the back, Giles,' ordered Charlotte, when the taxi had been sorted out and sent on its way and they were once more standing around Maggie's car. 'We two will have a nice girls' talk in the front.'

Girls! thought Maggie. Why doesn't she act her age? She started up the car and pointed it in the direction of the city centre.

'Well,' she said at last, 'you look just the same, darling. Haven't altered one bit. Is... is this kind of thing in fashion over here?' She fingered Maggie's jacket, an old cotton one that sagged at the pockets.

Maggie began to wish she had made time that morning to wash her hair and put on some make up.

'You know that I couldn't care less about fashion,' she retorted.

'Oh, but sweetie, it's so important to keep up with the times.'

'I don't see why.' She braked sharply as the lights in front of her turned red.

'You are a dear.' Charlotte patted her hand as it lay on the gear lever. 'It's so marvellous to have a daughter with whom one doesn't have to compete.' Maggie glanced over and caught her repressing a little smile of triumph.

'Who is this woman?' asked her mother. 'Why did she call you her daughter?'

Maggie shrugged. 'That's Charlotte's way. She thinks she's my mother, but I've always denied it.'

'I can see why,' replied her mother, looking Charlotte over. 'Miniskirt indeed! She's fifty if she's a day.'

'Never admits to more than forty-five. Her story is that she conceived me while she was still at her posh girls' school in Sussex. Giles was filling in there for a term as art teacher. They had to leave in a hurry.'

Her mother sniffed. 'Entirely unsuitable to be your mother.'

'I totally agree.'

'And what about him?' put in her father. 'Is it a trick of the light or is that a pony-tail under his hat?'

'It is.'

'Never would have been allowed in my firm. What line of business is he in?'

'He's a painter.'

'A painter?' said her mother. 'I wouldn't want him painting my house got up like that. Think of what the neighbours would say.'

'Not that sort of painter. He paints pictures for people to hang in their front rooms. He calls himself an artist.'

'An artist!' said her parents in unison. A mixture of awe and contempt passed over their faces.

'What kind of pictures?' asked her mother, cautiously.

'Tin cans, old boots, half-eaten meals. The stuff of everyday life.'

'Not much money in that,' commented her father.

'There was for Giles. He became extremely fashionable in the Sixties and he's been living off that ever since. They've a house in California and one in Kensington - oh, and a villa in Antibes. They spend the year flying between them.'

Her mother's face registered disapproval. 'I've always thought it simply greedy to have more than one house.'

'I quite agree.'

'Daydreaming again, darling?' Charlotte's voice broke into her thoughts. 'You take after Giles.'

'No, I don't,' said Maggie, automatically. She had been denying any resemblance to Giles, and Charlotte too, for that matter, for as long as she could remember. The lights must have turned green several minutes ago. She drove off amidst a beeping of horns.

Charlotte peered out of the window. 'I must say, this is rather a quaint little place, only...'

'Only?' said Maggie, ready to be defensive.

'Well perhaps a little drab, darling. Of course after the South of France, everywhere looks drab,' she added hastily. 'One misses the light, don't you agree, Giles?'

'What's that?' Giles was going a trifle deaf but would never admit it.

'I said one misses the light here.'

'Lighter? I think I have one somewhere.' He fished in the pockets of his yellow trousers.

'No, no! The *light*,' growled Charlotte. 'Ach, it doesn't matter,' she added in exasperation, as the lighter landed in her lap.

The taxi was waiting for them as they pulled up outside the Shelbourne.

'That'll be fifteen pounds, sir,' said the driver.

'Hang about.' Giles rooted around in his pockets and brought forth a twenty pound note.

'That's no use, it's sterling,' Maggie pointed out. 'Haven't you any Irish money?'

Since, with eerie predictability, neither Giles nor Charlotte had thought to change any money (indeed hadn't realised that the Irish had their own currency), she ended up paying for the taxi herself.

'Breezy, honey,' said Giles, by way of thanks. He strolled into the hotel, leaving Charlotte and Maggie standing on the pavement, surrounded by suitcases. I'm blowed if I'm carrying their luggage, thought Maggie. She went in search of a porter.

'Why don't you two go on up to your suite and get unpacked?' she suggested, knowing from experience what a tortuous process unpacking was with them. 'I'll wait down here and order us some coffee.'

'Decaff!' they roared, in unison. 'I never get a wink of sleep if I drink the real stuff after two in the afternoon,' explained Charlotte, who liked to pretend she was highly strung.

'Sandwiches?'

'Not for us. Never eat bread, darling.' Charlotte patted her non-existent stomach. 'Order us a salad.'

'Breezy, darling,' added Giles.

'Why does he keep on saying that?' enquired her father. 'Is he referring to the climate, by any chance?'

She had to hang about in the hotel lounge for three

quarters of an hour before they finally reappeared.

'This is very kind of you, darling.' Charlotte looked at the coffee pot, the prawns and the plates of salad.

'Not at all.' Maggie smiled. 'I told them to add it to your bill.'

'How are you off for dough, hon?' asked Giles. Without giving her time to reply, he went on, 'That's good. It's costing me a small fortune to keep three houses going. I sometimes wonder why we don't jack it all in and bum around India for a while, like the good old days.'

'I've no intention of starting that again,' said Charlotte tartly. 'My bumming days are over.'

'Trouble with you, Charlotte, is you've no sense of adventure, eh, Aurelia?' He winked at Maggie and began rolling a cigarette.

'*What* did he call you?' asked her mother.

Maggie flushed. 'I wish you wouldn't call me that here, Giles. Didn't you get my letter?' But Giles had lapsed into his usual cataleptic state, puffing away on his cigarette and staring blankly into space. She turned to Charlotte. 'Didn't you read my letter?'

'What letter was that, darling?' Absent-mindedly, Charlotte picked up and ate a slice of the brown bread which had accompanied their salad.

'The one where I told you that I've changed my name. I'm known as Maggie James here. It's going to get frightfully confusing if you keep dragging Aurelia into it.'

'But darling, Aurelia is such a pretty name and Maggie is dull, commonplace even. I can understand you wanting to change your surname, with your father being so famous and all that.' Maggie raised her eyebrows. 'Oh well.' Charlotte gave a little shrug of indifference. 'It's important to experiment with one's identity, I suppose. Speaking of which,' she moved closer to Maggie and dropped her voice to a confidential whisper, 'did I tell you Giles and I had a brief separation over the winter?'

Maggie shook her head. She wasn't surprised. Charlotte and Giles had been splitting up and getting back together all her life.

'He went off with some nubile adolescent - of course I knew that wouldn't last - and I met this perfectly ravishing Greek. Like a god he was. Tall and dark. Beautiful teeth. And guess how old? Twenty-two! Think of it, my dear, only twenty-two!' Charlotte rocked in her seat with delight.

'Charlotte, that's almost obscene!'

'Darling, you always were so old-fashioned. Besides, it was only an interlude, a small treat to myself whilst Giles got over his crush on the nubile teenager. And of course, apart from a few absolutely delightful massages, nothing actually happened.'

'Goodness me, why ever not?' exclaimed Maggie, curious in spite of herself, for usually in Charlotte's affairs a great deal happened, from all angles.

Charlotte leaned over. 'Aids,' she whispered. 'It's absolutely dreadful. Our friends are going down like nine pins. Giles and I have made a pact. Till they find some sort of a cure, we won't sleep, in the proper sense of the word, with anyone else.'

'You made that pact a long time ago,' Maggie pointed out. 'It's called marriage vows.'

'Darling, how sweetly conventional you are!' A shade of anxiety passed over her face. 'What worries me is, will he remember to keep to his side of the bargain, do you think?'

They both looked over at Giles who was staring comatosely at his plate of salad.

'It's the Greens,' he said suddenly.

Maggie glanced at the lettuce on his plate. 'You needn't eat it if you don't want.'

'I've been meaning to tell you, Aurelia...'

'Maggie,' corrected Charlotte.

'Hon, give me some credit. Don't always treat me as if my mind was completely screwed up. This is Ireland. This is our daughter, Aurelia. I am on top of the situation.' He turned to Maggie. 'I've been meaning to tell you, Aurelia. The Greens are where it's at now. Everyone we know is into cleaning up the environment, saving the whale, protecting the ozone layer. The problem I face is how to capture the new spirit of the age on canvas... in a way, yes... um.' It had been, for Giles, a very long speech and towards the end he had been running down in jerks, like an old-fashioned gramophone record. He lapsed into silence and took out his cigarette papers. By this time, a suspicious odour was drifting over the lounge. Maggie hoped none of the staff would notice.

'What are you talking about?' she asked, but Giles, though still physically present, had gone off into some mental landscape of his own.

'What is he on about?' she asked Charlotte. 'Ever since Thatcher got in, he's voted Conservative. So have you.'

'Oh, but darling, haven't you noticed how old the Cabinet have all got? Giles and I simply can't identify with them any more.'

'I can't think why not,' retorted Maggie rudely. 'It's about time you acted your age.' She had noticed, with satisfaction, that Charlotte was beginning to look a little raddled. Beneath her T-shirt, those pert little breasts of which she had been so proud were starting to sag.

'Pardon?' said Charlotte. 'What did you say?'

Maggie, who had remembered that Charlotte's favourite method of dealing with insults was simply to pretend she hadn't heard, gave up.

'Well, darling, what have you got planned to entertain us while we're here? When are we going to see some of your friends?'

Maggie blanched. 'Friends?'

'Yes, I was hoping you might throw a party for us...'

'A spontaneous happening,' put in Giles, returning to life for a second.

'...And introduce us around,' Charlotte continued. 'You know how I adore young people.'

'Charlotte, I'm thirty. Most of my friends are at least that. I don't know any young people any more.' Apart from my students, she thought, and I'm not letting either of you within a mile of them.

Charlotte shuddered. 'Don't remind me of your age, darling. Don't you think it would be kinder to me to admit to being only in your mid-twenties? Alternatively,' she added, considering Maggie over the top of her sunglasses, 'perhaps we could pretend to be sisters?'

'Not a chance,' muttered Maggie. 'Slight acquaintances, at most.'

'What did you say?'

'You heard. Where were you when I was growing up?'

Charlotte pouted. 'Darling, don't bring that up again. It's the past, it's over and done with...'

'What's past and gone can never be recalled,'

murmured Giles in a sing-song sort of voice, 'except, perhaps, mutton vindaloo.'

They ignored him.

'I'm a historian,' said Maggie firmly, addressing herself to Charlotte. 'For me, the past is never finished.'

'History!' exclaimed Charlotte, seeing her opportunity to change the subject and grabbing it. 'Are you still on with that dreary office job? Terribly worthy, of course, but isn't it time for a change?'

'That's right,' said Giles, 'keep on the move, Aurelia. Hang loose for a bit. You never had a proper adolescence.'

'Oh, you noticed,' she said, bitterly. She had not seen much of Giles during her teenage years, just stumbled across him now and again at parties Charlotte had taken her to in the school holidays. On her fifteenth birthday he had presented her with a pair of lacey, split-crotch panties. She had always suspected he had got her present mixed up with one to one of his mistresses. The panties had never been of the slightest use to her. She had ended up giving them to a friend at college who was into that kind of thing.

'Visit India, Aurelia, I should.'

'Why does he keep going on about India?' asked her mother. 'What's so fascinating about India?'

'Enlightenment and marijuana,' Maggie explained. 'He got in touch with his inner being out there.'

'I can't see that it's improved him much.'

'He lost it again in California.'

Charlotte patted her hand. 'Anyway, it's a good thing you kept on with the job because now you'll have a whole lot of nice colleagues to introduce us to.'

Maggie could tell she wasn't going to let go.

'OK,' she said. 'On two conditions. One, that you

152

don't let on you're my parents. You can be old acquaintances just dropping by.'

'Fine by me, darling. You *are* so terribly old, if you don't mind me saying so, to be my daughter.'

Maggie groaned and glanced over at Giles, slumbering catatonically behind a cloud of cigarette smoke. 'Impress that on him, will you? And secondly, that it's a small drinks party and you come dressed and behaving suitably.'

Only a very few friends, she thought as she left them in the hotel and headed back to Trinity, and only the most trusted. As parents went hers were, socially speaking, shocking.

In Grafton Street, she caught sight of Conor standing conspicuously in the middle of the road (less dangerous than it sounded for it had just been turned into a pedestrian precinct), talking into something that looked suspiciously like a remote-control gadget for switching television channels.

This is it, she thought, he's finally flipped. All that striving to get on in life, all that womanising, he was bound to feel the strain in the end. Come back Conor. I'll look after you.

'Hi.' He actually seemed pleased to see her; it made a pleasant change.

'What are you doing?' she asked cautiously.

'Phoning the office to see whether there are any messages for me.'

She coughed. 'Er... where's the phone?'

'Here.' He waved the remote-control device in front of her face. 'It's a cell phone. Forget answering machines, forget car phones, they're all *passé*. Cellular phones are the name of the game. Wouldn't be without it. I was hoping someone would notice me,' he added.

'I must be the first person in Ireland to have one of these.'

She tried to look suitably impressed.

'Lucky us meeting like this. I've been meaning to ring you.'

'Oh?' she said fearfully. By this time, she had given up hoping for anything good from Conor's phone calls.

'My house is getting too small.' She could have said, Why, Bridget's not that fat, but she refrained from comment. 'I'm thinking of moving. It doesn't suit my lifestyle any more to be living in a housing estate amongst a bunch of worn-out middle managers. I'm going for something more upmarket. There's a house in Castleknock I rather like the look of. *En suite* bathrooms, burglar alarm, remote-control garage door. I'm thinking of making them an offer.'

Selling the house, their house! She felt as if her past was being ripped away from her. She would no longer have roots in this country, or in any other country for that matter... Tears pricked the back of her eyelids.

'Can I come round and see it one last time?'

He stared at her. 'Why? There's nothing of yours left in it, is there?'

'No, but...' Only my memories, she thought.

He shrugged. 'You can come round if you want to, but let me know when... I'll be out a good bit over the next while.'

It means nothing to him, she thought. He is selling our past without a second thought. And I should be going there only to rake over the dead ashes of memory, by myself. I shall not go.

'You're looking depressed,' he said. 'What have you been up to?'

'Charlotte and Giles have arrived.'

'Really?' He gave her his full attention. She was used to this, the effect Charlotte and Giles had on some people.

'I'm giving a drinks party for them. Want to come?'

'To meet England's answer to Andy Warhol? Sure!' He paused. 'With or without Bridget?'

In despair she gave way. 'With. If you must.'

'Cheers.' He began fiddling with his phone again. 'See you around.'

'Yes.'

She walked into Trinity for her afternoon class wondering why meetings with Conor always left her feeling so bad these days. She was struck by a brief pang of nostalgia for her evening with Patrick. Things must be getting bad, she thought.

The next morning, she took Charlotte and Giles on a walking tour of Dublin. She met up with them in the Shelbourne and they made their way to the top of Grafton Street. Amongst all the brightly dressed young people strolling up and down, they no longer stood out in quite the way they had at the airport. That wasn't from want of trying, however. Charlotte was wearing a purple T-shirt dress which ended several inches above the knee, purple striped stockings, high-heel shoes and a large floppy hat. Giles wore dark glasses and complained of a hangover.

On the corner of Grafton Street they paused for a moment to watch a pale, sickly looking child in ragged shorts draw a picture of trees and cows on the pavement with different coloured chalks. He was copying the picture from a postcard. Beside him was an old tobacco tin. Maggie dropped some coins into it.

'I started my career doing that,' commented Giles, as they moved away. 'Every fine day I was sent out by my mother to earn my keep. I was only allowed to go to school when it rained. I made quite good money at it.'

'Did you, darling?' said Charlotte absent-mindedly, her attention taken up by the dresses in the window of Pia Bang. Maggie suspected Charlotte didn't believe Giles's story any more than she did herself. Giles made up a different tale every time about his origins. God knows where he really comes from, she thought. In her childhood she vaguely remembered him speaking with a broad Yorkshire accent. Now his accent veered erratically between West Coast, Home Counties and, when he was being especially pretentious, a kind of fake, French, Inspector Clouseau voice. Somewhere along the line, he had picked up a fake surname, too - Le Grys. They had all been Harrison till she was five.

'Hang on a minute,' said Charlotte, 'I must just...' She dashed into the boutique.

Giles wandered off on a mission of his own. Maggie leant against a wall, watching pregnant women and mothers recurring like decimals in front of her. Surely there had never been such a time for pregnant women... or perhaps it was just that she was noticing them more. She saw one woman carrying her baby in a harness suspended so precariously from her shoulders that the child was tilted sideways and its head poked out, unprotected. How can she be so careless, thought Maggie crossly. The child looked pale and tiny, no bigger than Maggie's two hands laid end to end. It made her feel like crying.

'Oh, look at him!' sighed Charlotte, returning from her abortive mission in the boutique. 'I can't leave him alone for a minute.'

Reluctantly, Maggie dragged her eyes off women with bumps and looked in the direction Charlotte was indicating. Giles was standing beside a lamp-post, chatting up two teenage girls in black T-shirts and leggings. They were both exceedingly thin and had masses of frizzy hair piled up on their heads. Their clothes made their legs and arms look like matchsticks.

'He was always a sucker for flat chests,' moaned Charlotte.

The girls were looking faintly uneasy. Reflecting that one instant out of her supervision and her family inevitably made a spectacle of itself, Maggie went over and pulled Giles away.

'Not the slightest response,' he complained. 'Do you think it possible they're virgins?'

'I expect they were wondering what on earth you were up to. You're old enough to be their grandfather.'

'Nonsense, Aurelia. You're being ridiculous!'

'If I'd had a child at the age Charlotte had me, it would be a teenager by now,' she pointed out.

'Would it really?' He stared at her. 'But then of course you were a mistake.'

'Thanks very much.'

'You were born with Charlotte's coil in your hand.'

'I have never in my life used the coil,' said Charlotte, heavily. 'You must be thinking of somebody else.'

Sensing tension in the air, Maggie guided them into Bewleys where a cup of coffee restored their humour.

'Pleasantly bohemian,' commented Giles. 'Lots of young people. Breezy.' He peered into a bookshop window. '*Galway Hookers.* That sounds promising. Shall we go to Galway, Charlotte?'

'It's not what you think,' warned Maggie.

They continued down Grafton Street. Out of the corner of her eye, she saw Conor pacing up and down, muttering into his cellular phone. She wondered whether he had taken up residence in this part of town. She hurried Charlotte and Giles past, hoping he wouldn't notice them (he didn't). She hadn't quite braced herself yet for the ordeal of presenting her parents to people; indeed they were, in her opinion, thoroughly unpresentable.

They passed a group of chattering students hanging around outside the language school.

'Ah, Gaelic!' murmured Charlotte. 'Such a beautiful language.'

'That's Spanish,' Maggie replied. 'The Irish don't speak Irish except in certain limited areas of the country.'

'What a shame.'

Tourists! thought Maggie. They always want the country to stay the same. If the tourists had their way, the Irish would still be living in thatched cottages, cooking on peat fires and fetching their water from wells. I don't know why Charlie doesn't simply turn Ireland into one huge folk museum and sell it to the Americans, she thought. Or perhaps a year-long summer school - Yeats, Joyce, Merriman, Humbert. At the bottom of Grafton Street, the wholly incredible sculpture of Molly Malone wheeling her cart of cockles and mussels seemed somehow to prove her point.

Giles stared at it in horror.

'What on earth was the sculptor thinking of? He...'

'She, actually,' murmured Maggie.

'...must have sculpted it from life.' He was aghast.

'Nonsense, dear. No real woman would have such an enormous cleavage,' said Charlotte. 'It's clearly a fantasy.'

'The tart with the cart, it's called. Come down O'Connell Street and I'll show you one you'll like better,' suggested Maggie.

In O'Connell Street, the shops were more tawdry, the people poorer and grim faced.

'It's not a very sexy city, is it?' Giles commented. 'Paris now is such a sexy city. You can sit in a café and feel the sex throbbing away in the air around you.'

'How unpleasant,' said Maggie.

'What turns Dubliners on, Aurelia?'

'Are you speaking to me? I'm Maggie.' But Giles's blank gaze showed her he was still not operating on the level of intelligence where she would have wished him. She gave it up. 'Religion and politics, that's what turns Dubliners on.'

'Bizarre. Who was O'Connell, anyway?' He stared up at the huge grey statue.

'That's history, Giles, it wouldn't interest you.' She paused. 'History - that turns Dubliners on, too.'

They passed some workmen standing beside a hole.

'The state of the Irish roads has not been exaggerated,' said Charlotte, peering down into it.

'That's not a pothole, that's deliberate,' explained Maggie. She pointed out the sculpture of Anna Livia Plurabelle lying against a huge concrete slab, her long hair rippling down over her outsize hands and feet to her toes. Water splashed around her... and Coke tins and paper wrappers and bits of orange peel.

'She looks most uncomfortable lying like that,' remarked Charlotte. 'It's a most awkward position to hold for any length of time. And, unless I'm mistaken, she has no cunt to speak of.'

'No, not in Ireland, she wouldn't.'

'Well, I like her,' Giles declared. 'Those marvellous Celtic features. Look at her eyes and that nose. She's a Jungian archetype.' He walked round it several times.

159

'Yes, it's easy to see that here we have expressed the heart and soul of Ireland.'

Maggie shrugged. 'Dubliners call her the floozie in the jacuzzie. What do you want to do now? Do you want to visit a gallery? There's one at the top of this street.'

Giles shuddered. 'Please, no. I never set foot in galleries nowadays. The past is dead. I don't want to be influenced by it. Turner, Constable, Stubbs... they ought to put a bomb under all that old stuff.'

'Don't talk about bombs, Giles darling.' Charlotte glanced uneasily over her shoulder. 'This is Ireland.'

Maggie returned them to their hotel for lunch and then left them to amuse themselves for the afternoon which, in Charlotte's case meant shopping and in Giles's, a lie-down on his bed and a smoke of a joint or two.

'Is this how they usually spend their days?' asked her mother, disapprovingly.

'Giles is looking for inspiration,' Maggie explained. 'It's a tiring business. And Charlotte, well, no one could accuse Charlotte of being idle. When she's in London, for instance, she has champagne breakfasts to attend, lunches at Harrods or Dickens and Jones, and tea at the Savoy. In between, she has consultations with her dietician, her beautician, her acupuncturist, her colonic hydrotherapist, her homeopathist, her chiropractor, her psychotherapist.'

'Is she very ill?' asked her mother, sympathetically.

'This is to prevent her becoming ill. Ever.'

Maggie walked towards her office, pondering on the drinks party she had so rashly promised. Where on earth was she going to hold it and whom could she invite at such short notice? She sat down behind her desk to think this one through. Conor's house was out of bounds... and anyway might be sold by now, she thought, with a pang. Fergus squatted in a horrid pokey little flat near the canal. Julian... but she did not think she wanted to ask anything of Julian ever again. There was only one thing for it. She rang Maureen.

'Maureen, I've an enormous favour to ask of you.'

There was a pause, a longer one than there should have been in Maggie's view, considering they had been friends for three years.

'Maggie, I've thought about that and I'm sorry, I really couldn't bring myself to. I'd like to. I know a more liberated woman would, but...'

Maggie stared at the phone in puzzlement. 'I haven't told you yet what the favour is.'

'Maggie, I know what you're going to say and I'm sorry, I couldn't.'

So much for friendship, she thought, a little hurt. 'It's only for one night, evening really. Actually, I was thinking about tonight, say between six and eight.'

'My, you have got your timing down to a fine art.'

'Well a couple of hours is all that's usually necessary for this kind of thing, isn't it?'

'I wouldn't bank on it. It took Art and myself four goes. You can't rely on films you know.'

Maggie frowned. 'What are we talking about here?'

'That film - *The Big Chill*. I saw it too. Where the woman lends her husband to her best friend for the night so that her friend can get pregnant. I'm saying in real life it doesn't work like that. It takes longer.' There was a controlled explosion on the other end. 'Why are you laughing?'

'Art?' gasped Maggie. 'You thought I was ringing you up to ask if I could go to bed with Art?'

161

'It's not that funny,' said Maureen, stiffly. 'I know he's losing his hair and getting rather staid and boring, but I had trouble hooking him, I can tell you. There were a lot of other women after him.'

Maggie sobered up. 'I'm sure there were, Maureen.'

'And he's proved he's up to producing healthy children... Well, if it wasn't that, what did you want?'

Maggie explained.

'Oh, the house! Yes, that's fine. It's only husbands I draw the line at in my reactionary bourgeois way. Art is working late, so we won't need to consult him. Will I be invited to meet these friends of yours?'

'Of course.'

'Jeepers! A party without my husband! My social life is looking up.'

Maggie invited Fergus, left a message on Conor's answering machine telling him where the party would be and spent several minutes wondering whether or not to invite Patrick. She dialled his number, let it ring for a few seconds, panicked and put down the receiver. After a moment, she picked it up and dialled again.

'Hello,' he said. 'I thought it might be you.'

She took a deep breath. 'I'm giving a party tonight. Would you like to come?'

'I made it a rule several years ago never to go to parties.'

'Oh.' She was half relieved. Come to think of it, he would have been bound to have seen through her game.

'I do drink coffee though.'

'Oh, yes.'

They arranged to meet later in the week. Strangely enough, it seemed like something she might look forward to, something apart from the muddle of her

162

everyday life. Then the thought of the party pressed in on her and she dismissed Patrick from her mind.

The numbers still looked thin. She decided to ask Julian - he had said he wanted to be friends. He informed her that he was engaged in writing several articles simultaneously, but would pop in if he found himself with a spare five minutes on his hands.

'And remember...'

'Don't worry, I'll keep Mum.' He chortled down the phone.

Was there anything in her recent past she regretted as much, she wondered, as that evening with Julian? After her class at four, she picked up some wine and nibbles and collected Giles and Charlotte from the Shelbourne. She was relieved to see that they were dressed quite soberly, Giles in a blue and white striped suit and Charlotte in a short, black dress.

'Right,' said Giles, rubbing his hands and looking more alert than he had done in a long while, 'let's hit this party.'

'All right. But just don't expect it to hit back,' she warned. They drove out to Rathgar.

Charlotte looked about her. 'Not bad, darling. The house has certainly got potential. Whom did you say it belonged to?'

Maggie introduced her to Maureen.

'I know this ever-so-clever interior decorator in London,' said Charlotte, kindly. 'Could do this place up a treat.'

'It is done up,' replied Maureen frostily.

'Charlotte, go and sit down,' ordered Maggie. 'Maureen and I will see to this stuff.'

They went through into the kitchen and began opening bottles and setting out cubes of cheese on plates.

'They're not at all like your usual friends,' Maureen remarked.

'No, they're not really my type. I met them in London years ago. Since then, we've rather lost touch.' Which is true enough, she thought.

'They look quite old, too.'

'Oh good, do you think so?'

The doorbell rang, waking Amber who had been in her cot upstairs. Maureen went to see to her whilst Maggie answered the door. It was Fergus and Anna, the latter looking just as Fergus had described her, tall and elegant, her copper hair done up in a plait. She was wearing a long, white dress, with leather boots and a leather belt. Maggie could see why Fergus had thought it necessary to invest in shoulder pads, but even with them, he looked absurdly short beside Anna, and he seemed to be strutting more than usual this evening.

Taking them into the living room and introducing them around, Maggie detected a gleam of envy in Charlotte's eye as she gave Anna the once over. Giles, as if he had been waiting in the interval for his legs and they had just arrived by special courier, shot out of his chair and offered her a joint. Anna politely declined.

'You're married?' she said, looking from one to the other, as if she was unable to fit them together, a problem Maggie had some sympathy with.

'On the whole, we are,' agreed Charlotte.

Giles made some sort of movement.

'I beg your pardon?' said Fergus.

'What?' said Giles.

'I thought you spoke?'

'Not yet. I may in a minute.'

164

As repartee goes, so far it isn't brilliant, thought Maggie. She poured out some wine. Fergus and Anna sat down on the sofa, holding hands. Maggie watched them enviously. Giles, having been unable to make any headway with Anna, retreated to the armchair and rolled a joint. Maureen brought Amber down to join the party.

'Sweet,' said Charlotte, keeping her distance. 'I didn't realise your friends had got to the stage of having babies, darling. I do hope you're not thinking of making me a grandmother?'

'Shut up, Charlotte,' hissed Maggie.

'Oh sorry, darling, I forgot.' She wandered off to cadge a joint from Giles.

Maureen nudged Maggie. 'What did she mean by that? Surely that woman's not your mother?'

Maggie laughed, uproariously.

'I've always pictured your mother as a gentle, grey-haired person.'

'That's exactly what she is, Maureen. A nice, conventional housewife living in Mill Hill. It's best not to pay attention to anything Charlotte says. She's in the early stages of senile dementia.'

'How terrible!' said Maureen, looking so truly shocked that for a moment Maggie felt a pang of guilt.

Conor, to her relief, came without Bridget.

'Naturally, art being her field and all that, she was dying to meet the famous Giles Le Grys, but she thought, since it was you giving the party, it would be morally wrong to come. She has high standards about that kind of thing.'

'It's a good job somebody has,' muttered Maggie, handing him a glass of wine.

'What?'

'Nothing.'

'Hey! A piece of good news! I've found a buyer for the house.'

'Oh,' she replied dully. Nowadays, Conor's good news never seemed to be hers.

'I say, is that Charlotte over there? Wow!' He rubbed his hands together. 'Introduce me at once. Perhaps it's a good thing Bridget didn't come after all.'

'Ah, Charlotte,' he said eagerly, shaking hands with her. 'I've heard so much about you. Didn't you used to be a model?'

'Briefly.' Charlotte fluttered her eyelashes.

'One can always tell,' simpered Conor.

Toad. Crawler, thought Maggie.

Maureen came and stood beside her. She looked at Fergus and looked at Maggie; and looked at Fergus and looked at Maggie.

'Maureen...' began Maggie, warningly.

Maureen screwed up her eyes. 'He'd do, you know. Ask him whether he likes children. Go on.'

'Maureen!'

'Then I will.' She marched up to the sofa where Fergus and Anna were still sitting holding hands. Maggie hurried after her, hoping to perform some sort of damage limitation. Gently, Maureen lowered Amber down into Anna's lap. She straightened up and glanced meaningfully at Fergus.

'There now, doesn't that look nice? Do you like children, Fergus?'

Fergus coughed. 'Um, yes. Not bad.' A shade of embarrassment passed over his face.

'She's lovely,' said Anna, handling the child with a practised air which caused Maggie a stab of envy. Like the wretched Bridget, this woman had everything,

166

lover *and* children. 'How old is she? Six months?' The two mothers went into a huddle on the sofa, discussing baby care. Fergus and Maggie hung around them, feeling redundant.

'How's your computer?' she asked, eventually.

'Feeling much better, thanks. I applied a vaccine.'

'No more morning sickness then?'

'No more morning sickness,' he replied.

Maureen, catching the tail end of this, looked up hopefully. Maggie glared menacingly at her. Maureen returned to her conversation with Anna.

There was a short pause while Maggie and Fergus eavesdropped on them. However neither could think of anything useful to contribute to the conversation.

'Come on,' she said, at last. 'I'll introduce you to Giles.'

'I've already been introduced to him,' objected Fergus.

'That doesn't matter. He won't notice. Hello again, Giles.'

Giles stared at her as if he vaguely remembered having seen her some place before.

'Enjoying the crack?' added Fergus, slapping him on the back.

A hopeful glint appeared in Giles's eye.

'As perhaps you know, Giles is a painter,' said Maggie, hastily.

'Artist,' Giles corrected her. 'Sometimes likened to Mr Warhol. You one of Aurelia's colleaguey thingies? Pleased to meet you. Breezy.'

'Yes, it is rather cool in here,' replied Fergus. 'What kind of thing do you paint?'

'Packets of cornflakes, record sleeves,' responded Giles, vaguely. 'I say, Aurelia, any chance of finding a decent record in this house - Santana, Cream, *It's A Beautiful Day*, perhaps?'

'I doubt it,' murmured Maggie. 'Maureen's given up necrophilia for Lent.'

Fergus grinned.

'Ah well.' Giles gazed blankly into space.

'There's talk of another general election over here,' said Fergus, conversationally.

Giles continued to stare into the distance.

Fergus nudged Maggie. 'Is he OK?'

'Oh yes, just his usual cannabis fog.'

'Why did he call you Aurelia?'

'Oh, you mustn't mind Giles. He gets muddled.' She drew Fergus to one side. 'You've heard of Alzheimer's Disease?' I deserve to be punished, going on like this, she thought.

'Greens are the thing,' said Giles, suddenly.

'Yes, all right,' she put in, briskly. 'We know all about that.'

Giles wandered off to make enquiries about Maureen's record collection.

Fergus raised his eyebrows. 'That fellow strikes me as being a few pence short of the full shilling. Is he really as mentally deranged as he appears, or is he pretending?'

Maggie shrugged. 'Life burn-out, that's what's the matter with him. Nobody wants pictures of Heinz tomato ketchup any more. Art has moved on and left Giles behind, I'm afraid.'

'Still, I'm glad you invited me. It's important to give Anna the right impression. She thinks the only people I know are boring academics.' Maggie winced. 'Foxrock is hard to live up to. You may just have rescued my image. That fellow's probably the most famous person

I've met in a long time.'

They were, as usual, charming all her friends, she thought dismally, staring at Charlotte and Conor sitting cross-legged on the floor on Amber's pink rug. It always happened. When they wanted to, they could ooze charm as an octopus oozes ink, sending it out in thick, cloying squirts. Oh, Conor, she thought, what does it take to keep you?

Julian called in. 'Can't stop. I'm in between articles. Ah, a baby!' he exclaimed, spying Amber on Anna's lap. He gave Maggie a deeply significant look.

'It's not mine, Julian.'

'Oh no, I forgot. They take nine months, don't they?'

He tackled Conor unsuccessfully about his Christmas Day article and left. On the doorstep, he said, 'I'd have liked to stay longer. It's this Northern work ethic. There's no escaping it. Gets me down sometimes. By the way, I'd keep an eye on that Conor, if I were you. He seems to be a terrible man for the women.'

'Thank you, Julian. I know.'

She went back into the living room and saw what Julian meant. Places had changed. Charlotte was now on the sofa beside Maureen and Conor was on his feet chatting to, or rather, chatting up, Anna.

'Fergus, quick!' she hissed. 'Go and rescue Anna or you may lose her.'

He glanced over. 'To Conor? Nonsense.' He thrust out his chest. 'What would she see in him?' He looked again. 'Well, perhaps, if you'd excuse me a moment...'

Charlotte came over. 'I like that Conor. He's been explaining to me all about his new cellulite phone. Now there's a man who moves with the times.'

'Oh, and that's good, is it?'

Irony was beyond Charlotte. She plucked nervously at the heavy gold bracelet on her arm. 'Darling, do you think any of your nice friends would have a little coke?'

'Coke? There's some in the fridge,' said Maggie, deliberately.

'Oh dear, Aurelia. What is the matter with you? You never were like anyone else we knew.'

'Thank God for that. I worked at it, you know.'

'What have you got against us?'

'You've let fashion dictate your lives. Look at Giles. He cultivated the kind of emptiness and inarticulateness that was fashionable in the Sixties and he's never been able to get himself out of it. I sometimes wonder whether he's all there.'

'Darling, don't be depressing.'

Their little skirmish ended there, because at that moment, Maureen and Giles came up.

'My health visitor tells me I should join an art class,' Maureen was saying. 'Do you think there would be any use in it?'

'Ah,' said Giles, in the kind of ponderous tone which made Maggie anticipate the worst, 'the true artist is a god, a priest. Can women be priests? Can women be gods? No. Women are trapped by their sexuality.' Maureen looked glum. 'They're at the mercy of their emotions. Therefore, the artistic impulse is undeveloped in the female sex. *Voilà pourquoi* there are no great women artists.'

'Or might it not be because, until now, the history of art has been written by men?' suggested Maggie, politely.

He gave her a vacant stare. 'Art history? Keep away from it.' He turned back to Maureen. 'No. Women like you get their fulfillment from being wives and

170

mothers. Isn't that so, Charlotte?'

Charlotte scowled. 'I never had any option. I won prizes for art at school. But you soon put a stop to that, didn't you, darling? Keeping up with you has been a full-time job.'

Maggie looked at her in surprise. This was a version of the past she hadn't heard before. She repressed a twinge of sympathy. It was too late now to begin rewriting history.

Giles ignored his wife's remarks. 'Take Bacon...' he told Maureen.

She looked puzzled. 'Bacon? Art likes a bit of...'

'Francis Bacon - now there's a great artist for you, an artist with balls. Can women have balls? That's the question you have to ask yourself... Mandy, Mavis, er... whoever you are.'

Soon after this, Maggie hurried them away.

The next morning she rang Maureen.

'Sorry for leaving you to clear up. I just had to get them away.'

'I must say, Maggie, they did seem a little odd. Still, at the moment I'm most grateful for any kind of social life at all.'

'Did Conor stay long?'

'No. After he'd run through Charlotte and Anna, he seemed to lose interest. He left soon after you. You know, Maggie, I can say this now. I never really liked Conor.'

'I know.'

'Oh... And Julian, as we saw, is a confirmed workaholic, but Fergus...'

'Maureen!'

'Ah well, he did seem rather attached to Anna.' She sighed. 'Pity. He'd make a good father. He spent quite a long time playing with Amber after you left.' Maureen always got sentimental over men who paid attention to her daughter. 'Hey ho! It's back to dreary old routine for me after that bit of excitement. What are they doing today?'

It turned out that they had decided to fly on to Shannon and all they wanted was a lift to the airport.

'I'd like to have stayed longer, but Giles is eager to move on and see more,' Charlotte explained, as they sat in the hotel lounge waiting for Giles to finish dressing. 'He believes there's something for him in this country. He feels in tune with the spirit of the place.'

'He said all that?'

Charlotte ignored this. 'He wants to paint the West of Ireland, the mountains and lakes of Connemara.'

'It's been done, with jaw-aching regularity, by practically every painter who's ever visited Ireland.'

'But not by Giles. Don't be so discouraging, darling.'

Maggie sat up. 'The truth is, Charlotte, that Giles hasn't picked up a brush for fifteen years and probably never will again. He's run out of subjects. Or talent. Or both. Why do you pretend all the time?'

'He knows it, darling. He knows he's finished. It's a terrible thing for a man.'

'Why do you allow him to fake it then? Why don't you get him to admit he's all burned out? Then you could stop this endless travelling around.'

Charlotte looked at her. 'Dear Maggie,' she said sadly, 'I don't believe that you can ever have been in love.'

'Is that why you stay with him? Come on, Charlotte, what's in it for you? He's hardly even all there any more,' she whispered, as Giles came into the lounge, stared plethorically around him and sat down in a chair. 'Look, he's forgotten all about us.'

'I have to stay with him. Our souls are knit together.' As Maggie raised her eyes to the heavens, Charlotte went on more quietly, 'All right, it may not be rapture, but it is comfort. And you have to remember that he stayed with me at a time when he could have gone off with any girl in London.'

'He was unfaithful,' Maggie pointed out, recalling the times she had been taken out of school to be company for Charlotte whilst Giles was embarked on a new affair. She remembered those awful, late-night soul-searching sessions when she had been forced to stay awake and listen whilst Charlotte explored her feelings from every conceivable angle.

'He always came back. Now it's my turn to stick by him,' replied Charlotte firmly, in the sort of tone that puts an end to further discussion.

They got up, went over to collect Giles who, to give him his due, seemed only mildly surprised to see them, and Maggie drove them to the airport. In the car all three of them fell silent. We have, as usual, run out of things to say to each other, thought Maggie. The only surprising thing is that it didn't happen earlier.

She became aware of Charlotte glancing over at her from time to time. Once or twice, her gaze lingered. She seemed vaguely uneasy about something. Oh well, at least we've escaped without a row, Maggie thought. And no one seems to have guessed their true identity. All in all, the visit had not been as awful as she had feared. But she was glad they were going.

At the airport, Giles, jittery about certain substances he had hidden on his person, kissed Maggie quickly on the cheek and hurried through into the departure lounge. Charlotte lingered behind. She looked at

Maggie, hesitated, then said rapidly, 'Darling, I don't know where Giles will want to be off to next. It may be another year before we see each other again. Can't you let bygones be bygones?' She leant forward and touched her on the cheek.

Maggie took a step backwards and stubbed her toe against the leg of a chair. 'Why should I?' she muttered.

'Sweetie, I know you think I made things hard for you when you were a child, but you must remember how young I was, much much younger than you are now, and terribly in love with Giles. To tell the truth, I was scared of losing him. He had so much energy in those days, he demanded my full attention. I couldn't cope with both of you. I had to choose. You always seemed such a serious, sensible little girl. I thought you would be the one best able to manage on your own. Giles needed me.'

'I needed you too! I was only eight when you sent me away to that wretched school. And left me there.'

Charlotte's eyes dropped. She examined her nails.

'Perhaps I made the wrong decision. But you have to understand, you seemed so independent, so well able to look after yourself. Giles is hopeless on his own. He gets into such muddles.' She looked up. 'You've turned out to be my only child. Don't you think I sometimes regret having missed out on your childhood?'

Maggie dug her nails into the palms of her hands. I will not give in, she thought. 'You'd better hurry or you'll miss that plane,' she said stiffly.

Charlotte leant forward and kissed her. 'Try to forgive me, Aurelia. Some time.'

She disappeared round the corner, trailing her three bags and a scarf.

MOTHER

Chapter Nine

Soon after this, Maggie began to have dreams. In one, an old man took her by the hand and led her into a garden where fountains played. Together, they circled the fountain and their faces were splashed by fine spray. He spoke these words to her: 'The unexamined life is not worth living - your view of yourself is derivative. Stop allowing others to impose their stereotypes on you. You must break free of the past.' Another night, she found herself standing in a prisoner's dock, on trial. The judge rapped on the table for silence. The prosecuting lawyer stood up. 'We are here to try your soul, Maggie James,' he said. 'It seems you have been guilty of wilful neglect.' At other times, Charlotte appeared before her. She was pleading for something. But she spoke so softly that Maggie could not hear her words.

The dreams made her feel feverish and shaky. The unpleasant sensations they left behind often did not dispel until lunchtime. On bad days, they lasted till she fell asleep again at night. The fact that she was able to piece together parts which came from recent conversations didn't seem to help. 'Fergus, do you believe that dreams can foretell the future?' she asked. 'No,' he replied. 'Because Anna's dreams are all of her children.' She asked Julian. 'It's generally thought,' he said, 'that dreams compensate in some way for our waking lives. They express things we are afraid to admit openly. In that sense, they probably can foretell the future.' She was not reassured.

She met Patrick for coffee in Bewleys, just before he left for the West of Ireland. He looked taller and thinner, more vulnerable, than she had remembered. For the first time in her life, she found herself feeling vaguely protective towards a man. She told him, because he asked about her plans, that she intended to have a child in the near future.

'Are you wise enough to have a child?' was all he said. He had no children himself.

'And you,' she asked, 'what are your plans?'

He stirred his coffee. 'My immediate aim is to grow a beech tree.'

She was uncertain whether to laugh or not. As always, he was confusing her.

'It's one of the most difficult trees to grow,' he continued. 'It needs a lot of light.'

'Why a tree?'

He looked sad. 'Something that will last into the future... like your child.'

'What about your books?'

He shrugged. 'Literary fame can't be relied on. Fashions change. Even Shakespeare was out of favour in the eighteenth century...'

She told him about her dreams, omitting the one in which Charlotte figured.

'If you're dreaming like that, you're not being honest with yourself. You're denying something and it's surfacing in your dreams. What are you denying, Maggie?'

She looked down. 'I don't know.'

'You're floundering. Like this country of ours.' He leaned back in his chair and considered her.

She looked up in surprise.

'Term will be ending soon. You'll have a bit of time before exams start. Why don't you come and stay for a week or so in the West?'

'But...' The sight of his hands, lean and brown around his coffee cup, sent shivers down her spine. For this reason, she said, 'I couldn't...'

He shook his head. 'The idea seems strange to you now, but I've a feeling that very soon, you'll be wanting to get away for a while.'

She wondered briefly if he was referring to McGregor and whether he had heard anything new, but her thoughts were too taken up by his extraordinary invitation to enquire.

He took his dog-eared notebook out of his pocket, tore off a page, scribbled down his address and handed it to her.

'But...'

'What now?'

'Won't I be disturbing you?'

He gave a short laugh. 'I live on my own, something of a recluse. I rarely have visitors.'

'Then why...?'

'Don't ask so many questions. You should learn to accept things as they happen. And don't leave it too long,' he added.

She saw him off on the train, vaguely promising to visit him when term ended. She did not expect to keep her promise.

For the last two weeks of term, she was left on her own a lot. Fergus was busy with Anna, Julian was away at his conference in Birmingham and Maureen was fretting over Amber who had developed a mysterious cough. One day she saw Conor and Bridget walking arm in arm down Grafton Street. She was about to run in front of them and make some ribald comment. Instead she turned away. It didn't seem worth it any more, playing the clown. She gave up her plans of revenge, not because she was above it, as Patrick had suggested she should be, but because she simply hadn't the energy any more.

She wished he was there to talk things over with. It wasn't that she was attracted to him or anything like that, of course (for heaven's sake, he was even older than Charlotte). The thing was he simply knew more about life than any of the people she hung about with. His going away had left her with an absence, a kind of yearning, she didn't know for what.

The day she met Paul in a pub off Grafton Street for the promised after work drink, the newspapers announced a crisis. An election had been held but there was as yet no government. The Irish people had been unable to agree on whom they wished to govern them.

'The country is going to the dogs,' said Paul gloomily, shaking his head. He was wearing the double-breasted jacket with the shiny gold buttons again. This time he had a white polo-neck jumper on underneath. Not an improvement, Maggie thought.

'Aren't you too hot in that lot?' she asked, rather rudely. She was wearing a short, denim skirt and T-shirt, the weather having become unexpectedly mild.

'You never know when it might take a turn for the worse,' he replied, glancing anxiously out of the window at the perfect blue sky. 'I had thought of bringing an umbrella.'

He was getting to be quite a challenge.

'The plane wasn't delayed,' she brought out, with a certain amount of satisfaction.

'Beg pardon?'

'The plane I was running off to meet the day you moved in. It wasn't late. You feared it might be.' You insisted it would be, she thought.

'Indeed? Most unusual. I wonder what went wrong?' He leaned forward and inspected his beer glass. 'Not the cleanest of places this, is it?' He took out a handkerchief and wiped the rim. 'I have my doubts about the toilet arrangements, too.'

'How are you settling into the flat?' she asked hurriedly, biting her lip quite ferociously to keep from laughing.

'Very comfy, thank you.'

'None of those drawbacks you were worrying about?'

'Ah, those.' He gave her a most serious look. 'I've made out a list. I'm having half an hour with Mr Nolan tomorrow.'

'Oh?'

'It won't be enough.'

'Oh.'

'I know a place where we could get something to eat,' he said suddenly. 'But you probably wouldn't like it.'

She rose to the challenge (besides, she had absolutely nothing else to do). 'Try me.'

The restaurant was called Annabel's and he had been right, it wasn't her sort of place, though she was determined not to give him the satisfaction of knowing this. It was the kind of restaurant where middle-management brings its wives to celebrate a birthday or a promotion. The men were all in suits, the women wore what Conor would have called party frocks, little-girl dresses with puffed sleeves and flouncey skirts, pulled in at the waist with gold or silver belts. Even

181

Charlotte would have had more taste, she thought. They were all, without exception, wearing high-heeled shoes. Quite, quite hopeless for escaping from rapists. The thing was though - she stuck out a mile. She looked down at her grubby, denim skirt. 'I'm afraid I'm underdressed.' She smiled.

Paul did not return her smile, but nodded slightly, looking at her through half-closed eyes. 'First rule if you want to get on in life: always dress appropriately.'

'See?' said her mother. 'I keep telling you that a little more effort in the clothes line would do you no harm at all.' Shut up, mother, she replied, automatically.

'What if I don't want to get on?' she countered.

He shrugged, apparently not thinking that a question worth answering.

They stood hovering about the entrance, looking so grimly determined to enjoy themselves that they had difficulty getting a waiter. Eventually, one did deign to notice them and they were led over to one of the little tables set round the tiny square marked out for dancing. On the other side of the square a group was playing; a 'band' Paul called it.

'You don't like it,' he said, studying her expression. 'I knew you wouldn't.'

'Nonsense! I love it.' She tugged a smile onto her face, resolved not to let his pessimism win the day. 'Shall we order?' She felt a sudden desire to speed the evening along.

'The food is nothing special.' He picked up the menu. 'But the plates are clean and I've never yet got sick after eating here. Touch wood. Also, you can rest easy in your mind - the toilet arrangements are immaculate.'

'Well that's a relief.'

'Exactly. May I suggest the set menu? Safety in

numbers and all that.'

'Can't be worse than my cooking, at any rate,' she murmured, looking about her. She found the atmosphere sapping, certainly not conducive to the type of bright, witty conversation she was used to having with Conor and his friends - which now Bridget would be sharing. The restaurant made her feel middle-aged and serious. Paul was a serious person.

Over the avocado vinaigrette (avocado a little underripe), he told her about his accountancy job, his colleagues, his prospects for promotion. Over the coq au vin (which he dithered about eating till she assured him that no cases of death by salmonella poisoning had actually yet occurred in Ireland), he went further back and recounted his early struggles which included night-shifts in the jam factory to pay for his college education. His family lived in a working-class suburb.

'You see, I was determined to get on,' he said, gazing at her with dark, serious eyes. 'I mean to have the best in life and I want my wife, when I decide to marry, to have the best too. Quality of life's all-important, you know.'

Perhaps to show he meant business, he sent back a plate of chips on the grounds that they weren't the French fries he had ordered. She was mortified.

'It's quite normal,' he assured her. 'You have to insist on your rights. I don't mind paying, but I do expect good service.'

Over the black forest gateau she began to get bored. There was a heaviness about him that she was not used to. She sneaked a glance at her watch. Half-time, she thought, and the wind's in our backs in the second half. Then she felt ashamed. I have become frivolous, she reflected. Ireland has made me frivolous. I'm thirty. It's time I grew up. 'Yes, it is', agreed her mother. 'Paul seems a nice boy, willing to provide. I can't think what more you could want.'

'You're looking sad.' He reached across the table and took her hand. 'I've been watching you. You often look sad when you go out of the house on a morning. Why?'

She shrugged. 'Oh, this and that.'

'You should be happy. You deserve to be happy.'

'No one *deserves* to be happy.' She removed her hand. 'Happiness is an exaggerated emotion bearing no obvious relation to the facts.'

He appeared not to take this in. 'I shall make you happy, now that we're together.'

'Together?' Her voice rose in panic. 'What does that mean?'

'I... well...' he stammered. 'I thought this was a date. A sort of trial balance.' He recovered himself and smirked.

She leaned across the table. 'I don't have dates. This is simply a neighbourly meal.'

'Oh.'

He looked dismal. 'I'm not good enough for you, is that it?'

'Of course not,' she said sharply. 'My family aren't that well off themselves as a matter of fact. My father...' Not that again, she thought. She lapsed into silence.

His eyes narrowed. 'I don't believe you. You speak posh.'

'All English people, especially Southerners, sound posh in Ireland. It's something to do with our loud voices.'

'I'm not clever enough for you then, I suppose?' He sighed and dabbed at the corners of his mouth with his napkin.

'I don't go around examining people's IQs,' she retorted.

'Oh? I thought that was part of your job?'

She noted nervously that he was beginning to get sarcastic. 'Can you wonder?' said her mother. 'The way you go on.'

'Well, if it's not those things, what is it?' he persisted.

'I'm just not looking for anyone at the moment.'

He stared at her. 'Of course you are. Everyone is. How old are you?'

'Twenty-ni...' No, that was Charlotte's trick. 'Thirty,' she admitted reluctantly and guiltily, as if owning up to a particularly appalling crime.

'There you are then. Your stock is depreciating. You'd better hurry up.'

'Hurry up and do what?' She glared at him across the table.

'Settle down.'

'What a terrible idea.'

He ignored this. 'Marry, start a family. Look at me. I'm only twenty-four and already I'm planning ahead.'

'Good for you.' Now there's what I call a sensible lad, said her father.

Paul wagged a finger at her. 'Solid accountancy is what you need, in business and in life. Thirty's a dreadful age to be still a spinster. You can't just drift, you know.'

'Why not?'

He sighed. 'I don't understand you. Don't you believe in happy endings?'

She thought of Conor. 'Not any more,' she said.

There was a silence. She couldn't help thinking that his silences greatly improved the conversation.

'I don't suppose you want to dance?'

'I would have,' she said, completely fed up with him, 'only I'm afraid my joints have seized up. Arthritis. At my age, it's a bugger.'

He sighed again. 'We'd better get the bill then.'

She insisted on paying her share. At first, he got quite shirty, acting as though his masculinity was being called into question, but when she pointed out that they were unlikely to have another meal together and it was as well to keep the books balanced, he took her point.

Outside, they walked in silence towards their respective cars.

'I knew this evening wouldn't be a success,' he said, as she got into her car.

She smiled. 'Well, look on the bright side.' She switched on the engine. 'For once you were right.' She drove off. 'I can't understand you,' said her father. 'I thought you were looking for a secure, stable, normal relationship?' There's normal and normal, she retorted. I've never been so bored in all my life.

Perhaps as a result of this evening with Paul, it began to come home to her how much she was skulking around the edges of people's lives, an observer rather than a participant. She remembered the restaurant full of couples and felt the impact of Paul's word 'spinster'. He might, despite his dismal personality, turn out to be right. She might very well be heading for a lonely old age. She couldn't help having a sneaking suspicion that society was on his side, supporting couples, making it difficult for single people to find a place for themselves.

On the last day of term, she was meditating on such matters in between frantic efforts to finish her marking, when Niall came to see her. He hovered in the

186

doorway in his green cloak, looking pale and tense.

'Dr James,' he said, hesitantly. 'Can I speak to you for a moment? I've a bit of a problem.'

'Mm.' She pointed with her pen to a chair.

He sat down, drawing his green cloak around him. There was a short silence during which he studied his feet, the carpet, the curtains, her left shoulder. Finally he burst out,

'It's my girlfriend, you see. She's pregnant.'

'Oh.' She hadn't expected that. Exams or next year's reading list, not something so personal. She had rarely in fact had a student come to her with a personal problem. They generally went to Lallie for that sort of thing. She looked at him. There were dark rings under his eyes and he was shivering. She remembered guiltily that the last time she had seen him, she had attributed his pallor to drugs. Wondering whether she would be up to this, she put down her pen. 'Tell me about it, Niall. Take your time.'

'She's a student too... law.' He twisted his hands in his lap. 'Christ, it was a shock. Something must have gone wrong... well anyway, she's pregnant,' he repeated dully.

Maggie suppressed a twinge of envy. 'How long have you known her, Niall?'

'A year or so, on and off. I like her, but neither of us wants to get married or anything like that. It isn't that kind of relationship. We just hang around together.' He paused. His hands were trembling. 'It's her family, you see. They keep phoning me up and going on about marriage. Marriage! It'd ruin us. My parents are the same. In fact they've chucked me out,' he ended, miserably.

Maggie frowned. 'Don't they realise you've got

exams coming up?'

'Oh, they realise all right. They say I should have thought of that before.'

'So where are you living now?'

'I've moved in with some mates of mine. They rent a flat in Adelaide Road. I'm dossing on their living room floor.'

'Not great for revising. Have you spoken to your tutor? Perhaps he could help with accommodation.'

He grimaced. 'My tutor is Dr McGregor.'

'I take your point.'

For the first time since he entered the room, his eyes brightened. 'The thing is,' he fiddled with the edge of his cloak, 'we were wondering about an abortion. But we don't know any addresses in England...'

A wave of anger swept over Maggie. A baby on the way, a new life. Didn't they know how lucky they were? Abortion on demand was just the kind of thing Charlotte and Giles supported. Indeed she remembered Charlotte joining demonstrations once or twice in London and hinting that if abortion had been easily available in the Fifties, Maggie herself might not be here now (always adding, 'But of course I've never regretted having you, darling.') She glanced across at Niall and saw that beneath the green cloak he was shivering. How old was he? Eighteen, nineteen at the most. Too young to be faced with this sort of decision. And vulnerable. Her anger died. It wasn't fair to throw her personal situation at him. She had always, in theory, supported women's right to choose. Nevertheless, theory was one thing, practice another.

'What does your girlfriend think of abortion?' she asked. 'I hope you're not bullying her into this?' He shook his head. No, she thought, Niall wouldn't bully.

'And what about her parents? They aren't going to be too pleased if you go through with it.'

'We won't tell them. We'll wait till after the exams and go over together "on the boat",' he replied, grimly repeating a phrase that had been bandied about during the amendment campaign. 'They'll chuck her out. But then they said they'd chuck her out anyway, if we didn't get married. On her own with a kid, there's no way she could continue her studies. She'd have to bring it up on welfare and charity. What kind of a life is that? But they don't care. They've even had the priest round trying to persuade her that marriage is her only option.' He put his head in his hands. 'I feel so guilty,' he muttered. 'She's so bright - she got a First last year - and now she's talking about dropping out of Trinity altogether.'

'What do you think would be best?' she asked, with a gentleness which surprised herself.

He raised his head. 'She's very ambitious, much more than me. She's hoping to become a barrister. She doesn't want the baby, she's just afraid. She's a Catholic... was a Catholic. The nuns... you never really leave them behind.'

Setting her own feelings on the matter to one side, Maggie tried to think through the problem from all angles. 'An abortion would be expensive. How will you manage for money?'

'I've some left over from working in the States last summer. I was going to buy a stereo.' He twisted his hands together. 'Christ! It's a nightmare. We're both on tranquillisers.'

She sighed. 'Listen, if you're convinced this is what you want to do, I could get you an address.' Lallie was bound to know of a good, safe, London clinic and at

189

least that would balance out the choices, give them something to set against the priest. 'About accommodation... I would go to the accommodation officer and see what she can do for you. You should be a priority case with exams coming up. If that doesn't work, well, there's a chance I might be away for a week or so, you could borrow my flat to study in. It's quiet at least.'

'Thanks, Dr James. I didn't know who to go to.'

She waved aside his gratitude. 'And stop taking tranquillisers,' she said, as he went out of the door. 'You'll never make a proper decision whilst you're on those things.'

She realised how very little she knew about her students. Perhaps Paul was right, perhaps she only saw them in terms of intellects - to be tested, selected and graded, like Bird's Eye peas. Now suddenly this human tragedy had erupted, demanding more from her than a purely intellectual response. Yet, in a way, her response had been an intellectual one, for her emotions in this case were all in the other direction; for life, and the child.

At lunch, she asked Lallie for the address of a London clinic. They went back to her office and Lallie dug one out for her. She handed it over with a look of sympathy.

'It's all right, Lallie,' said Maggie, hastily. 'It's not for myself.'

'No, of course not,' Lallie replied. 'Aren't men beasts?'

That evening, she had an end-of-term drink with Fergus who was killing time while Anna visited her children. Maggie told him about her conversation with Niall.

'It's illegal in Ireland you know, to hand out addresses of abortion clinics.'

'I know.'

'You'll catch it from McGregor if he ever finds out,' he said, comfortingly. 'I'm not sure I approve either.'

'Look, I don't need this. I was only trying to give them a choice. Personally, I hope she has the baby.'

'So do I. The adoption agencies are running low on supplies.' He passed a hand over his face. 'Sorry, kid, didn't mean to attack. I get nervous whenever Anna's visiting her children.'

'Poor Fergus.' She took a sip of Smithwicks. 'How is it all going to end for you?'

'Ach, I don't know.' He tugged at his beard. 'It'll be messy, whatever happens. This bloody country's laws, they leave people like us in limbo. No chance of a divorce unless ould eyes filling could be persuaded to go and live in England, which I doubt. So they'll have to work it out between themselves about the children. He's being exceptionally stingy at the moment. Won't let them come and stay with us on the grounds that I'd be a corrupting influence on them.' He groaned. 'Anna thinks it's because he's afraid of losing them.'

'It sometimes happens.'

'I'm not playing Dad to them. That wouldn't be right.'

'How would you like having children around?' she asked, curiously. 'It would be quite a change for you.'

'Me? I'd love it.' He grinned. 'We'll need a bigger place though, and that will only be possible if I can sell the house in Lucan, and that will only be possible if Gráinne agrees to move out.'

'Jeepers! Your life is complicated. Will Gráinne agree, do you think?'

'As my mother says, why should she? Gráinne, as my mother never fails to point out whenever I visit her, taught me to drive, supported me financially when I was an impoverished research student, cooked for me, cared for me. Why should she move out?'

'You're not in good standing with your family then?'

'I was reared in the Church of Ireland tradition. No saints, no incense, no gambling, smoking, drinking or passion. On Sundays, Da wasn't allowed to wash the car and we kids weren't allowed to play out in the street. My relationship with Anna is the grown-up equivalent of playing out on the streets on Sunday.'

'Mm. I see.'

He shifted restlessly on his stool. 'Enough of my troubles. What about you? Still fussed about this promotion interview?'

'Yep.'

'Term's ended. Why don't you get away for a bit? We'd be off now too, if it wasn't for Anna's children.'

'Where do you suggest I go?'

'England? Visit your parents?'

'Um, I think not,' she mumbled.

'Not much of a holiday, eh? I thought they were pretty decent, your folks?'

'They are,' she said hastily. 'Actually, I have another invitation.'

'Oh? From whom?'

She hesitated. 'Patrick Brophy, as a matter of fact.'

'Good God! You're not going to visit him, are you?'

'Fergus! Why do you dislike him so much?'

'I don't dislike him personally. I hardly know him. It's all this unity claptrap in his books. Some mornings I wake up and wish the North had been towed out to sea over night and dumped. We're getting on quite

192

well down here, thank you very much. We can't afford the North's economic problems.'

'But if there were something more than economics?'

He gave her a sharp look. 'He has got you hooked, hasn't he? OK, so economic growth and monetarism are ideas we borrowed from the English. What do you put in their place? The vague sort of spirituality and cultural identity Brophy spouts on about? Too wishy-washy for me, I'm afraid. I agree that capitalism isn't an end in itself - though it's often taken to be nowadays, by people like your friend Conor for instance - but it's important enough. I wish they'd get this election sorted out and decide who the government is going to be,' he added anxiously. 'I'm afraid, with all their messing, the punt's going to slip.'

'So the struggle for independence was for nothing then? Just to turn out the same as England?' It's like wanting to be an independent woman and ending up living like a man, she thought dismally. 'To be successful, Ireland must become like England?' To be successful, women must be like men?

He shrugged. 'I don't see what's wrong with that. The sooner we come to terms with how dependent financially we are here on England, the better.'

She fingered her beer glass. 'There must be a way round it. To become a competitive nation without losing the Irish identity. To be an independent person without losing one's essential womanness, to be feminine without losing one's freedom... Julian thinks that men and women will become more alike in the future.'

'That's just the sort of rubbish he would come out with.' He grinned. 'I like a woman who knows how to cook.'

'You're no help at all. You're a retrogressive chauvinist. And where does that leave women like myself who never had time to learn to cook properly?'

'Oh you. You don't fit into any proper definition of a woman. You're just an oddball.'

'Thanks.'

That night she dreamed that a stranger took her by the hand and led her along a forest track, over streams and boulders. He held her arm as they jumped over stepping stones. He pushed back the branches of the trees so that they would not scratch her face. Eventually, they reached the centre of the forest, a clearing in which stood a tiny ruined church. 'There is no male or female,' he told her. 'The sexes are about to be reunited after centuries of separation. You also must unite the male and female parts of yourself. Don't let the female side of you remain diminished.'

She woke with every muscle in her body taut. Her face felt as if someone was stretching the skin so tightly that, if she tried to smile, it would surely split. She feared she might be going mad. The voices inside her head had started up again, warning her that she was slipping behind in her work, giving way, like a woman, to her emotions. She needed someone to interpret her dreams. And she knew of only one person who could do that, who would take them seriously.

Chapter Ten

She cycled along the bumpy road, the sea on one side, the mountains on the other. Pure madness, she thought. He might not remember me, he might have gone away. She had been unable to get through on the phone and had come anyway, leaving the keys of her flat with the departmental secretary in case Niall should need them. 'Typical of you,' said her mother crossly. 'You get some mad scheme into your head and go haring off without a thought for anyone else.' Shut up, mother, said Maggie.

She cycled into the village of Ballybrack and stopped at the Post Office.

'Could you tell me the way to Patrick Brophy's house, please?'

The hard-faced woman behind the counter looked at her suspiciously. 'A mile out of the village and the first road on the right. But he never has visitors.' She paused, her hands on her hips. 'And you'll get short shrift if you're a journalist come to talk about his books.'

'I'm not.'

'Well, you'd better take him this bottle of whiskey while you're about it. He'll be running low, I expect.'

She would rather have brought him flowers.

The whiskey bottle bounced up and down in the basket as she cycled out of the village.

'Alcoholic!' sniffed her mother.

'Patrick is not an alcoholic,' said Maggie, firmly. 'He's

merely fond of a drink. There is a difference. Especially in Ireland.'

'Why Patrick?'

'Because he's a man who's done things. He has lived. Because he's simple and because he's complicated and because he will leave me free. Because a child is better than a beech tree.'

'You're making no sense at all.'

'You just wait and see.'

She stopped outside the tiny red-brick cottage. A long, winding path with yew trees on either side led to the front door. She pushed her bike up the path and knocked. There was no answer. She took off her rucksack and left it and her bike propped up against the wall and went round the side of the house. He was standing on the lawn talking to a black-faced sheep. They both looked up as she came round the corner.

'Wretched bloody sheep, eats all the flowers. Get along out of it.' He kicked it lazily. The sheep raised its head briefly, then resumed its nibbling. 'No discipline around here, that's the trouble. Come inside and have a drink.'

They went round to the front of the house again.

'Oh, you came by bike, did you? Not all the way from Dublin, I hope?'

'No. I took the train as far as Galway. You don't seem very surprised to see me,' she commented, as he led her through the tiny flag-stoned hallway and into a room on the right. It had a huge desk and was lined with books from top to bottom.

'I had a feeling you would turn up soon,' he replied. 'I would call it magic, only you don't believe in it.' He took out a bottle and two glasses from a cupboard by the fireplace. The bottle was nearly empty. He poured the dregs into the two glasses and threw the bottle into the waste-paper basket with a sigh.

'I brought you another one,' she said. 'The woman at the Post Office in Ballybrack suggested it.'

'Good old Mrs Healey.' He handed her a glass. 'Is she still gossiping about me?'

'She told me you didn't like visitors. I could go away again if I'm disturbing you,' she added.

'Now where would be the sense in that?' His fierce blue eyes crinkled into a smile. 'You've only just arrived. Relax.'

She smiled back, at the same time thinking that he looked thinner and more unshaven still than when she had last seen him. Again, she felt a strange impulse to take care of him. He was wearing an old pair of trousers and a shirt patched clumsily at the elbows. Knotted round his neck was a red scarf. She glanced about the room. A dusty pipe and tobacco pouch lay on the mantelpiece. Books and letters littered the floor as they had done in Dublin. There were no photographs of his wife; but on the walls, in between the bookcases, hung several sketches of a young woman with long black hair and sad, large eyes. 'She's very beautiful,' murmured Maggie. Despite the sadness in the eyes, it was a strong face, with strong, pre-Raphaelite features.

'She's my Muse. Was.'

She noted the past tense with satisfaction. 'Watch it now,' said her mother.

'Are you still writing about Job?'

He shook his head. 'No, I've given that up.'

'What? Completely?'

He shrugged. 'I need a rest. It was coming out flat.'

'So what do you do all day?'

'Oh, this and that.'

No clues there, she thought.

'What about you?'

'Me?' she said. 'I'm such a depressed area I should think I'll qualify for an EC grant shortly.'

He grinned and put down his glass. 'Come on, I'll show you the garden before it gets dark and then I'll cook you a meal. What's the matter?'

'I don't want to put you to any trouble.' Had he really expected her to come here, she wondered uneasily. How much was she going to be in his way?

'Nonsense, you have to eat and there's nowhere else for miles around that serves food. You've come to the right place. Besides, it will do me good to mix in a bit of food with the whiskey.'

The garden wound down through fir trees to a pebbly beach and the sea which lay glinting white in the half light. The lawn, she noticed now, was dotted with wine bottles upended and pushed down into the soil.

'Is this some kind of penance?' she asked. 'Are you making yourself keep count of the bottles?'

He smiled. 'It's to deafen the moles. A humane way of killing them, I'm told.'

'I thought there were no moles in Ireland?'

'There are in my garden.'

At the bottom of the lawn, just before it gave way to the taller grass which fringed the beach, was a huge, grass-covered mound.

'I see what you mean about moles.'

'Foolish girl! It's a funeral mound. I'm not allowed to touch it. The villagers believe that to disturb it would bring bad luck.'

'Superstition!'

'Magic.' He laid a hand on her shoulder and she was alarmed to feel a small shiver of desire run through her body. 'There's a place in France, a Carthusian monastery high up in the Alps outside Grenoble, where the monks live under a vow of silence. The monastery stands in a hollow between two mountains, surrounded by forest. I visited it once and felt something magical about the place, a sort of power. The old monks knew what they were about when they chose their sites. Look at Glendalough - what could be more mystical than that?'

'With all the American tourists in their checked trousers and pac-a-macs? Come off it, Patrick!'

He shook his head. 'You have to abstract, look up. You'll see the trees, the round tower, the mountains... there's a spirit in that place. No one knows how to look up nowadays. They're too busy staring sideways at what their neighbours are doing. Everything depends on your point of view. As long as people look on the world as atheists and pose questions as atheists, they will get the answer that there is no God. But if you look at the world spiritually...'

'Yes?'

He shrugged. 'You'll see patterns.'

'I don't see patterns,' she objected. 'I see a world running down into chaos, governed by chance, and completely without meaning or purpose.'

'Maybe then you aren't asking the right questions?' He pressed her arm. 'Come on. It's getting cold. Let's go back and eat.'

She sat on a chair in the kitchen, watching as he fried steak and mushrooms on the Aga. It was an old-fashioned kitchen with a stone floor, too few cupboards and strings of onions hanging from the ceiling.

'Have you planted the beech tree yet?'

He pointed to a small pot on the window sill.

'It's in there. It starts as a nut, grows a shoot, which becomes a twig, and then it's time to plant it out.'

She peered into the plant pot. 'Looks like a lot of old weeds to me.'

'Tut. You need patience and trust.'

'Trust?'

'In nature,' he replied, skilfully turning the steak. 'I have a feeling you could do with trying that, letting go a bit. You give me the impression of being the kind of person who's always planning things - a child, career, revenge...'

'I've given that up.'

'Glad to hear it.'

He turned the steak out onto plates, opened a bottle of wine and they sat down to eat at the small, well-scrubbed, wooden table. She found herself watching his hands again. What was it about them? She felt a kind of lost yearning inside.

'So how is life in Dublin?'

'The same,' she replied, through a mouthful of steak, 'only worse. My parents came to visit.'

'Ah. Your nice, ordinary, safe, proud parents?'

She blushed.

'Come off it, Maggie, who are your parents? Or perhaps you came by stork?'

'They're a pair of left-overs from the Sixties called Charlotte and Giles,' she said bitterly. 'She stuck me in a boarding school when I was eight and forgot all about me. I wasn't even allowed to call her mother. Giles started off as a pop artist. Then, when he got rich and famous, he went on the cocktail-party circuit doing commercial portraits of bankers and their wives. He still called it art. Nowadays, he's given up painting altogether, though he won't admit it.'

'I see.' He fingered the wine glass. 'And the accounts clerk?'

'A voice inside my head. One of several.' God, she thought, I sound schizophrenic.

He leant forward. 'What do they say, these voices?'

'Oh, they nag on about how I should find a man and settle down and have kids. Or they tell me that kids ruin a career and that I owe it to myself to keep on with my job.' She smiled. 'Actually, I've become quite fond of them.'

'Nevertheless, they're trapping you,' he said, seriously.

She frowned. 'Trapping me? How?'

'Because, don't you see, they're part of your social conditioning, these voices. They're echoing what you think society is telling you to do.' He paused. 'No wonder you're in pain. Your personality, or part of it, is trying to break through the prison you've built around it.'

Prison. For some reason, the word made her think of Paul.

'I believe women will always have such voices, until they become more certain of their identity,' she said firmly.

'No, Maggie. Don't cling to them. Let them talk themselves out. Let yourself be healed.'

'Healed?' She was shocked. 'Do you think I'm sick then?'

'In a way.' He ran his long, thin fingers through his hair. 'Do you know, I cured Mrs Healey's bunions once? She knew nothing about it, of course. I wonder

201

whether it's possible,' he added quietly, 'that one can be loved too much by God?'

There was a silence. Maggie felt uneasy. The people she hung around with thought it in poor taste to talk about religion... and Patrick talked about hardly anything else.

'Have you got your man back?' he asked, suddenly.

She shook her head. 'I can feel Conor and I growing further apart. Our personalities don't seem to fit together any more. We meet without linking. It's as if someone had mixed two jigsaws together and taken out half the pieces. Conor's round where I'm jagged.'

'Good simile,' he said, rather coldly she thought. She felt perplexed. Why were conversations with him always so unpredictable?

He showed her to the spare bedroom. It was furnished simply with a single bed, a rug and a chest of drawers. On the whitewashed walls hung more sketches of the woman with black hair. I could be jealous of her, she thought.

'Sleep well.' He ran a finger down her arm. She felt shaken inside and hollow with desire. She glanced up at him. For a moment he met her gaze, then he looked away. 'In case you're wondering, you can stay as long as you wish. You won't be disturbing me.' He went out abruptly, shutting the door behind him.

Left alone, she felt confused again. Why had he invited her here? What exactly did he want from her? Questions throbbed in her head, preventing her from sleeping. Eventually, around five o'clock, she fell asleep and dreamed of Conor. He swung her up into his arms and carried her, laughing, down Dame Street. She woke up and burst into tears.

Patrick spent the morning reading. Determined not

to be a nuisance to him (for then he might send her away and she needed time out of Dublin, to think), Maggie wandered along the pebbly beach for a while, breathing in the fresh sea air, getting the city out of her lungs. Then she cycled down to Ballybrack for some milk and bread.

'You still there?' Mrs Healey sounded disappointed. 'There's a couple of letters for him here. You may as well take them with you.'

She glanced at the postmarks. One was Dublin and the other Australia. She put them into her basket and cycled back. The sea was green, speckled with white. Here and there along the road, she came upon a thatched, stone cottage. More frequent were the ugly modern bungalows with wrought-iron gates, crazy-paving walls and square windows placed in a line from one end to the other. She had read somewhere that all these bungalows had been copied from a Spanish prototype imported by a hairdresser from Galway. That hairdresser has a lot to answer for, she thought. She saw no one, apart from some children playing and a man out walking his dog. He lifted his cap to her.

She took the letters into Patrick's study. 'Ah,' he said, putting on his spectacles, 'my ex-wife. She writes once a year, regular as clockwork, demanding an increase.' He didn't say who the other letter was from.

Having persuaded him to let her do some cooking, she went into the kitchen to prepare a salad. Half an hour later, when he still hadn't come through, she went to fetch him and found him standing by the window holding a letter in his hand, the one that was not from his wife.

'Never marry,' he said. 'My wife's view of marriage was deep-pile towels and wall-to-wall casserole dishes.

203

That's what comes of not believing in magic. Let's have lunch.' He threw the letter down on the desk.

'I hope you won't be bored here,' he said, as they ate the salad she had prepared and Mrs Healey's brown bread. 'I lead a very quiet life. I don't even have a car.'

'I'm enjoying it. It's good to get out of the city for a while.'

'So long as you don't develop spongy brain cow syndrome.'

'What on earth is that?'

He laughed. 'Easy to see you're not a country woman. It's a disease cows get if they're fed recycled chicken droppings.'

'Sounds disgusting.'

'It is. A lot of what goes on in the countryside is disgusting.'

'And yet you stay?'

'Oh, I stay. At least...' He looked down at his plate.

'What?'

'Nothing.' He pushed away the plate. 'Can you amuse yourself? I'm going to lie down for a bit.'

'Of course.'

She gazed after him as he walked out of the kitchen. What was it about him that made her want to take care of him? It was absurd to feel like this. Someone like Patrick didn't need looking after - certainly not by her. Being with him had made Maggie feel how hopelessly naïve she was, inexperienced and shallow. It's the people I hang about with, she thought. No, she had nothing to give a man like Patrick. It was he who could teach her a thing or two.

In an attempt to understand him better, she took one of his books out into the garden and read for a while, sitting on the lawn amidst the upended wine bottles. It was a novel of political intrigue with an ambitious young politician as its hero. Subtly, it made a plea for a united, socialist Ireland. It had been published twenty years ago. Patrick had obviously been carrying these ideas around for a long time.

The black-faced sheep turned up for its afternoon snack of sweet peas. 'There'll be hell to pay if the boss catches you here,' she whispered. But the sheep took no notice. She wondered who the woman in the sketches was. She looked quite different, younger, gentler, from the photograph of his ex-wife on the mantelpiece in Dublin. She wondered too what had been in the letter from Dublin and then again why he had invited her here. Too many mysteries, she thought. 'Too much curiosity,' retorted her mother. You still there? 'I'm keeping an eye on you.' Oh go and talk to Mrs Healey, Maggie growled.

When she went inside to prepare dinner, she found Patrick watering the plant pot on the window sill.

'I'm worried about this tree,' he murmured. 'A shoot should have appeared by now.'

'It's important to you, isn't it?'

'I want to leave something behind on this earth. No, it's all right,' he added, as she made a move towards the fridge. 'You got lunch. I'll do dinner. Equal division of labour. I think the EC has passed some laws about it.'

His sleep seemed to have refreshed him. He looked years younger than he had done at lunch. Surprised at this observation (it wasn't the kind of thing she usually noticed about people), Maggie sat down at the table and watched as he got out a pan and began frying the chicken pieces she had bought that morning in Ballybrack. 'There're your books,' she said, after a few minutes. 'They'll make you famous.'

'Oh, fame. When you're a writer, you have to accept the fact that the jury's out till after your death. No, fame's a chance - and it usually comes for the wrong reasons.' He washed a courgette and added it to the frying pan. 'I wanted to be a politician and I ended up becoming a novelist because it was the only way to get my ideas heard, socialism as a practical proposition having been out of favour for rather a long time in Ireland.'

'I know. I started one of your books this afternoon.'

'Oh?' He seemed surprised. 'Which?'

'*The Hustler.*'

He winced. 'I'll find you a better one.' He turned the chicken over in the pan, hesitated, then said, 'How are your voices?'

'Still there. I need them.' She stared at him defiantly. 'I don't want to become like Charlotte and Giles.'

'So you're prepared to let the past determine your future?'

'Doesn't it always? I chose to study history precisely because it's a closed subject to Charlotte and Giles. I didn't want to be like them, creatures of the moment.'

He set out the chicken and courgettes, the cheese and soda bread, and the bottle of wine they had started at lunch. They sat down to eat.

'You can't go on defining yourself against the past, you know.'

'I can't change the past, however.'

'No, but you can change how you view it. Hobbes said we make a future out of our conceptions of the past, but the reverse is also true. Everyone needs a narrative for their lives. Yours seems to be breaking down. Why not rewrite the past?'

'That needs forgiveness and... understanding.'

'Hallmarks of an historian, I should have thought.' He smiled. 'Think of something good about your mother.'

'About Charlotte? Impossible! She was a bad mother. I don't want to be like her.' Really he asked too much of her, she thought, irritated.

'How can you hope to be a good mother yourself while you feel this way about her?'

'That has nothing to do with it.'

'Hasn't it?'

There was a pause.

'OK, maybe not a bad mother, but a mother too soon,' she said reluctantly.

'Good, start from there. Rethink your life. Put yourself in her place. That's the only way to make progress.'

'Progress?' she snapped. 'I don't believe in it. No self-respecting historian does.'

Patrick grinned. 'No self-respecting English historian. The Irish may, I think.'

'I thought you'd given up on Ireland?'

'I'm becoming more optimistic again. You know, when I looked about me on my last trip to Dublin, I found the city had changed. There's a new spirit of confidence about the place. The Irish are beginning to stop defining themselves against England. They're starting to emphasise things in their tradition which will make them stand for something different from the other European nations. Coffee?'

'Yes, please.'

He lifted the pot off the Aga and poured her a cup.

'Yes, this country is coming awake. I feel more hopeful than I have done for a long time. Ireland is finally getting rid of her emotional dependency on her past, is becoming quite different from England and is self-confident about it. Ireland is maturing.' He grinned. 'What about you?'

She grimaced. 'I cannot forgive. I cannot forgive them for abandoning me all those years. I spent the holidays in school, for God's sake, whilst they did the cocktail circuit.'

'Look, I know heredity is involuntary colonisation...'

She laughed. 'That's quite good.'

'...but you can't simply reject your parents. You must somehow find a way to work them into your life.'

She shook her head.

'Oh Maggie, Maggie,' he murmured. 'I don't want to leave you like this.' He leant forward and brushed her cheek with his hand. His touch made her shake inside.

'Leave?' she said.

'Yes, I...' He ran a hand over his face. 'Never mind. Want a whiskey?'

She nodded. They took their glasses into his study. It was still light and from the window she caught a glimpse of the sea glimmering between the fir trees. He sat down in an armchair and she sat opposite him, cross legged on the hearth rug.

'You know, I used to be like you, ambitious, sharp, not caring a bit on the outside, inwardly torn apart by doubt and self-criticism...'

'Then?'

'Then I met Sara.' Maggie started and felt suddenly fearful. There was a note in his voice, a note of tenderness, she had not heard before. 'My wife had buggered off to Australia. I travelled the world, giving lectures and readings. There were parties, casual relationships. And at the end of it all, twelve years ago,

I met Sara. You may have noticed sketches of her around the place. She was about the age you are now. She came to live with me here, causing a scandal in the village. Mrs Healey who used to come here to "do" suddenly stopped coming...' He pulled a wry face and fell silent.

'Sara?' she prompted, feeling a twist of jealousy in her guts.

'Ah, Sara.' He looked down at the carpet. 'It was incredible. I had had to wait till I was nearly fifty to find out what love was - but when it came, there was no mistaking it. It was all the things poets have ever written about it, all the things I had dismissed as crap... We lived here together, spending the days much as you and I did today, reading, writing, gardening. Occasionally, we went up to Dublin or over to London for the theatre...'

'What happened?' She couldn't help asking. She had to know. 'Where is she now?'

He poured himself another whiskey.

'She wanted a child. Like you, she felt time was running out. There were complications. Jesus, it was frightening. They asked me to choose. How can one choose between someone you've never seen and someone you've lived with and loved? Of course I chose her. They gave her anaesthetic but it went wrong. She died. The child died with her.' He looked up. 'That was eight years ago. In all this time, I've never made love with another woman.'

She felt the tears come into her eyes. 'How can you believe in a God who allows such terrible things to happen?' she whispered.

'Oh I believe in Him all right.' He clenched his hand. 'Sometimes I argue with Him, sometimes I get angry and shake my fist at Him. But I've never stopped believing in Him. When I'm angry, I put on Beethoven's Fifth. There's a lot of anger in that first movement, a lot more than I'll ever be capable of feeling...' He paused. 'And you? What do you do, Maggie, when you're angry?'

'I clown around. It gets on people's nerves... Or I hear voices inside my head, which gets on my nerves.' She hesitated. 'What did you mean yesterday when you said I'd built a prison around myself?'

He ran his fingers through his hair. 'I think you're a bit like this country of ours. You've suppressed the soft, intuitive, feminine part of yourself in order to get on.'

'Had to. At work, they find it easier to deal with chaps.' She pulled a face.

'Clown! Seriously, though, you shouldn't let yourself be imposed upon by other people's ideas about yourself. Listen to what your feelings tell you.'

She plucked at the rug. 'They tell me I'll have to work harder to keep up with my male colleagues.'

'It's only part of you, you know, that voice. An old part perhaps, which is determined not to be given up without a struggle.'

'And,' she glanced at him, 'they tell me to have a child.'

'A child must be planned for, longed for...' He fell silent. 'Perhaps after all, a beech tree is a poor substitute.' He looked at her. 'Would you have my child?'

'I think I would,' she said softly.

They sat looking at each other.

'Maggie, I can't...' he began, then shook his head and said in quite a different tone, 'Tut. Is there no sense in you at all?'

She tilted her chin. 'I make my own kind of sense.'

He glanced at her. 'Well, maybe that's right.'

They lapsed into silence. He looked over at his desk. 'Do you want to work?'

He hesitated. 'Well, I...'

'It's OK. You don't always have to entertain me.'

She stood up. He caught at her hand and held it tight for a moment. He seemed on the point of saying something, then apparently changed his mind. He released her hand. She felt vaguely let down.

'What will you do?'

'Walk.'

He smiled. 'You're an easy guest.'

'I mean to be.'

She went for a walk in the garden. As she drew near the house she saw, through the lighted window, Patrick standing by his desk, re-reading his letter. She went up to her room without disturbing him.

Out in the garden she had come to a decision. She must let this relationship, friendship or whatever it was going to turn out to be, develop at his pace. For the first time in her life she had met someone whose judgement she trusted more than her own. Patrick's knowledge of life was larger, much larger, than her own. She undressed and got into bed.

The next morning, she woke to the sound of Beethoven's Fifth Symphony.

Chapter Eleven

Later in the day, Maggie cycled into Ballybrack to buy some food and a newspaper. On impulse, she phoned Conor.

'What's the matter?' asked Patrick, the moment she walked through the door.

'Conor - he's bought a new house and asked Bridget to move in with him.' She put her bags down on the table. Damn, damn, damn. She realised that part of her had been hoping Conor would miss her whilst she was away. Instead, he had sounded delighted that she was having a holiday. It wouldn't be long before she overstayed her welcome with Patrick, and the thought of returning to her empty flat and the promotion interview filled her with dread. 'Perhaps I'll move back to England,' she muttered. 'I don't fit in here.'

He took her face in his hands and tilted it upwards.

'You can't give up the entire Irish nation because of one man. Go back and fight.'

She sighed. A tear ran down her cheek. 'I feel so empty inside.'

'It will pass. Believe me.' He released her. 'Listen, I was thinking of hiring a car and driving around the area for a bit. Before you decide whether to leave it or not, you should see the best of our country. I expect you've never visited Donegal?'

'No.'

'Right, that's what we'll do.'

So they hired a car for a few days and drove up

through Donegal, along deserted roads with craggy mountains rising sheer on either side. Here and there they came upon a farmhouse encircled by three or four trees, like an enchanted oasis in that barren landscape. He pointed out a well which was said to have magic powers and a stone which had healing properties. He took her to Glencolumbcille.

'Do you believe in prayer?' she asked him.

He shrugged. 'When I pray, coincidences happen. When I cease to pray, they don't.'

'So you pray?'

'Yes.'

They stayed overnight in small bed and breakfast places and once in a gate lodge by the sea. Often in the evenings she was left by herself in the sitting room as Patrick turned in early. The driving tired him, he said. She noticed that, even for a man in his sixties, he didn't have much stamina.

They talked about life and books and people they knew. They did not talk about love or the past. We are to be simply friends then, she thought, not knowing whether to be relieved or disappointed. After Conor could she face the effort of starting a relationship all over again - and if she felt like that, how much worse, she thought, must it be for Patrick with all his memories of Sara?

There were times, though, when he gazed at her across the table or took her by the arm to point out something to her, when she had to catch her breath, he looked so ridiculously handsome. Perhaps after all he was out of her class. She should stick to her own level - Paul? Between herself and Patrick it couldn't be a relationship between equals. He would always be ahead of her in years and experience.

213

They returned to his house in the evening and wandered out into the garden, hand in hand. Patrick was fond of taking her by the hand, a thing Conor had never done, reserving all his physical intimacy for their times in bed. It was a small thing, but she realised how much she had missed it, that holding hands.

Now they were back home - Patrick's home at least, for she had still not found hers - Maggie felt more at ease with him than she had ever done before. They walked together through the dark and hushed garden. He stopped beside an oak tree and stood behind her, his arms around her.

'The ancient Teutons imagined that the spirits of their ancestors lived in the trees and that if they went out into the forest when they were unhappy and confused, they would gain comfort and insight. They believed the pattern of the branches weaving in and out symbolises life's underlying symmetries.'

'That tree has half its branches broken off,' she protested, pointing to a Sitka spruce. 'It's not at all symmetrical, or even beautiful.'

He kissed the back of her neck. 'The Teutons would have said that ugliness too has its place. For life is never perfect, though it can be complete. I have always believed that we have an allotted number of experiences and that as we look back, at the end of our life, perhaps even at the very moment of our death, they will all fall into place. Then we will see the pattern we have been groping after all our life.'

She thought of the people she knew - of Conor and Maureen and Fergus - none of them thought in terms of order and patterns.

She leant against the tree, facing him. 'There is a certain beauty in what you say, but as for me, I can't...

believe like that.'

He passed a hand over his face.

'Perhaps you're right. Perhaps it's only an illusion, or maybe earthly eyes are too feeble... Did you know that the ancients believed in a music of the planets which mortal ears are too weak to hear?' They began walking back towards the house. 'It all comes down to faith. Each of us decides the reality we shall see... whether it's order and beautiful symmetry, or... chaos and darkness.' He seemed to be speaking more for himself than to her.

Suddenly, something clicked in her brain. 'When you said you were leaving?' she began, half fearfully.

He looked at her.

'So you've guessed, finally... Well, I would have had to have told you if... I was in Dublin for tests when I met you. They were confirmed in the letter you brought me last week from Ballybrack.' He glanced away. 'Four months, if I'm lucky.'

She gasped. An icy cold feeling ran down her spine. 'Aren't you afraid?'

'A little. But eight years of solitude makes one less unwilling to leave.'

She felt as if someone had just punched her very hard in the stomach. She could find nothing to say. She had not been prepared for this.

They went inside and had a final whiskey.

'I'm on the last lap, Maggie. Would you want a child by such a crumbling ruin of a man?'

'Would you want such a clown, such an unbelieving clown, to bear your child?'

He held her face in his hands. 'You are a clown, but you're also brave and honest. And I find in the end that I would like to leave something of myself behind.'

215

So now she finally knew. 'Did you invite me here for this?' she asked, placing her hands over his.

'Perhaps. I was surprised myself when I invited you. But when I thought about it, it seemed right.'

'Does this seem right?'

He nodded. They made love there, on the carpet in his study, slowly and gently. He came inside her with a shudder and a groan, as if some demon was trying to tear his very soul out. He called her Sara. She tried not to mind. Afterwards, they went upstairs and lay for hours on his bed, looking at each other. 'Your hair is the colour of ashes,' he said. His eyes seemed tired. They were creased at the edges. They made her feel sad. She looked up at the sketch of the black-haired woman hanging on the wall opposite. 'I am jealous of her,' she thought.

The next morning, she sat in the sun, feeling its warmth on her arms and shoulders. For one brief moment, she saw past and future melt away, leaving only the golden, marvellous present. She winked knowingly up at the sun. It was a day to climb a mountain, punch the sky in.

But then she went inside and was faced again with the sketches of Sara. She stood in his bedroom, staring at her. This was the woman he had lain beside for four years, whose long hair he had stroked, whose body he had caressed as, or perhaps more, lovingly than he had caressed her own. A union of two souls, he had said.

'What are you doing?'

She jumped for she had not heard him come up the stairs.

He followed her gaze. 'This afternoon, I'll take them down.' He put his arms round her. 'We'll live in a time warp. No past or future, just us here and now.'

They made love again that night.

But though they could make efforts to suppress the past, it was not so easy to ignore the future. A few days later, he broached the forbidden topic.

'Do you have the courage to go away, knowing we might never meet again?' he asked her one night as they lay in bed.

She rolled over onto her stomach.

'I could stay,' she said. 'I could look after you.' She was afraid of mentioning his sickness directly for he had not spoken of it again himself. He was proud.

He looked up at the ceiling.

'No,' he replied at last. 'Babies and death don't mix. One thing at a time. You will have your thoughts on a new life. Besides, you haven't spent your life with me. I have no right to impose the burden of my death on you.'

'I wouldn't mind,' she said, though she had never watched anyone die before.

'Someone once wrote that we should prepare for death, turn it over in our fingers, taste it, smell it. That's what I must do - retire in solitude and silence to prepare myself. You will make it harder for me to leave this life, Maggie. I'm fond of you already... if you stay here, I shall not want to die.'

She switched off the light so that he would not see her tears.

Now she was convinced. His most important relationship would be with Sara. She had come too late; the thought of death was setting limits on his feelings for her. And her love for him would have been deeper, she felt, if only she could have understood more - about his past, his ideas. She began to feel angry and bitter. But that was no help to him.

The next morning, she ran into the bedroom straight from her bath and shook her wet hair over him as he lay dozing. Drops of water fell on his face and shoulders. He opened his eyes and smiled. 'You're such a clown.' She stuck out her feet and pulled a clown face.

They invented games, lovers' games.

'Do you like me more than a piece of broken glass you're about to tread on with your bare feet?'

'Yes. Do you like me more than a greasy chip paper that's been dropped in the gutter?'

'Yes.'

'That's all right then.' She sighed contentedly and kissed the tip of his nose.

But she could not prevent his thoughts returning to the future.

'Will you tell the child?' he asked her.

'When the time is right, yes.'

'What will you say?'

'That you were - are - an extraordinary man and that she/he can be proud of you. And I'll give the child your books.'

'I must make a new will,' he said.

'Only for the child.'

'If that's what you want.'

'Yes.'

'I am fond of you,' he said.

'And I of you.' She squeezed his hand.

'What about Conor? You know I'm beginning to get a little jealous of him.'

She shook her head. 'I don't know. I can't tell what I feel about him right now.' Oh, why couldn't we have had more time, she thought. We scarcely know one another.

But the date of her interview was drawing near.

'I could stay,' she said again.

'No. You've your future to think of. Go back and fight for it.'

'Will you write at least?'

'Every day if you like.'

'I do like.'

He pulled her to him. 'I'm falling more and more in love with you, Maggie. You must go. I'm beginning to bear a grudge against God. It wouldn't be right to die angry with Him.'

'The angels would have to play Beethoven's Fifth as you marched through St Peter's gate.' She grimaced.

He shook his head. 'When you are gone, I will have plenty of time to make my peace with Him.' He stroked her hair. 'One day you too will believe in magic.'

'Not a chance.'

On her last evening, she made a meal of all his favourite things - steak and salad and apple pie.

'I suppose you think it will be all right in the end,' she said crossly, turning the steak in the pan. 'That we'll all meet up in heaven or something. It's going to be pretty crowded though, with your ex-wife, Sara, me and the child. Even you must see that it's going to be awkward.'

She transferred the steak to a plate and set it in front of him.

'I've never subscribed to the view of heaven as a cocktail party where you meet all your old friends,' he said, taking up his fork. 'I believe in purgatory.'

'Purgatory! I thought that faded out long ago.'

'All the people I have ever seen die seemed to me to be entering on a period of darkness. I can't explain it exactly. I've always thought of purgatory as a time when the soul loses its hold on earthly things and becomes purified in some way, in order to draw closer to God.'

She shivered. 'Sounds horrid to me.'

'I think it probably is fairly horrible,' he murmured. 'A period of separation from God.' He laid down his fork.

'You're not eating any more?'

'It's wonderful. I... I can't.'

She knew then that the illness was starting to bite.

'In the morning,' she said, summoning up all her courage, 'I'll slip away. No goodbyes. We'll pretend I'm just going into Ballybrack.'

That night, she cradled him in her arms till he fell asleep.

Their last night together. She lay awake in the dark, trying to get her mind round the idea of his death, trying to make herself realise that this warm solid body touching hers would one day be nothing but dust. It was impossible. His breathing, steady and quiet, seemed as if it would go on forever. And when her mind did for a moment take in the idea of his death, the next minute it had shied away, numb with panic. It is a good thing I am going, she thought, I should be no help to him at all.

She left very early, whilst he was still sleeping. Lightly, she touched his face. It was beginning to have the drawn, dull look of someone in pain. 'Goodbye, Patrick,' she whispered.

She took her bike out of the shed and began cycling furiously. By the time she reached Galway, the wind had dried the tears on her cheeks. She put the bike in the goods carriage and sat huddled in a corner without speaking, all the way to Dublin.

220

Chapter Twelve

She arrived in Dublin feeling that nothing would ever be the same again. She dumped her bike in the hire shop and turned in the direction of Trinity to collect her keys. She wondered whether Niall had made use of her flat and what his girlfriend had decided to do. Walking through the Front Square, she came across Conor sauntering around with headphones on his ears. He introduced her to his new Sony Discman.

'Well,' he said, 'enjoy your holiday?' Without waiting for a reply, he went on, 'I've been booted out of the men's group.'

She made an effort. 'Why?'

'Didn't empathise enough.'

She looked puzzled.

'George was cut up over this woman and wanted us to spend hours listening to the latest bulletin on the state of his emotions, how it all went back to the way his mother had brought him up, etcetera. In the end, I told him to snap out of it. We've all been rejected at some point or other.'

'Indeed.'

'You just have to make the best of it.'

'Quite.' She looked at him. It was a little strange to be with him now. He no longer felt like hers. Perhaps she was finally learning to put a distance between them. Nevertheless, she couldn't help asking, 'How is the new house? Has Bridget moved in yet?'

He shook his head. 'She's staying put for the

221

moment.' There was a pause. 'Well, have to be off. Just wrangled an interview with the woman who runs the Women's Health Clinic. Wears incredibly short skirts. See you around.'

'Yes.'

The second person she met was Lallie. She was carrying a cat basket, on her way to the vet.

'Thank God, if there is one, that you've come back,' she said. 'Not a moment too soon. There are all kinds of rumours flying around about you.'

'About me?' It was impossible. Apart from Fergus, she had told no one that she had been staying with Patrick.

'They say McGregor is gunning for you over this promotion interview. Apparently he's peeved about some advice you gave one of his tutorial students.'

'Oh God.' How on earth did he find out? she wondered. Surely Niall wouldn't have spilled the beans?

'I say, are you all right? You look banjaxed.'

'I... I'm OK, Lallie.'

'Remember, if there's anything I can do, give me a call. It mustn't become a habit to throw out staff.'

'Thanks, Lallie.'

Feeling that life in Dublin had become quite unreal, she went into the Arts Building and retrieved her keys from the secretary. 'That Niall fellow did borrow them in the end,' the secretary informed her. 'Generous of you. I wouldn't let him anywhere near my house. You'll be smelling sweaty socks and pot for months.'

She decided it would be a good idea to track down Niall and find out how much McGregor knew. Her interview was the day after next and she wanted to be prepared. She went into the students' bar which, now that exams were ended, was filled to overflowing. Seamus was there, his arm round Fionnuala's waist. His spots had almost cleared up and he had apparently managed to shave that morning without cutting himself. He winked when he saw her. Fionnuala blushed and crossed her legs.

'Seamus, have you seen Niall?'

He shook his head. 'He went off after the exams and hasn't been seen since.'

They did go over to England then, she thought. And McGregor knows. Shit.

She collected some exam scripts to mark at home. The flat had been left looking quite neat, with only faint traces of sweat lingering in the air and none at all of pot. 'Clearing out his mind before exams,' she thought. She spent the rest of the day marking exam scripts, trying to shut out thoughts of Patrick. Seamus looked as though he would make a First. Fionnuala, even taking into account her unscholarly habit of overdressing, got a solid II.1. Niall scraped a bare pass. His mind had obviously been on other matters.

When she finished marking, she wrote a long letter to Patrick. 'I'm sure I'm pregnant,' she ended. 'I'm off to the doctor tomorrow to have it confirmed. Haven't stopped thinking of you all day.' Going out to post it, she passed Paul on the steps. He threw her a frosty look. Hostility at home, hostility at work, she thought. I shall become a little paranoid.

The next morning, she went to the doctor's. The test was positive. She was indeed pregnant. She beamed at the doctor in delight. He looked at her curiously. 'You're not married and you're pleased?'

'Very.' She smiled.

He shook his head in disbelief.

When she got home, she found a letter had arrived from Patrick. He proposed leaving money in his will for her to buy a flat. 'Think that it's for the child, if you won't accept it for yourself. It's difficult to bring up a child in rented accommodation.' The black-faced sheep was still eating his sweet peas.

She wrote back that she was indeed pregnant and that her voices had gone. 'It's the child. It has made me stronger.' But after she had posted the letter, she began to feel panicky. She was finally pregnant. In nine months she would give birth. What could she have been thinking of? It seemed to her now that despite all her resolutions, she had embarked on this without sufficient preparation. Oh God, she thought, how on earth am I going to cope? I must talk to someone. I must see Maureen.

As she drew up outside the house in Rathgar, she noticed that the climbing roses over the door were starting to bloom. Art's car was in the drive. This is what life is about, she thought. A home, a family, roots. It gave her a nice warm feeling in the pit of her stomach. She got out of the car. As she walked up the garden path, she became aware of voices raised.

'You bastard! You frigging selfish bastard! You promised you'd stay here this afternoon and help me clear up this bloody pig sty.'

'Look, don't blow your top. It's not my fault. I have to be back at the office. I've an appointment.'

'Typical! Fucking typical! I bet you arranged it on purpose.'

'Don't swear in front of Amber. And just remember who earns the money round here.'

'I'll swop any day. You can stay at home with the brat. See how you like it!'

'Call yourself a mother?'

She was hovering on the doorstep, wondering whether to press on and ring the bell or beat a hasty retreat, when the door opened and Art appeared.

'Hello, Maggie,' he growled. 'What are you doing here?'

Without waiting for a reply, he pushed past her, strode over to his car and backed out of the drive amidst a screeching of gears, narrowly missing the gatepost.

'Jaysus! Men!' shouted Maureen, giving him the two fingers. 'They make bloody sure they have it all their own way, don't they? Come inside, Maggie. The place's a dreadful tip, I'm afraid. We took Charlotte's advice and had the decorators in.'

There was new wallpaper in the living room. The carpet had been rolled back and the floor was covered in newspapers and old rags. The furniture was swaddled in plastic sheeting. By the window, Amber lay gurgling happily in her cot. Maggie went over and gave her a kiss.

'She enjoys a good row now and then,' Maureen explained. 'It relieves her of the responsibility of making all the noise. Sit down, Maggie, if you can find somewhere to sit, that is. I'm going to leave all this exactly as it is. He's not getting out of it that easily.'

'How's the seven month colic?' enquired Maggie, removing a plastic sheet from a chair and sitting down.

'Completely cleared up,' replied her friend, happily. 'Jeepers, was that a time! I never want to go through that again, I can tell you. Well you saw me, Maggie. It got to the stage where I was needing a bottle of wine a day to help me cope. Cope? For Christ's sake, I used to teach maths at Leaving Cert level. I reminded myself of that one day. It's amazing how your confidence evaporates when you're stuck at home all the time with a crying baby. The mere thought of standing up in front of a class now gives me the shivers. I should think carefully, Maggie, about having a child. You learn things about yourself you'd rather not know. Ah well,' she glanced fondly over at her daughter, 'I suppose it was all worth it. Would you like a cup of tea? I can't offer you anything stronger, I'm afraid. Since Amber's given up colic, I've had to give up the afternoon boozing. No excuse for it.'

'Tea's fine.' And anyway, now that it was confirmed, she supposed she was off alcohol for the next nine months.

They went through into the kitchen. Maggie leant against a cupboard, watching Maureen prepare the tea, and wondered how she was going to break her news.

'It sounds as if you're becoming reconciled to motherhood?' she suggested, tentatively.

'Oh well, you know, some days it's not so bad, now that she's stopped that dreadful crying and is starting to sit up and take notice. Then I ask myself, do I really want to go back to shouting at a classful of adolescents, dealing with bloody-minded parents and spending my evenings marking, when I can fill my days here exactly as I please? Mind you, I don't tell Art that. I make him think it's all a great sacrifice. He's just got promotion again. Very sheepish about telling me. But the strange thing was I didn't feel envious at all. Not a bit. Sugar?'

Maggie shook her head. They took the tray back into the living room.

'You know, Maggie, sometimes I wonder whether it might not be a good idea to have another one and get it all over and done with at once. Only children often

226

turn out to be odd. You were an only child. Art was an only child. I'd stop after two,' she added hastily. 'Wouldn't want to over-populate the world.' She looked at Maggie. 'Anyway, what about you? Have you thought any more about Fergus?'

Maggie blushed. 'Maureen, you're not going to like this. I'm very grateful for your help and all that, but...'

`Oh my God! You're pregnant already!'

`'Fraid so.'

Maureen clapped her hands in horror. Amber burst into tears. 'Put a sock in it, Amber,' ordered her mother, picking her up out of the cot and cradling her on her lap. 'Now tell me all about it,' she said sternly. 'You owe me that much, since you've gone and done it so sneakily behind my back.'

Maggie told her.

'It's crazy,' said Maureen, 'but rather beautiful too.' She looked as though she might be about to cry. 'Oh Maggie, you'll have such a lovely time. Don't mind what they say about the sickness, the early stages of pregnancy are wonderful. You lose weight and look frail and interesting and vulnerable. You pick like a sparrow at your food and your cheekbones begin to take on that hollowed-out look ballerinas have. Men in the street will come rushing up to help you carry the shopping. I remember Art became so protective...' She fell silent, recollecting that her friend's position was rather different from her own.

Not feeling up to explaining, indeed not knowing, how she was going to cope by herself, Maggie changed the subject and told Maureen about Niall.

'I'm afraid I'm going to get stick for it at the interview tomorrow. Do you think I did the right thing?' she asked, anxiously.

'Between you and me, Maggie, and since there isn't a man around, I can say that I've never been sure what to think about abortion. But if they'd really made up their minds, I don't see how you could have done anything else. It wasn't as though you were actually advising them - just making the option realistic, and safe. You'd have felt a lot worse if they had ended up in the hands of some back-street abortionist over here.'

'Mmm... But will McGregor see it like that? I wonder. I must say I'm surprised at Niall. I'd have thought he'd have had the cop on not to tell McGregor. Oh well, it'll be over soon enough, I suppose.' She stood up. 'Thanks for the tea.'

'Baby clothes,' said Maureen as she showed her to the door. 'I've got stacks of then. No point buying them new - they just grow out of them.'

'Thanks. And when I've finished with them, I'll hand them back to you,' Maggie called over her shoulder. 'You'll probably be needing them by then.'

Maureen grunted. 'Tomorrow I'll have changed my mind.'

It's different for Maureen, Maggie thought, driving back to her flat. Amber had a ready-made family waiting for her, with parents, grandparents and cousins. A child needs a framework. What had she to hand on? A family history of bitterness and separation and misunderstanding. She thought of the scene at the airport, remembering, guiltily, that she had rejected Charlotte's olive branch. Charlotte had all but admitted her mistakes and she had refused to listen. Or forgive. Oh, what the hell, she thought sourly, getting out of the car. Charlotte and Giles will never change. Yet for the sake of her unborn child, perhaps she should make one last effort?

228

She was reflecting on this as she crossed the hall and stumbled upon Paul in a tight clinch with a girl up against the banister.

'You want to watch it,' she growled. 'That banister's likely to give way at any moment.'

They sprang apart. Paul bent down anxiously and inspected the bottom of the banister. 'No, no. I think it's all right. I must remember, though, to draw our landlord's attention to it.' He straightened up. 'May I take this opportunity to introduce Sheila?' he said, with a little air of triumph.

Sheila had freckles, pony-tail and a decidedly limp handshake. She was wearing a short, pink, cotton dress which made her look absurdly young. At any rate he won't be able to taunt her with the word 'spinster', thought Maggie, watching them disappear, arm in arm, into Paul's flat. She went over to the phone and called Fergus. They arranged to have coffee together after her interview the next day.

'I shall need cheering up,' she warned.

'You're not the only one,' he muttered and rang off.

On her way to the interview the next morning, she bumped into Prue in the street. At first Maggie didn't recognise her, she looked so changed. She was wearing a tailored navy suit with a neat little silk blouse and a string of pearls around her neck. Ballsbridge clothes, thought Maggie.

'Hello, darling. Thought any more about the women's group?'

Maggie reflected guiltily that at this moment, Prue's 'bumph' was lying at the bottom of her rubbish bin.

'Well actually, Prue, I've been so busy and... well... the fact is, I'm pregnant and...'

'Pregnant? Oh my dear, how unfortunate.' Prue's

eyes flickered for a moment over Maggie's left hand. 'Aren't men absolute bastards?' She took Maggie's arm and said, in a low voice, 'You don't, er... I mean... I have the address of a nice little place in London, perfectly safe...'

'Thanks, Prue, but we're very happy,' replied Maggie, patting her stomach.

'Well, if you're sure...' she said doubtfully.

'I am.'

There was a pause.

'You're quite right about the women's group, darling. No need to rush things. Some of the women might be a bit, um... I mean, well you know how things are in this country. I don't mind, but...' She gazed over Maggie's left shoulder. 'Call me any time you want a little chat,' she said hastily and moved on.

So much for social progress amongst the middle classes, thought Maggie, knocking on the door of the interview room.

'Come in.'

There were ten men sitting round a green baize table so large that she could barely squeeze into the room. She felt sick, panic-stricken, and of course she had a headache.

'Do sit down.' The Provost made it sound as if she would normally be expected to stand and he was conferring a great favour on her. He was a small, thin man with weasly black eyes. There was a yellowish tinge to his face, or perhaps it was the light? On his left, sat Dr McGregor; on his right, Professor Gardener who was carefully studying the notes in front of him. Or appeared to be doing so.

There were a few pleasantries from the Provost on the weather, the state of the roads, public transport, etc.

Then he began.

'Now, Miss...'

'Dr,' interrupted Professor Gardener. She shot him a look of gratitude. At least someone in the room seemed to be on her side.

'I stand corrected,' said the Provost, looking anything but chuffed about this. 'Dr James, your research seems satisfactory enough, more than satisfactory. Your record of helpfulness within the department perhaps less so...' He paused to consult his notes.

Maggie jumped in to defend herself. 'I had certain suggestions for changes, Provost, which were not approved of.'

Dr McGregor glared at her. She glared back.

'They were not approved of,' he said, his sandy hair standing on end like a question mark, 'because they were unworkable.'

'I didn't think so.'

Dr McGregor wriggled his eyebrows at the Provost, as if to say, 'What can you expect from a woman!'

Professor Gardener shifted his gaze from his notes to the portraits of various dons from the past lining the walls. They were, of course, all men.

'But what is more worrying,' continued the Provost, his weasly black eyes glinting in a way that disturbed her, 'is the moral stance you have adopted on certain issues. Take the question of the strike last year. Trinity pays you to think. I cannot possibly comprehend how you could consider going on strike from that.'

'Not to mention the disloyalty to the students who entrust us with their futures,' put in Dr McGregor.

'Quite,' agreed the Provost. Eight heads nodded around the table. Professor Gardener contemplated a mark on the ceiling.

'Not of course that that would bother Dr James who cancels classes at the drop of a hat.'

'If you are referring to the class I think, Dr McGregor,' she quavered, 'I cancelled that because I was not feeling well.' Christ, she thought, he'll never understand morning sickness.

'Sometimes I think there's too much of this not feeling well in Trinity.' Dr McGregor sniffed. Several faces round the table looked uneasy.

'I hardly think we can blame Dr James for cancelling one class,' put in Professor Gardener unexpectedly, then turned pink. 'And so on and so forth,' he muttered.

'I agree,' agreed the Provost. Eight heads nodded. Dr McGregor looked the other way and appeared to be swallowing a large, invisible pill. 'However, there is this other matter to which Dr McGregor has kindly drawn my attention. A tutorial student of his to whom you apparently gave advice of - well - of a personal nature.'

'I think we should be more explicit,' said Dr McGregor, thrusting out his jaw. 'One of my students went to Dr James because he had got a girl into trouble.' Into trouble! thought Maggie. This is becoming surreal. 'Instead of referring the student back to me, as would have been proper, Dr James took matters into her own hands and advised him to persuade his girlfriend to go over to England for an abortion. As we all know, they are disgracefully lax about such matters over there. They went and I've been informed by the girl's parents who are friends of mine - I play golf with her father - that she has been utterly traumatised by the whole experience. As indeed one would expect.'

Maggie mentally cursed golf, the one ecumenical pastime in Ireland.

Dr McGregor continued, 'Here's a bright student with her career in ruins because of some irresponsible, illegal and, I'm sure you will agree, morally dubious advice from Dr James.'

Nine shocked faces around the table. Oh baby, she thought, how do you fancy life on the dole?

'These are serious allegations, Dr James,' said the Provost. 'As you are no doubt aware, to give referrals to abortion clinics in England is illegal under the Irish constitution. Strictly speaking, you and the student concerned could be prosecuted.'

Patrick's words rang in her ears. 'Go back and fight.' Holding on to the edge of the table and feeling very much like the Guilford Four, she gulped and said, 'I disagree with Dr McGregor's presentation of the facts. The student concerned emphasised that he did not feel able to consult Dr McGregor on this matter. I didn't enquire into the reasons. I did not advise the student and his girlfriend to choose abortion. I merely pointed out the various options and gave them the address of a reliable London clinic. I thought on balance it was safer than letting them fall into the hands of a quack. The decision was entirely their own. They are adults, after all. I got the address from a friend,' she added, as an afterthought.

The Provost, looking more jaundiced than ever (perhaps it wasn't the light), pursed his thin, pinched lips, hummed and hawed for a few moments and then said, 'It's a difficult situation. I shall have to look into it more closely. Trinity can't afford to get a reputation for breaking the laws of the state. That will be all, Dr James. We'll notify you in a few days' time.' His weasly eyes stared at her, unblinking.

As she rose to go, she glanced over at Dr McGregor. He was looking extremely smug. Well baby, she thought, I did my best. I was polite, cautious, even-tempered. But will it be enough?

There was one last card to play. She knocked at Lallie's door.

'Come in.'

Lallie had a kitten on her lap and was feeding it milk from a baby's bottle. 'A stray,' she explained. She looked at Maggie. 'How was it?' she asked sympathetically. 'Bad?'

Maggie nodded, sank into a chair and recounted the interview from the beginning. By the time she had finished, Lallie was livid.

'Traumatised! What nonsense. What propagandist rubbish! Of course the girl is upset. Abortion is not something anyone takes lightly, despite what the Pro-Lifers say. And it hasn't been helped by her family's attitude. I saw Niall this morning and he told me all about it. They've thrown her out of the house, of course. Parents! But she's definitely going to continue with her studies. In fact I'm working on her application for a grant from the university's emergency fund now. And Niall said to say thank you for your help.'

'Thank heavens McGregor didn't find out I lent Niall my flat. He'd probably accuse me of trying to seduce my students. He seems determined to see me off.'

Lallie shrugged. 'He hates women, that's all. And it's part of his duties as a Freemason to ensure we don't get jobs.'

'McGregor's a Freemason? I thought he was a Protestant?'

'The Protestant Church in Ireland is riddled with

masonry,' explained Lallie. 'And they're all committed to excluding women and appointing their own. They have to be kept sternly in check. I expect he's got a nice little Mason lined up for your job. Well, he shan't be allowed to get away with this if I have anything to do with it.'

'You see, I wouldn't mind so much if it was just for myself.' She hesitated. 'But the thing is, Lallie, I'm pregnant and I need to hang on to this job.'

'Pregnant!' exclaimed Lallie in horror. 'Whatever did you go and do that for?'

'You have cats, Lallie. I wanted a child,' replied Maggie firmly, looking pointedly at the kitten on Lallie's lap.

'OK. OK. I've never understood the urge to procreate, but I gather it's quite common.' Lallie smiled and stroked her kitten's ears. 'Well now, action is required. The first thing we must do is organise a little demonstration in your favour. Don't worry,' she added, as Maggie looked up in alarm, 'nothing that will get their backs up. Just a small gathering on the steps of the Common Room at lunchtime tomorrow.'

'Do you think I should have let her?' asked Maggie anxiously, over coffee in Bewleys with Fergus half an hour later.

'Can't do any harm,' he replied. 'McGregor seems to have gone a bit far this time. I'm all for keeping women in their place, but...'

'Fergus!' Then she noticed he wasn't smiling, that in fact he was slumped in his chair, an expression of defeat on his face she had never seen before. 'Fergus, is anything the matter?'

'Anna's gone back to her husband,' he said glumly. 'Ould eyes filling has got the better of me at last.'

235

'Oh Fergus, I am sorry.' She seized his hand and squeezed it.

'Ach, it was always on the cards that she'd go back. She missed her children. And then if I'm honest I have to say that I couldn't offer what he could. She'd got used to a certain style of life in Foxrock. On a lecturer's salary, I couldn't compete.'

'But if she really loved you...?'

'Money wouldn't matter?' He shook his head. 'Don't make that mistake, Maggie. After a certain age, it always matters. And then, as you know, I come from Dublin 22. I have working-class habits. I eat baked beans straight from the can. She found it quaint at first...' He sighed. 'The irony is that Gráinne had just agreed to us selling the house in Lucan. She's moving over to England. She has relatives in Liverpool.'

'She's picked up the pieces then? I rather admire her for that,' she risked.

'Yes.' He looked down. 'I'm beginning to realise that Gráinne submerged her personality in mine during our marriage. She's much more independent - and lively - now.' He looked up and winced. 'I could almost start to fancy her again.'

'But you won't?'

He shook his head. 'No. I'd be afraid of hurting her again. Once is enough.' He was silent for a moment. 'Anyway, I was looking forward to moving out of that pokey little flat by the canal and getting a place with a decent garden where Anna's children could play when they visited us.' He fingered his beard. 'Ah well, shit. I guess, like you, I'm not cut out for family life.' He gave her a wry smile. 'Rootless we are.'

Should I tell him, she wondered; will he understand?

'It's not like you to be hankering after family life,

Fergus.'

'No, well, it's not something I usually talk about but, yes, I would have liked a child. By Anna. Gráinne couldn't have any, you see.'

'I never knew you wanted children,' she said softly. 'You never said.' Maureen wasn't so far off the mark after all, she thought.

'Well, there was a kind of loyalty to Gráinne. And then I suppose I didn't expect you to understand. You're not the maternal type. It's simply that there comes a time when a man feels he'd like to leave something more of himself behind in the world than a book on the French Revolution.'

'I do understand, you know.'

He glanced at her. 'Yes, perhaps you do. You've changed a bit, become softer perhaps. Like our Norman.' He moved restlessly in his chair. 'Excuse me. I can't be feeling well, going on like this. Life has a way of jumping up and surprising one, hasn't it? I'll be functioning properly in a day or two.' He cleared his throat. 'Let's change the subject, shall we? I can't deal with these soul-baring conversations for long. Perhaps I need a dose of Conor's men's group.'

'Oh God, no, not that! But you will support me at the demo tomorrow?'

He nodded. 'Of course. Though you'll understand now why, personally speaking, I'm not greatly enthusiastic about abortion - despite the fact that the Micks try to make out that all Protestants want abortion on demand.'

'What a bigot you are, Fergus.' She toyed idly with her coffee spoon. Should she tell him or not?

'They're the bigots! It's to their advantage, you see, to represent all Protestants as secularists so they don't have to face the issue of religious pluralism. If we're all secularists, we're clearly 'baddies' and they don't have to bother to explain why they won't tolerate a different code of ethics from the one which comes out of the Vatican. Then, when they've swallowed us all up, as they will do by the middle of the next century, religious tolerance will cease to be an issue in the Republic. We will be an entirely Catholic state. A neat solution. For them.'

'Why aren't you in favour of joining up with the North then?' she asked, fighting to give him some feedback. Her thoughts, meanwhile, wandered off in a direction of their own. She felt a dull ache, a longing for Patrick that was already becoming familiar. She wrenched her attention back to Fergus. 'A united Ireland would at least have the advantage of swelling the Protestant population.'

'Ach, truth be told, no one down here wants unity, except perhaps Patrick Brophy,' he added.

She twitched, nervously. Fortunately, Fergus didn't seem to notice.

'We can't afford the North,' he continued. 'Unity, when it comes, will be forced on us by the demands of the British electorate. The Brits - sorry, the English - will pick up the tab for a while, say ten years at the most. And then what? Bankruptcy, I'd say.'

'Perhaps the Americans will step in.'

'Only if it's in their interest to do so. And just think of what that would mean - hamburgers and the moral majority.' He shuddered. 'I'd prefer a confederation with the English to becoming the fifty-first state of America.'

'So freedom doesn't come into it? Unity will be dictated by the political situation in another country?'

'Exactly.' He stirred his coffee. 'You know, McGregor and his cronies in the North should be making their plans for unity now. If they leave it too late, they'll have nothing to bargain with. Perhaps it's already too late. The Anglo-Irish agreement has abnormalised the Ulster Prods - the forces of history are seeming more and more to be against them. Mind you, they could make a start by finding themselves some attractive spokesmen... sorry, persons.' He straightened up. 'I say, I do feel better. Nothing like a political discussion for reviving the spirits.' He finished his coffee.

It's now or never, she thought. 'Um, actually, Fergus, I've been doing my bit for pluralism recently.'

'Oh?'

She swallowed. 'Fergus, how would you feel about being an uncle?'

He stared at her. 'Maggie, you're not... ?'

'Yes, I am.'

His eyes widened. 'Golly, as you English would say.'

She spread out her hands, smiling at the expression on his face. 'I was fed up of being a chap, you see.'

'Pregnant! You! I'd never have thought it.'

He digested the news in silence for a couple of minutes.

'It was planned?'

'Yes.'

'You're getting married?'

She shook her head. He looked at her with narrowed eyes.

'It's not Conor's, is it?'

'No.'

'Good, I wouldn't trust any child of his as far as I could throw it.'

He gazed at her. She could almost hear his brain

ticking over.

'Oh God, I know. Patrick Brophy!'

She nodded.

'But you can't! He's a frigging Catholic!' He put his head in his hands. 'This is ecumenism run riot.'

'He's not really a Catholic, not any more.'

'Once a Catholic, always a Catholic. It hangs around in the genes.'

'But remember that any Catholic blood will be diluted by my English secularism.'

He groaned. 'Poor child! An English Catholic! It's a contradiction in terms.'

'There are some around, however.' She laughed. 'Well, are you going to exercise a blow for pluralism, or not?'

He stroked his beard. 'Uncle. It's a serious business,' he said solemnly. 'Responsibilities.' He swelled out his chest. 'But I think I'm up to it.'

She grinned at him. 'That's the spirit.'

'Besides the child will need someone to put the Protestant point of view to it if it's to have any chance at all of counteracting those Catholic genes.'

'Fergus!'

'And the first thing I shall do, as a responsible uncle,' he said, as they walked out of the café together, 'is ensure its mother keeps her job by joining in that demonstration tomorrow.'

'Spoken like a true pluralist.'

Chapter Thirteen

The next morning, a letter arrived from Patrick enquiring how the interview had gone. His handwriting had become shaky, almost illegible. She folded up the letter and put it into her pocket.

On her way to the car, she met Paul in the street.

'I hear you've got into trouble.' He smirked.

Goodness, she thought, how news travels. But he was pointing to a snippet in the *Irish Times*. "University lecturer faces dismissal. Demonstration planned for one o'clock today." My God, Lallie, she thought, what have you done?

'Sorry about you losing your job,' he said.

'I haven't lost my job quite yet,' she replied, frostily. 'They're still deciding. So one can always hope.'

'Do you think that's wise? By the way,' he leaned forward, confidentially, 'I think you should know... Sheila's given the go ahead for a merger.' As Maggie continued to look puzzled, he added impatiently, 'We got engaged yesterday.'

'Oh? Oh. Congratulations,' she said feebly.

'So I'll be moving out soon. Pity for you. If I'd stayed, I might have persuaded Nolan to fix the place up a bit.'

'There's nothing wrong with it.'

'Um, do you think so?' He glanced at his watch. 'Must push off. Shame about your job. Still, you win some, you lose some.' This was true, she thought.

Arriving in front of the Common Room steps shortly after one, Maggie was touched to see how many of her students were gathered there. Some were holding placards. Others were handing out leaflets or sitting around in small groups, chatting. She noticed Seamus amongst them. He was looking quite different, had discarded his sports jacket and tie in favour of a pair of grubby old jeans and a T-shirt. There was no sign of Fionnuala.

'Seamus!' she exclaimed. 'What's happened to your clothes? Why haven't you shaved? Does Fionnuala approve of this? Where *is* Fionnuala?'

He shrugged. 'Fionnuala! Boring! She believes in Thatcherism, the survival of the fittest and dismantling the welfare state. Appalling stuff - can't think what I saw in her.' He moved closer. 'The Workers' Party fully supports your stance in favour of abortion, Dr James. We're all for making it legal in Ireland.'

'I'm not taking a stance in favour of abortion,' she protested. 'I just want to keep my job.'

'Maggie!' Lallie called her over and handed her a pile of leaflets.

'What on earth have you been telling them, Lallie? They think they're demonstrating to legalise abortion in Ireland!'

Lallie smiled mysteriously. 'I can't help it if some radicals misinterpret the story, now, can I?'

'Lallie!'

'It's the numbers that count, believe me,' she replied, handing a leaflet to an elderly gentleman who was trying to fight his way into the Common Room for his post-prandial cup of coffee. It was Mayhew. He stopped beside Maggie.

'Gangway, gangway!' shouted Lallie. Mayhew was swallowed up in the press of students around the door of the Common Room. Then the door opened and

Fergus came out, followed by several of their colleagues.

'I've rounded up support,' he said. 'I promised you'd stand them all a drink when your promotion comes through. You'd better not have one, though.' He winked at her. 'This is the most fun I've had for a long time, with my clothes on.'

Behind Fergus, came Julian. 'You've changed your tack,' he boomed at her. 'Given up the baby idea, have you? Jolly good. Anyway it all fits in very nicely. I was thinking of writing an article on MC - middle-class - attitudes to abortion in Ireland.'

'This is not about ab...' began Maggie.

'Julian!' shouted Lallie. 'You can make yourself useful for once by handing out some of these leaflets.'

Nearby, Maggie spotted Norman. His hair had got so long now he had tied it back in a pony-tail. Fond as she was becoming of Norman, she wasn't at all sure that his presence here would help her cause. He looked less like an ex-policeman than a... what? She was trying to work out who he reminded her of when he beckoned her over. Turning his back on the rest of the gathering, he rolled up one leg of his jeans.

'What do you think?' he asked sheepishly.

'About what?' It looked like a normal male leg to her. She looked again. No it wasn't. He'd shaved it. 'Very nice,' she said lamely.

'Is it the right shape, do you think?' he whispered. 'I lie awake at nights worrying about it.'

'Oh, I shouldn't do that,' replied Maggie, whose attention had been distracted from the no-doubt-important matter of Norman's leg, by the sight of Bridget O'Doherty coming across the Front Square. 'Sleep's frightfully important. Keeps you on an even

243

keel, if you know what I mean.' She stared at him doubtfully. Did Norman know what she meant?

He sighed. 'Of course I can never be a mother.'

'No? Well no, naturally not...' What on earth was he on about?

'You think - drop the "n" and that's all there is to it. But it's more complicated than that, a lot more complicated.'

What was he rabbiting on about?

'So you see I had to come and support your stance on minority rights in Ireland.'

'What?'

Bridget was now at the foot of the Common Room steps. Maggie just had time to wonder how many causes Lallie had drummed up support for and what Norman's leg had to do with minority rights in Ireland when Bridget tapped her on the arm.

'Hello,' said Maggie coldly and, she hoped, in a dignified manner. 'What are you doing here?'

Bridget stared straight ahead. 'I thought I ought to tell you, because he probably won't, that Conor and I have split up.'

'Split up?' Strangely enough, Maggie was not as pleased as she thought she would have been.

An expression of embarrassment crossed Bridget's face. 'It was becoming obvious that I had exchanged one career-absorbed man for another. My daughter and I are going to live on our own for a while. That's why I'm here,' she added. 'I fully support your decision to bring up your child on your own. I think it's scandalous that Trinity is trying to sack you simply because you're pregnant.'

'Lallie!' said Maggie, through clenched teeth.

'Think of the numbers,' replied Lallie airily. 'The

committee will only count heads. They won't bother to enquire what precisely we're demonstrating about. A lot of useful causes are being supported here today, one way or another.'

'Clearly.'

Suddenly a cheer went up. Niall, with his arm around a girl, had joined them on the Common Room steps. Maggie presumed this was his girlfriend, though she was dressed more like a Ukrainian folk dancer. Someone on the student union committee made a speech in favour of abortion, congratulated Niall's girlfriend on her courage and honesty and likened Ireland's laws to those of Nazi Germany.

Maggie shuddered. 'Christ! I hope McGregor isn't listening!'

'He never listens to students,' Lallie assured her. 'Don't worry. Trust me. I know what I'm doing.'

'I hope so,' muttered Maggie. Poor baby, she thought. What kind of a future will you have with your mother on social welfare? She thought again of Patrick's words, 'Are you wise enough to have a child?' She looked around at the hopeless tangle of misunderstandings wilfully created by Lallie from the kindest of motives. Who was it said the opposite of good is well-intentioned, she wondered. She thought back to her interview the previous day. Was this the best she had to offer her child? A sort of clever sharpness, an ability to get on, to manipulate people?

'There are two sorts of people,' Patrick had said once, 'those who think that the world is empty, that nature is silent and that objects have no significance apart from the arbitrary and subjective ones bestowed by ourselves. Some very great books have been written on this theme. Out of the hands of the philosophers, though, this belief can quickly degenerate into the notion that the world exists only for our benefit, to be used and exploited. The second kind of people see the world as enchanted, filled with intermediaries between God and humans - angels, the stars, the movements of the planets across the sky; everything to them has a significance divinely, not humanly, bestowed, and each part of creation, down to the smallest movements of a butterfly's wing, fits into the overall scheme. The Elizabethans called it the great chain of being. This view of the world gives dignity to humans and at the same time humbles them, for we are assigned a precise place in the chain, mid-way between the angels and the beasts. We are seen as having evolved out of the earth and owing a debt to it. A modern version of it is the Green Peace movement. Which would you prefer,' he had asked her, 'a universe with meaning and purpose woven into its structure and which we are part of, or one that is purposeless, governed merely by chance, and which may drive you to despair?'

She felt for the letter in her pocket.

'Lallie, I'm going away for a while.' She scribbled an address on the back of one of the leaflets. 'Let me know what happens.'

'You're not going over to England as well, are you?' asked Lallie, anxiously. 'We're talking major propaganda here.'

'Don't worry, Lallie, I won't let you down.'

That afternoon, as she was back in the flat packing her suitcase, Conor phoned.

'I hear you're pregnant.'

'Who told you that?'

'Prue.'

Ah, Prue. 'Yes, I am. Isn't it great?'

'I think it's a terrible idea. You're surely not going to have it? Prue knows of a...'

'Yes, she told me.'

'What about your career? Have you thought about that?'

'I'll manage.'

There was a silence.

'Bridget and I have split up.'

'I know.'

'Oh, you know.' Pause. 'Look, I've been thinking. How about if we got back together again? I have this huge house - the mortgage is crucifying me, by the way. Perhaps we could come to some arrangement? Did I tell you it has remote-control garage doors?'

'Yes.'

'Well... what about it?'

She hesitated and for a moment the world stood still. 'You wouldn't want me pregnant, Conor, would you? Waddling around the house at eight months. I wouldn't look very attractive, would I?'

Pause. 'Um, I don't suppose you would.'

'You'd start fancying other women again.'

'Um, I suppose I might.'

'So...'

'OK. Take care then.' He rang off.

He didn't try very hard, she thought. He didn't even ask who the father was. She stayed by the phone. She had one more call to make before she went away. She took a deep breath and dialled California.

'It's Maggie.' Silence. 'Your daughter.'

'Hi there, darling!'

'You didn't stay long in Ireland.'

'Giles ran out of inspiration after two days. Still, it was a fun trip. How are things with you, Aur...

Maggie?'

'Fine. I'm expecting a baby.'

There was a distinct pause on the other end. Then, 'How nice for you, darling.'

Maggie flinched. 'Is that all you have to say?'

'What do you expect me to say, sweetie? Do you have a good obstetrician over there? You must take extra care with your diet from now on. Will they let you give birth underwater, do you think? Or what about hypnosis? I've heard it's very good.' She hesitated. 'You know, darling, that if wasn't for Giles, I'd fly over and keep you company for a bit.'

'I don't expect you to come over. Aren't you the least bit excited about becoming a grandmother?'

'Oh, darling, can't I just be an aunt or something? Grandmother sounds so old and not at all like me.' Charlotte chuckled, her deep, throaty, sexy chuckle.

Maggie was silent.

'Look, sweetheart, have to fly. We're off to an opening. I'll send you over some baby clothes. You can get the sweetest little things here. Lots of hugs and kisses - and from Giles too, of course. He'll be delighted.'

If he remembers who I am, Maggie thought glumly. The phone went dead. She stood in the hall dangling the receiver in her hand. What more had she expected? Charlotte would never change. She had to be taken on her own terms. Maggie supposed that would be the adult way of going about things.

Chapter Fourteen

Patrick answered the door in his dressing gown and slippers. His face looked gaunt and grey and he had lost more weight but there was welcome in his eyes.

'How did you know I was needing you?' he said, pressing her so close she could feel his ribs.

'Magic?' she replied.

'I told you you would end by believing in it.'

If not me, then my child, she thought. Yes, if she couldn't believe in it herself, she would like to pass it on to her child. So that its world would not be empty.

He sat down on the stairs with his arms around her. 'I would never have sent for you.'

'I know. Pride.' She softly kissed him. 'Well, now I'm here and I'm not leaving.'

'Good.'

This time, she thought, there will be no limits on our love.

She unpacked her things, took one look in the fridge and tore down to the village before the shop closed. Sheepishly, he admitted that food was not figuring largely in his life at the moment; he was living on tea and whiskey. 'Oh, and pills,' he added.

Later that evening, the doctor called in to replenish his supply. She seemed pleased that Maggie, anyone, was there to keep him company. As she was leaving, she drew Maggie to one side.

'I was about to book him into hospital. I would have done, if you hadn't arrived. You know that it will get very much worse. Will you be able to cope?'

'Yes.' Behind her back, Maggie crossed her fingers.

'I could send round a nurse?'

'No, we'll manage on our own for as long as we can.' She couldn't bear the thought of a stranger in the house, looking on at their last bit of time together.

'Good. I've a feeling he would prefer that. I'll drop round every day and see how you're getting on.'

'Are you still angry with God?' she asked that night as they lay in bed unable, either of them, to sleep.

'No, I've made my peace with Him now. It's strange,' he added, 'lying here with you, I feel as if I'm in a kind of half-way state, a sort of dream world, between life and death. The ancient Celts knew it well... an elusive in-between place, like mist or twilight. Things are becoming less and less real for me. I feel... detached.' He fumbled for her hand. 'Not from you though. I am freer now to love you since I made my peace. He's given me back to you.'

'For a while.' She grimaced into the darkness, wrestling with her anger at God, at life. 'Don't you ever feel trapped?'

'I've come to think of freedom as a paradox. The more I become aware of the mysteries of fate, the freer I feel. In tune, rather than fighting against them. It's a question of co-operation. And God Himself isn't a static being. He fights alongside us.'

She lay in the darkness and struggled to understand. 'So you would say it was fate or destiny, not chance, which brought us together?'

He kissed her shoulder. 'Yes, I would.'

'Then where does freedom come into it?'

'God isn't a chess player, moving us around like pawns. We have our part in this. It wouldn't have worked if we hadn't wanted it to. God acts in the world by being believed in.'

'I didn't believe in Him,' she objected.

'Ah, but I did. And you must admit that it has been good for us, given us both exactly what we needed.'

'Has it? For you, I mean?'

'Oh yes. I would have been very... desolate now, without you. I was wrong to separate birth and death. They are two halves of the same process. It's comforting to me to know that after my death will come a birth.'

She turned over on to her stomach, switched on the light and gazed at him. 'I will try, you know, Patrick, try to make the child yours as well as mine.'

'I know.' There was a pause. 'I'm going to leave this house in trust for the child. I'd like to think of you both spending time here. After all, I don't want my heir to have half its brain cells missing because of Dublin's lead pollution.'

'Country bumpkin!'

'City slicker!'

She looked into his eyes which were so blue and so intelligent and found herself wondering how someone so full of life could be on the point of dying. She laid her head on his shoulder, ceased wrestling with her thoughts and slept. But in the morning when she woke and saw the grey shadows on Patrick's face, she wondered whether she would ever in her life sleep so easy again.

Later that day, a letter arrived from Lallie. 'Demonstration a success. The job is yours. Told you so. Love, Lallie.' Fergus had added a PS. 'We're waiting for our pints.'

'You're safe now, baby,' she said, patting her

251

stomach.

There was a flurry of letters in *The Irish Times* supporting or condemning the students' pro-abortion stance. Maggie, scanning the newspaper each morning, saw that Lallie was having the time of her life. She had a letter published practically every other day. After three weeks or so, the correspondence faded away, without anything having been decided.

All that summer she stayed with Patrick. At first they went for strolls along the beach, then they sat in the garden and finally, as even that got beyond him and he became house-bound, she brought the beach and the garden to him in the form of brightly coloured stones, sea shells and wild flowers which she heaped in vases about the house. She learned to limit her life to his. She got used to the words 'for the last time' echoing in her mind.

Life became haphazard. They slept at odd hours, just whenever he felt tired. There came a time when he could no longer make love. It didn't seem to matter. What they had between them was deeper than physical. There was passion, but there was something else as well, too deep to put into words. Often they stayed awake through the night, listening to music in his study and waiting for the dawn to break over the sea. And through it all, they talked and talked. She felt she was learning a lot of things very quickly, enough for a lifetime. She felt proud of herself, proud and touched that such a man should choose to spend his last few weeks with her.

One day the parish priest came to call. To her surprise, Patrick invited him in and spent half an hour talking to him in his study. But he refused the priest's offer of Mass.

'If the Church had been less rigid, I'd have considered going back,' he said, when the priest had left, 'but as it is...'

'Aren't you afraid?' she asked.

'Yes, of course.'

In bed, awakened by a nightmare, she clung to him angrily. 'How can you be so certain that anything lies beyond the darkness?'

He fingered a strand of her hair. 'I just prefer to think that something does, that's all. I'm not sure, sometimes, whether I believe in personal immortality. The process - life itself - is eternal; that I believe. And through death, we become part of it, part of the grain and the rain, as we make way for the next generation. I sometimes wonder whether that's what giving up your life for others means - making a sacrifice of yourself so that life can go on and the human race evolve.'

At other times, they spoke of Ireland.

'Ireland is coming to stand for definite things in the world,' he said. 'Neutrality, independence, sympathy with the exploited and the oppressed. The long struggle to find its identity is almost over. The Irish are moving forward to determine their own future, without reference to the past.'

'I think,' she said, 'that you get more absurdly optimistic by the minute.'

'Funnily enough, I do feel quite optimistic. It must be love.'

'Yeuck!'

Her mind became a camera - this picture I will remember, she thought, watching Patrick sitting in a chair looking out over the garden, and this one and this one... All these pictures will I pass on to our child. Oh, she thought, catching her breath, I love him so much and there is so little time.

He began to have fevers. He tossed and turned in the bed, murmuring about people and places she didn't know, till the doctor came and gave him a shot of morphine and he lay quiet again. She bathed him, changed his sheets, made cups of tea and held them to his lips, in the process drawing on resources she didn't know she had and which she saw would stand her in good stead when she became a mother. Learning to submit her will to his needs, it was a preparation for motherhood. Patrick had been right, they had become inextricably linked, his dying, the child growing inside her; they couldn't be separated.

When he was moved into hospital, Maggie went with him. He lay very still and pale in the huge bed, scarcely breathing. 'He's sinking fast now,' whispered the nurse. She spent the last night with him, holding him in her arms. He died just as it was getting light.

The funeral was a small one, a few villagers, the priest and his brother, John, who came by train from Dublin and stayed overnight at the house. She was glad of his company. Going back to the house for the first time without Patrick was every bit as desolating as she had expected it to be.

'Patrick wrote to me about you,' said John, looking at her with eyes so like his brother's that she wanted to cry. 'If you are ever in need of anything, let me know.'

'A godfather?' she suggested.

'Willingly.'

His death left her feeling stunned, blank, and at the same time restless. She wandered aimlessly about the place like a lost soul. Then gradually, as the initial sharp grief subsided and she began to feel the first ghostly flutterings of new life inside her, Maggie grew to love the house, for it seemed to her that something of Patrick's spirit still lingered there. She decided that every summer she and the child would leave the city behind, come out to the West and for a few months live a different kind of life. Together they would keep the memory of Patrick alive. It seemed the most important thing she could do with her life - that and bringing up their child.

Fergus came to visit. He scolded her for cycling.

'You ought to take more care of yourself, in your condition,' he said, with all the seriousness of an uncle-to-be. He had brought with him half a dozen books on babycare. When he caught her standing on a stool to dust down a cobweb, he went straight to the village and charmed Mrs Healey into coming back to clean for her.

In October, Maggie moved back to Dublin. In February the next year, her baby was born. She called her Sara Charlotte and began to see that it might be possible to forgive.

THE END

For a full list of **Attic Press** books please send for a *FREE* copy of our current catalogue to:

Attic Press
4 Upr Mount Street
Dublin 2

Tel: (01) 616128
Fax: (01) 616176